Mirrors and Dreams

C R Saxon

HCS
HATTON CROSS STEAMPUNK
PUBLISHING

First Edition
Copyright © 202 C R Saxon
www.hcspublishing.com
All rights reserved.
ISBN: 9781955644037

Acknowledgements

To my amazing, supportive, and totally awesome husband and alpha reader: Thank you! Thank you for helping me make this book a reality. I love you oodles!

Thank you to my wonderful beta readers – my two most loyal in particular: Tammie and Kelly. And thank you to everyone who helped get this book published.

To everyone reading this, thanks for giving my story a shot. I hope you enjoy it!

Unseen Scars:

Cost of Victory

Mirrors and Dreams

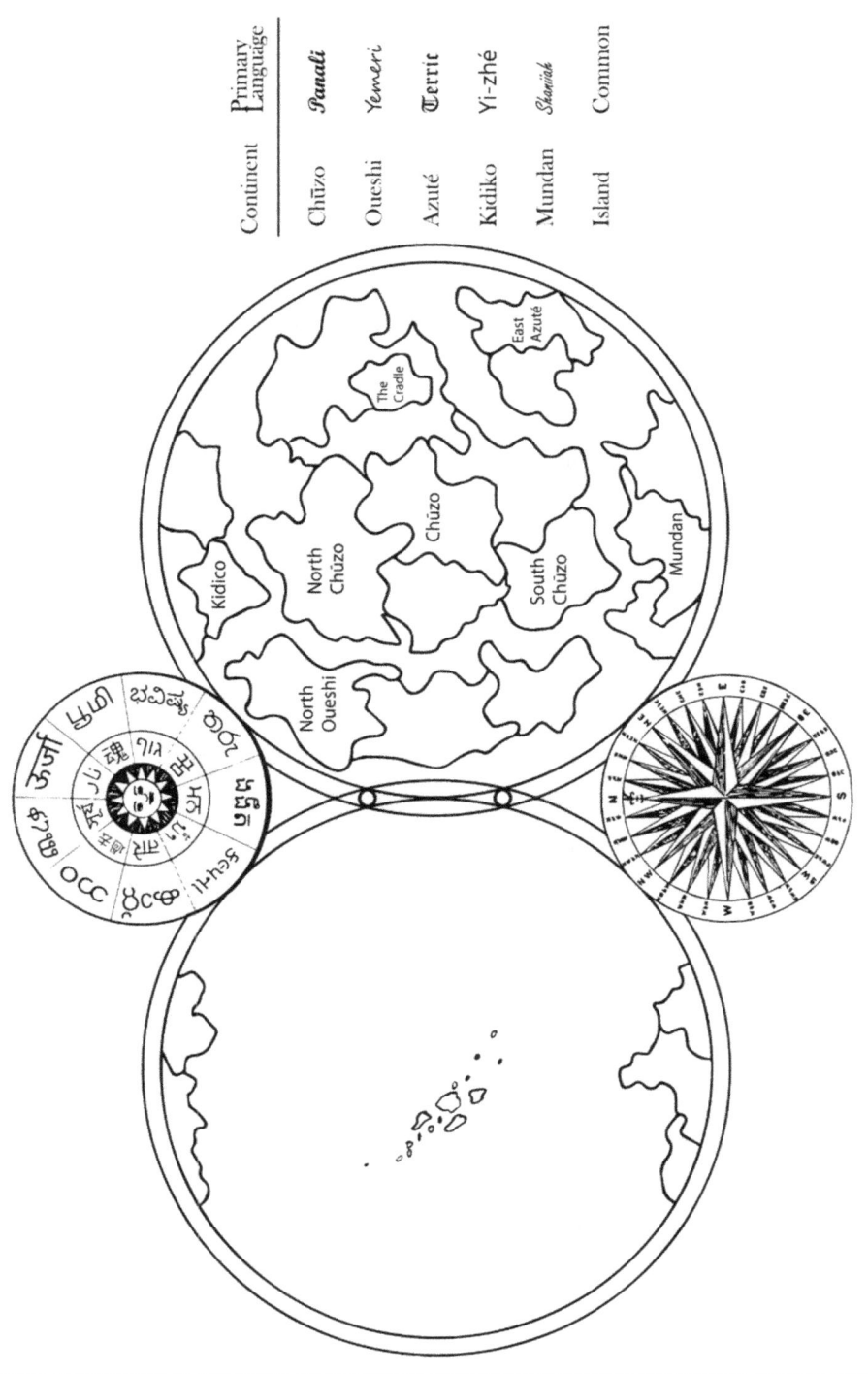

Continent	Primary Language
Chūzo	*Panali*
Oueshi	*Yemeri*
Azuté	*Terric*
Kidiko	Yi-zhé
Mundan	*Shaninsh*
Island	Common

THE CHARGES

 Humawit
Earth

 Zavun
Sun

 Û-ya'în
Water

 Iinamĭ
Heart

 Saikun
Fire

 Śarī-a
Body

 Shēnó
Life

 Dyzlar
Stars

 Ogani
Dreams

 Wézi
Moon

 Dashū
Souls

 Pigosa
Darkness

 Erviv
Wind

 U-Ech
Mind

 Kámua
Past

 Umbacano
Imagination

 Ajulagrá
Future

 Táqua
Energy

ABILITIES

 Athletes run faster and farther than Olympic humans. They're stronger and more agile with superhuman stamina. Athletes are often trained as Fighters to fulfill future political duties. Athletes and Fighters both are small and lean.

Fighters have less stamina than Athletes but greater fine motor control, process and react faster, and are ambidextrous. They're unable to digest animal proteins.

 Healers control the energy inside of living things. They expertly manipulate cells and encourage them to die or grow. Reading living energy allows them to "see" what's going on inside organisms and what has happened to the body.

Energists control and manipulate the naturally existing energy around them. Though they can access living energy, they risk killing the creature they pull the energy from. They're born without hair pigment.

 Artists stimulate and maipulate brains through visual stimulation using images, movement, and sculpture they create. Their art carries their intended messages to the viewer regardless of how abstract the idea or differences between viewers.

Weavers stimulate and manipulate brains through auditory stimulation. By telling stories and creating music, they seemingly alter reality for the hearer. A Weaver's voice triggers this stimulation unless they consciously choose not to. They're born with vitiligo.

 Thinkers' minds constantly work to understand the world around them to the deepest detail. Though Thinkers try to focus on one specific interest or two, they'll study and contemplate anything that grabbs their attention. Nothing bothers them more than not being able to understand.

Tinkerers are driven to use their knowledge to create. Their minds have an uncanny ability to easily figure out and understand what's needed to bring their ideas to life, but they have difficulty processing the world outside their head. They're born with unusual eyes.

 Telepaths constantly experience the minds of those nearby, making their brains more resilient against illness. They process mental stimuli at superhuman levels while engaged in everyday activities. With effort, they can access deeper parts of a person's mind and can even force simple commands.

Mind Talkers choose to access another's mind and can reach forgotten and hiddend parts. They can easily manipulate and control a mind they've accessed. They're born with hypotrichosis.

Languages:

Common – Generally used by the majority of the world

Oŭndo (**Ō-ōon**-dō) – Considered an extinct language; origin unknown

Yuchio (**Yōo**-chi-ō) – The Grassland's traditional language

Elemental voice – regardless of the language spoken the hearer can always understand.

Titles:

Dinta (**Din**-tä) – North Oueshi "lesser prince"

Nuwa (**Nōo**-wä) – East Azuté "queen"

Nu (**Nōo**) – East Azuté "king"

Zi (**Zē**) – East Azuté "prince"

Inoa (**E-nō**-ä) – West Kidico "general's daughter"

Mwā-tonô (**Mwä-tō**-nō) – Unknown origin "heir of Tonō"

Tonō (**Tō**-nō) – Unknown origin – a name from legend

Kōjomä̀ (**Kō**-jō-mä) – Unknown origin – means nothing nice

Jinku (**Jin-Kōo**) – Oŭndo for trainee or heir

Kalj (**Kal**-j) – Heir to the Emperor of Kidico

Rā-yŭmon (**Rä-yōo**-män) – A title Oya refuses to claim

Chapter 1

They could've died...

Would've died...

If not for Oya...

My incompetence nearly killed them...

The package was small – not even the length of his palm. Yet the challenge was overwhelming. Two forced healings in two months left Ferdinan's body depleted. Weakness and fatigue followed him everywhere. But his injuries were nothing next to his apprentices'.

What are weeks' worth of daily healings doing to Yuyu? Elbie's hands were mostly healed, but still being treated. *Even fixed, what are the long-term repercussions? How much have I limited them both?*

Such grand, monstrous things you've accomplished!

Monstrous? Did that come close to describing his sins? The countless names of all he'd failed bubbled up – taking over his mind. As he had for months, Ferdinan clenched his jaw and waited for the memory to pass. There was no stopping them or that voice. But he'd found a bandage for one of them.

Inserting the fully charged earpiece, he tapped it. Forbidden music from Oya's cube shielded against that voice. *Oya... She hasn't visited much... Is she sick of me? Did she make real friends?* Metallic notes magnified the pain of that thought. *I never should've called her 'friend.' I was wrong...forcing my desires on her...*

His face twisted. The wrapper's crinkling brought his attention back to the little bar. His stomach corkscrewed. Green tinged his lips. *The histories...* He looked at the screen containing the information from Oya's cube. But when he picked it up... It felt like he was being lectured. Like the histories were upset with him...with his progress...

The odd comfort he usually got reading through the seemingly infinite information wasn't there when he turned on the screen. Or scrolled through the amazing treasure. Neither did he recognize any of the items. Normally he couldn't *not* find something he was thinking about. But now...not even languages he knew appeared.

Sighing, he looked back at the bar. It mocked him.

Opening the little package made him gag.

"Nutrition bar" was misleading. It was more of a supercharged multivitamin. Nutritional values, taste, calories, how long they took to bake – Ferdinan knew everything about them. These were made to suit his tastes – unlike the calorie intensive version he created for a general palate. *Ugh...this is the best I can do?* A Tinkerer focused on medical products couldn't make these any smaller or easier to eat?

The bar hovered at his lips. One bite. Two for politeness... But... Ferdinan's free hand clenched into a fist. Forcing it past his teeth, the skeleton compelled himself to bite down. Drums filled his ears, emphasizing how full his mouth felt. Was chewing possible?

Looking down...barely an eighth of it was gone.

Gagging, he forced his jaw to move. *I deserve worse than this!* A burnt, half-crushed Yuyu filled his mind. *I deserve so much worse...*

He couldn't visit her. The Healers refused to tell him anything... Though...he was a student, not her guardian...but... Her first two years on the islands, he was her mentor... But traveling to Isolation to check on her... *What right does a coward have to any information?*

A revolting mush filled his mouth – blocking his throat. *Swallow!* His first attempt failed. *How does anyone find this enjoyable?* His second try came during an uncomfortably long lull between songs.

Pathetic. How are you still alive?

The intrusion made him choke. Violent coughing set every nerve in his healing body aflame. The choice was allowing it into his belly or risk choking. Seeing the remaining amount left Ferdinan pale.

But he repeated the process. *I must find something better than music to keep that voice under control...*

During an epic battle with the third bite, the skeleton found himself face to face with an intruder.

"What're you doing?" Jon raised an eyebrow.

Lobster red, Ferdinan turned away – hiding the uneaten portion of the bar. "It's rude entering unannounced."

"You weren't answering. Did you turn off the chime?"

2

Ferdinan blushed harder. No, he hadn't. Between the music and focus required for this task... "What do you want?"

"Snack time...but...you're eating?"

A darker shade of red flooded his face – making him dizzy.

"If you're already eating...then... What is it?"

The swaying room forced Ferdinan to sit. "Nutrition bar."

Surprise held Jon in place. "I have to see it."

"See what?"

Frowning, Jon shrugged. "The bar? What kind do you like?"

Purpling, then suddenly paling, left Ferdinan feeling more ill. "It doesn't matter. What did you bring?"

"As long as you're eating, it's fine."

"You made it." *I don't need any more attention from the school.*

"That's never stopped you..." Jon put the plate down.

Closing his eyes, the skeleton forced back a cringe. The situation was offensive. But...minus the sauce...the food wasn't disagreeable.

What will they demand next? And when? If not for healing from the fire, they would've already laid out more demands. *I need to appear cooperative so they leave me alone...* "Thank you."

Jon let out a breath of relief. "Anything you want or need?"

"No, thank you. This is more than sufficient."

"Then...um...how're you feeling? Your skin?"

Silence fell. Both boys averted their eyes.

"Between your brother and the cream you made, it's healing well." Gaze fixed on the window, Ferdinan hid his face.

"Are you still in pain?"

"I'm not comfortable..."

Nodding silently, Jon looked away. "That's better than before..."

"Yeah." Awkwardness paralyzed them, but the music offered a strange kind of comfort. If only he could run. *Please leave me alone.*

3

Chocolate brown eyes searched for a clock. "Oh."

"What?"

"Sorry... I have a meeting with Healer Bær and..." Jon stood. "What sort of 'official' business could Xhou have with me?"

A small smirk tugged at Ferdinan's thin lips. *You earned your lab a year ago.* "Could be anything, knowing Xhou Zi."

* * *

Strong, golden hands shifted from defense to offense – thumb of the forward hand tapping the ring finger three times.

I'm not ready to defend yet! Even his apprentices could beat him after so much time in "quarantine." But against Captain Rutoric?

Rutoric flew before the golden Prince could breathe. The first strike was slow. *He's going easy on me...* Annoyed, the Athlete took the charity – blocking it with ease. A few more easy strikes came.

Then the warmup started.

Even with his lifelong mentor – and second father – going easy on him, the Prince was coated in sweat and panting hard.

The beatdown didn't let up. Zephyr's time in that torture aside, Rutoric was stronger with significantly more years of experience. And the man was a true Fighter. One narrow miss after another. With each, the man moved a little faster. Until one hit solidly in the gut.

Stunned. Unable to breathe. Zephyr staggered. *Move!* At their best, an Athlete couldn't stand against a Fighter in combat. Multiple personal trainers. Countless hours practicing. It didn't matter.

Losing to Rutoric wasn't usually bitter. The rare times he landed a strike or surprised the man were golden. But now he felt disgusted.

Why didn't I fully inherit mom's mutation...? A boulder masquerading as a fist grazed his cheek. Yet, Rutoric wasn't going half as hard as he could. *I'll never be good enough for him to fight me seriously.* His eyes couldn't even keep up with the Captain's, his mom's, and Aunt Tenalia's movements when they fought each other.

Feet that'd been on the ground were in the air. Zephyr's back hit the hard floor, stunning him. Padded or not, everything felt like stone when rammed into it by a Fighter. *I'll never succeed.* Seeing what his mom, aunt, and the Captain could do... Not inheriting the secondary trait of his mother's mutation condemned him to failure at birth.

Worse, Zephyr was the last born of the original line of Fighters. The main family. *Why did I end the line?*

Staying down was tempting. *How many times have I lost today? I'm getting worse.* The lie Athletes told themselves hit the Prince.

"With hard work and training, no one would see the difference." This lie kept Athletes striving for Fighters' skills and knowledge – all to fulfill their positions in life.

I don't want to move...but it's my duty. Zephyr rolled to his side and forced himself back to his feet. *I wish that lie was true.* Then he might have a chance. But no amount of hard work would allow him to overcome. Rutoric charged. It was the same for all abilities.

No Artist would best a Weaver at wordsmithing.

No Telepath would best a Mind Talker at mind delving.

No Healer would best an Energist at mass energy manipulation.

No Thinker would best a Tinkerer at creating.

And No Athlete would best a Fighter at combat.

One fist landed. Then another. Zephyr couldn't breathe.

Drive, ambition, will...didn't matter. A fist grazed his shoulder. Some things were simply impossible due to circumstances of birth. Another came. The Prince jumped back so it couldn't land solidly, but it still stole his breath. A heel rammed between his ribs and hip.

"*Agh!*" Zephyr stumbled on land and out of those thoughts.

What am I doing? All abilities have an advantage. Zephyr dropped into a defensive stance, but didn't maintain it. By the time Rutoric realized, the man was flying forward.

Knowing coal eyes watched the golden Prince advance. The first strike was a test, but Zephyr cartwheeled to the side anyway. A thickly muscled leg swung. He rolled toward it and flattened himself to let it pass overhead before leaping to his feet. With each attack, he dodged and weaved in an erratic dance. But it wouldn't last long.

A battle between a Fighter and an Athlete was a game of attrition. Athletes had more stamina, could run longer distances, and change directions more swiftly. Fighters didn't expend as much energy, could process details more effectively, and strike faster. If this were a fight for survival, the Prince would've bolted...but this was training.

Minutes passed as seconds. And he didn't stop moving. *Don't look at me like that. I know I'm cheating.* To improve, he needed to train like a Fighter, not an Athlete. But he was tired of being inferior.

All movement stopped. Captain Rutoric dropped into a defensive position Zephyr had never broken and gestured, "Attack!"

Onyx eyes widened over a golden grin. A second chance. *I'm sorry. I'll do it right this time.* The Prince leapt. Blow after blow. High, low, front, back, feint... Nothing breached the impenetrable fortress of Captain Rutoric. The closest he came was when he grazed the man's collar – revealing a barely hidden circular birthmark.

Not once did the man flinch. Rutoric waited for Zephyr to wear himself out – blocking his attacks as if shooing away an annoying fly.

I'll never win... Something filled his lungs and strangled his heart. It wasn't just fighting. He wasn't capable of winning... The elf's words echoed in his mind, making him grimace. *What is that elf?* A dream, delusion, symptom of a warped mind? It wasn't apologetic in the–

Rutoric's hand landed on his chest and bodily threw him *into* the ground. Even if he wanted to get back up, neither his body nor the Captain was about to let him. Strong hands pointed at Zephyr before crossing and swiping away. Rutoric tapped the Prince's golden forehead and rotated his hand forward and back.

Panting. Dazed. Onyx eyes closed. His second father pulled him up to sit. Palm down, he sliced back and forth through the air before tapping the side of his head. "Nothing's on my mind. I'm just fighting."

Thick fingers pinched together at the tips before a thumb was thrown over his shoulder.

"I'm not obsessing!" Zephyr's head dropped. Hands danced with his mumbled apology. *Admitting my thoughts will make you worry more...* After the last couple months... But the man didn't let up. *The elf...* Zephyr swallowed hard. Telling a Chūzite about her wasn't wise. But a royal Grassland's warrior... "I...I keep having the same dream."

Rutoric's palm rotated from facing the Prince to facing himself.

Flushed cheeks deepened. That dream was ridiculous.

The Captain drew Zephyr's eyes to him. Fist over his heart, Rutoric raised an eyebrow in challenge.

"No..." Zephyr's chest tightened. Rutoric was the one he could speak to without reservation. But... *Is talking about her a mistake? After finally escaping quarantine?* He took too long thinking. The Captain's weight pinned Zephyr's chest to the ground.

A finger tapped the side of his mouth before pointing to Zephyr.

"...can't..." escaped his lips – signaling his surrender.

One swift motion and the man was kneeling beside him. Using both Yuchio and the Grassland's sign was habit for Zephyr. "Every night the same dream. A woman comes and asks why I'm angry."

* * *

"*Ooof!*" Oya fell back – landing on nothing. Above was a torn and tattered net. And beyond that a magnificent galaxy of light and thought and brilliance in total disarray. "Still here, young one?"

"Yes," echoed in the disrupted galaxy beyond the torn net.

Yuyu's getting louder... But she'd yet to see the girl. Neither had the galaxy above returned to any semblance of order. A smirk glowed under inhuman green eyes. Countless frayed ends swayed. Waiting.

Back to work. Oya jumped to her feet and slowly turned. A once orderly mesh now draped chaotically... *The brain's fascinating.* She'd spent countless hours roaming minds, but this was the first brain. And even from here she could see the mind beyond. *Which next?*

Small holes were repaired quickly. But the largest mocked her. Every time alien green eyes caught sight of it, Oya wanted to stop and fix it. But the smaller holes were better for practicing. There was less damage she could cause with the little ones. Still... *I need to fix it...*

Confidence wasn't something Oya lacked. But if she didn't fix that big hole right... *It'll kill him if she doesn't wake up the same...* And not just her dear friend, but many others on and off the islands. It wasn't a matter of simply reconnecting the ends like most of the other holes. Large portions of the mesh were missing...or frayed beyond repair. She'd have to completely rework that section of net.

She searched for the other large hole. "It's getting closer."

"Thank you. I don't like it here."

Unlike the giant hole – this one was barely large enough for her to slip through. *What can I do....?* Golden-brown hands ran over the breaks. Words. Oya blinked. *How can she talk to me if this part is damaged...?* Reaching past the tear... Faces. *Faces? Why would words connect to faces?* And not some words. All. Any face with one word connected had them all. *I don't understand...*

Past faces were emotions...no...*one* emotion. One Oya couldn't describe. It was between trust, understanding, and another thing... Like the emotion tied to...familiarity. Not the pleasant or pain of the familiar. The existence. The connectedness that held no opinion.

Once again, she brought her hands to the broken ends. And again, all she found were words. *Why are words here....?* There were no experts on the brain or mind anymore. But Oya was certain this wasn't right. Wouldn't emotions connect to people before words? And words to general knowledge or experiences? Why faces?

That left the giant hole. If this one didn't make sense... Walking over, she reached out. Restoring a path between memories was simple. But the hole of faces and words and this monstrosity were deeper. Delicate fingers took hold of the broken ends.

A world full of knowledge punched her. Knowledge whole, broken, and incomplete. Letting go, Oya stood frozen. The words and faces made more sense. *I don't have to understand, just see how it connects.* Breathing in, she took hold again. There was so much it was dizzying! *Push past. What does it connect to?*

How long she stood there, Oya didn't know. But she found ends and patterns. That first hole though... "I know it's early, young one. But there's something I need to check. I'll return soon."

"Please no! It's dark...and lonely..."

"If I stay, you can't escape the dark. Can't hold those you love."

"...I...please...please don't be long."

"I'll return." Closing her eyes, Oya brought herself into focus.

When she opened them, she was sitting on Yuyu's bed. The adorable girl laid perfectly still. Tight, dark curls stood starkly against the pillow. A strange piece of metal blinked on her forehead. Tubes came and went from the small body.

"I'll figure it out."

Chapter 2

Sunshine warmed him. It was the most wonderful feeling – aside from working without restriction. Elbie looked at his hands. If he hadn't seen... There wasn't anything to suggest they'd been damaged.

No scarring. His nails grew in quickly. Beside some stiffness... *When can I use them again...?* Healers Herrard and Nammie were doing a great job. But ideas were piling up. He wanted to build!

Returning his attention to the screen, Elbie continued reading. Though mismatched eyes kept drifting to his hands. *Amazing...*

"How do you study like this?"

Looking up, Elbie smiled. His suitemate floated above. Snow white hair swayed and impossibly black eyes glistened. "This is the only way to study. Going to training, Haoyu?"

"No. Master Tuel had an assessment." The Energist drifted to sit next to Elbie – elbows on knees and head in hands. "I'm bored."

"You don't have any schoolwork?"

Haoyu grimaced. "I can't believe you haven't taken a break."

"I've been on break for weeks." Laying back, Elbie let the soft grass cradle him. "Can't wait for it to be over."

"Being unable to work isn't the same as a break." Haoyu leaned over to give Elbie a disapproving look – careful not to touch him.

True... He wanted to build. His hands wanted to create. But no matter how he pestered them, Healers Herrard and Nammie refused to rush. Logically, Elbie knew this was the best for him. Lifting his hands to float above his head, he studied them. Aside from stiffness...

If he justified using them, he could make them worse, impacting the rest of his life. How many people would he then disappoint...?

"Are you ok?"

"Hm?" Elbie lowered his hands to rest on his belly.

"You've been staring at your hands for ten minutes."

Huh? Focusing...his arms were a little tired, but nothing like holding them over his head for that long. "It wasn't ten minutes."

"Maybe." The Energist lifted off the ground to float over his island brother. "But it was a while. I thought you fell asleep like that."

* * *

"What you're doing, Oya," a tall man in a floppy fishing hat walked up and sat beside her on the sand, "are you sure it's wise?"

Oya winked at the orbs in her peripheral and looked up at the starless twilight sky and full moon. "Is doing nothing better?"

"Even if you could make the girl's brain look the same, doesn't mean it is the same. That it'll work the way she needs it to." Concern coated the Fisherman. "This isn't a cut. It's the most complex organ."

"Why do you think I'm studying others?! I'm making sure."

"And how is that going?"

That question cooled Oya off. "The girls her age...their brains aren't the same. And Elbie...flames took over..."

"Shouldn't that be warning enough?"

"And it's better to do nothing?! In this world?!" Sand kicked up when Oya jumped to her feet. "Doing nothing dooms her to a life of nothingness. It'll kill my friend and destroy everyone who loves her!"

"If any of it isn't perfect, that nothingness would be paradise."

Oya took in the world of purple-gray. A world that never changed. "If I do something wrong, she won't realize there's nothingness. And that's better than being trapped in it."

Oya looked at the silver thread wrapped around her hand. A few more strands were weaved into it – but nothing next to what needed to be collected. *I'm too frustrated to work on her brain tonight...* But this task... She'd been neglecting it while helping Yuyu. Letting out her frustration on that was fine.

"Don't worry. I'll make sure."

"It's not just the girl. It's affecting you too." Before she could wave open the door to the silver roads, the Fisherman stepped in front of her. "You can't tell me you don't feel it."

"It doesn't matter. And it's not worse than this," Oya held up the strings she collected. "Helping Yuyu doesn't change my future."

No answer came, though the man looked desperate to give one.

A *snap* summoned the road's entrance. "Keep watching him."

Defeat sighed out of the man. "The infection's returned. If it takes over again..."

Oya turned away. "I know."

"You've noticed the change in his mind as well."

"Yes."

The Fisherman stepped in front of her again. "Are you sure?"

"You only live once – I'll make it great for my dear friend."

"A lucky few live twice."

"How's that lucky?" Shadows darkened Oya's countenance. Walking past him, she stepped onto the first silver road. "I made three promises. I'll keep them all."

"Isn't that an admission of who you are?"

He's trying to delay me... "I needn't admit anything."

"Why is it so hard? Even the veil you wear is impenetrable." The Fisherman gestured to Oya's façade. "Are you scared of the truth?"

Inhuman green eyes and a Cheshire grin turned back to him. "I don't want to think about it. Why let my reflection remind me?"

"And when someone finally sees under the veil?"

A sad chuckle left her. "I pity the soul so broken to see past it."

Silence fell. It suited her twilight beach perfectly. *A world that never changes...* The calm ocean. Various shades of twilight purple painted the sky and beach. A consistent gentle breeze. There was no life. No stars. No time. *But then...it's the empty spaces that're the most beautiful.* The only thing breaking the view was a giant moon shining silver-white against the gray background.

This place separate from time...how perfectly it suited her. *How often have I come here? How many hours have I lived in this place? When did I first arrive?* Oya sighed and returned her gaze to the silver roads. *It was bright and colorful at first... How long ago was that?* Not that it mattered. This was the last metamorphosis the beach would see. ...until the next person came. *The next person...*

There was so much to do. Rescuing Yuyu from her damaged brain. Finding every connection that woman tainted. Making her dear friend happy...healthy... *And Zephyr too... There's so much...*

Focus on what I can do right now. Stepping forward, Oya made her way to the Kōjomà.

* * *

Music bounced around the lab but it didn't drown out the truth.

Xhou couldn't help Yuyu. *His* charge. Yet, Ferdinan saved her.

And he sat doing nothing! *I have no right being angry.* Unlike the skeleton, Xhou understood his place as a scientist and didn't impinge on the world of healers. But...it was like jumping into the ocean with an open wound. Everyone. The boy would gladly...

Xhou shook that line of thought from his head. It wasn't helping. Nor was it leading anywhere pleasant. Herrard refusing to tell him anything about Yuyu only made it worse. His suitemate was the Healer's Lead and the main student assisting Healer Bær.

No. Stop it. Focus on Elbie. I can help him. Every day he made sure the small boy wasn't blaming himself. He was keeping Elbie from becoming like Ferdinan. *He* did that.

Ugh... How juvenile am I? I'll be a young man in a matter of days and I'm still thinking...feeling like this...

If only his mom would send more for him to do! But she refused... She wouldn't let him leave school early. Wouldn't let him help from afar...

Clenched fists bashed the desk he was unsuccessfully working at.

Blue-black eyes drifted to his sister's picture. *I couldn't do anything for you. I'm sorry... I'm so sorry... You deserved better.*

The mounted screen *beeped* – reminding Xhou of his session with Master Loucé. *It's morning...? When did that happen?* Xhou sighed. *What's the point?* The sessions were as useless as trying to sleep. Nothing either of them said or did would change anything for him, so why steal time from someone who could be helped? Pulling up a new box, the Science Lead considered his reply. *I'm tired of canceling...* But the appointments were made despite his wishes.

Xhou turned back to the picture. She was beautiful. But in his mind all he saw were her charred, twisted remains. *No. Think about something else.* But what replaced that image were thoughts of his devastated country. *No! Something useful! Something you can control!* But all he saw were his sister's remains. It was a never-ending cycle... *Stop it... I've got work to do and people to care for...*

Setting his jaw, Xhou spun the most magnificently mundane lie – filled with partial truths and warped realities. And when he finished, he was satisfied Master Loucé wouldn't pester him for another session. He was well adjusted and had all the resources any Nu could ever want...

The latest reports of his country flashed through his mind – sending a shiver down his spine. But he didn't want to think about that. Everything was beyond his control or already taken care of.

But there was one thing he hadn't found yet.

I need to know... This desire annoyed his island brother. But it was something he could do. No matter how useless he was, he'd find the scientist who saved his country.

Besides, what sort of Nu doesn't properly thank the one who saved his people? But...finding a starting point had proven problematic. *Work backwards. Who sent the message about the cure and instructions to make it?*

Pulling up a search box Xhou went to work.

And he didn't stop until the screen blurred – nearly falling off his chair. Drooping eyes turned to the window. It was dark again. But that didn't matter. He couldn't stop. If he stopped...well, he wouldn't sleep anyway.

Standing, the Thinker jogged in place – until another *beep* interrupted his exercise. *Now what?*

Looking up at the mounted screen, Xhou saw a waiting call from Herrard. *Why's he awake? I'm here so I don't keep him up!* The Healer needed to sleep so he could get Yuyu better. *Why won't he tell me how badly she was hurt?*

There was no point reading the message. He knew what it said. It was the same arguments they'd had for weeks. Opening a new box on the screen, Xhou sent a short message. "*Yes. I ate dinner. No. I'm not answering. I've got a large project to get through, and you need to rest your body so you can work tomorrow. Good night. Sleep well.*"

Jeopardizing Yuyu's recovery...! A little insomnia's nothing to worry about! Heal my charge! Make her better! It took grabbing his head to stop those thoughts.

The scientist. Focus on finding the scientist.

Chapter 3

A *beep* from his mounted screen cut through the music. Putting the histories aside... Every thought and worry Ferdinan was useless to fix flooded in. His apprentices. That voice. His Prince. Even eating this stupid nutrition bar felt impossible. Everything crushed him – pushing him further toward ultimate failure.

Returning to the near endless information was tempting. But if it was the Duchess's report of his Prince's progress...

Pulling up the message, Ferdinan smiled. *Master Fulason.* The man always had dozens of projects to work on or brainstorm...

Blueprints, ideas, questions...

For nine years, Ferdinan helped with whatever popped into the Master Engineer's head. All because of a child's bet. That's what earned the man's respect... Though...his father being a Lashi helped.

Guilt filled him. A useless son had no right taking advantage of a highly regarded title. Inheriting the Duke's mutation couldn't justify such greed. But...for inventing, the world recognized Duke Samultz as "Lashi." All the times Ferdinan used Lashi Samultz to his advantage... He disgusted himself... *I'm a terrible son...person...*

The attached blueprints were interesting. Building machines to build machines was Master Fulason's specialty. One Ferdinan took advantage of too many times... The guilt grew – crushing him...

Another *beep* came – this one followed by silence.

Are you really so great? Freak.

Ferdinan swallowed hard. *I know what I am.*

Really?

I know! I don't know how to change...

Pathetic. What good are you? Why do you exist?

I don't know! I'm sorry... I wish I didn't.

The world wishes you didn't.

Swallowing, Ferdinan braced himself until the unwanted memory subsided. *I should've never been born.*

Your family could've enjoyed a good, capable, reliable child instead of being cursed with your filth.

I know. I'm a disappointment...a defect.

You aren't even that much.

Transparent blue crystals turned to the window. Ferdinan chewed his lip to keep it from trembling as he switched out earpieces. *It's right...why do I exist? Everyone would be happier, safer if I... No... I can't fail everyone that way... It's not allowed. Stop wanting-*

A crazed smile popped into existence an inch from his face. "*I want to play with my awesome friend!*"

Ferdinan jumped back – his healing body unhappy at the sudden movement. *How does she do that?* A soft smile took over his lips. *She came back.* He didn't deserve it, but... Whatever he did to drive her away, he'd make sure not to do it again.

"*You'll never clear your mind in here.*"

Clear my mind... Great idea. "Shouldn't you be in class?"

"*You aren't, why should I be?*"

"I finished my core classes."

Exotic green eyes swallowed Ferdinan whole – telling him it was her secret, not his. "*Where to?*"

"*My island.*" That answer came without a thought.

"*So early in the day?*" she teased.

"*I don't care.*" Ferdinan grabbed a set of cuffs. "*Let's fly.*"

"*Ha!*" A golden-brown wrist showed off an activated cuff.

Partially healed skin objected as he eased himself out the window. But he didn't care. Neither did he wait for Oya before shooting off into the sky. "*Catch me if you can!*"

"*Haha! Cheater!*" she laughed and rocketed after him.

Ferdinan sped up until he could barely breathe. Passing air nearly drowned out the music and he felt that voice scratching at the back of his mind. *Go away or I'll make you.* He nearly heard amused laughter. *Even if death is the only way, I will get rid of you.*

An impossible nothingness slapped his arm, startling him out of his thoughts. Oya stuck her tongue out and zoomed off.

"*You won't win so easily!*" Forcing a smile, Ferdinan pursued – shaking off the lingering void of her touch.

Despite his declaration, she won. He let her. Winning didn't matter – only an endless race. Every time Oya bolted toward the island he blocked her path, forcing her further out. It was fun... If only they could fly faster. But that meant giving up breathing...

Was the damage to Yuyu's lungs repairable? Will she struggle the rest of her life...? An impossible void encased his hand. It pulled him down to the island and dragged him to a shady clearing.

In the center of a laid-out blanket sat a beautifully carved wood box. "*How often do you steal my violin?*"

A mischievous grin emphasized Oya's giggles as she opened it. "*Only when you haven't played for a while.*"

Fire consumed his face. Moving hurt...so he'd been neglecting her undeserved gift. "*Then I should play for you now.*"

"*Yay!!*" Exotic green eyes brightened – nearly blinding him.

He took the violin and bow from her. "*Any requests?*"

"*Play everything!*"

"*I don't know about everything, but I'll play what I know.*" Reaching up, Ferdinan turned off the earpiece.

That's a short concert.

◊

His little joke made her giggle. If only Ferdinan's bleeding chest and darkened mind would heal. *How much of his silliness is an act? How much of his life is a performance?* Boney hands lifted the bow.

Oya sucked in a breath – waiting for him to strike the first note.

Show me your heart, dear friend.

17

A smile painted itself across his face and mischievousness flashed in those nearly transparent blue crystals. A lively jig sprung to life. Laughter rang out as her hands clapped in time. Jumping to her feet she danced. Anything to keep him playing.

For a tune so joyful, each note was saturated in agony. Vigorous playing couldn't burn away his anxiety. Fear and uncertainty drowned his music. It grew with each song he played. And each time she praised him; those emotions intensified.

I'll leave you a world of happiness – whatever it takes.

* * *

"Are you sure?" Worry filled his mother's voice. "You don't have to push yourself. I want you completely well first."

"I am, mom." Hugging her...his mom's body felt weak and frail. But the Prince knew better. Like Rutoric, she was an actual Fighter and had beaten both of them on more than one occasion. But...even next to him she was tiny. Protecting her was all he could think about. "I love you, but I'll grow complacent if I stay."

"It's ok, I'll beat that out of you later." A delicate smile enhanced her worry. "Are you sure you're ok? You haven't been yourself..."

His hands moved with his mouth. "I've already fallen behind. Catching up in your thirteenth year is difficult."

"You've always excelled; you've nothing to worry about."

"Maybe–"

A knock interrupted them. Both bowed when the General walked in.

"Tenalia, I apologize. I thought you were arriving later," the Queen straightened.

"No need, Am'ria. A meeting was canceled. I apologize, but I need to brief my heir." Looking from mother to child, the General added, "Was I interrupting anything?"

"No." A sad smile stretched Am'ria's lips. "Only my failed attempts at getting him to stay longer."

Turning to the Prince, Tenalia raised an eyebrow. "You turned your mother down?"

"Yes, ma'am."

"Good. You understand your place."

"Yes, ma'am."

Apologetically, Tenalia turned to the Queen. "Mind if I steal your son?"

"Of course not, sister." Giving the General a hug, Am'ria left her son's room, closing the door behind her.

"How may I help you, General?" Zephyr tapped his sternum and extended his hand to his aunt.

"Sadly, this is a family matter." Tenalia made her way to the sofa.

Zephyr sat next to her. "What's on your mind, Aunt Tenalia?"

"You missed a lot." The events of the Family Week celebration rolled off Tenalia's tongue. "Those burns were gruesome, but that's not what concerns me."

That selfish child? Impossible. Zephyr's fists clenched and wouldn't move. Tenalia said she saw it happen, but he couldn't believe it. "What concerns you?"

"He's covered in scars." She watched Zephyr closely for a reaction. "You didn't know?"

The Prince's hands answered along with his tongue. "I haven't seen his skin. He doesn't swim and always wears multiple layers. But he's clumsy, so I'm not surprised."

"Those weren't self-inflicted. And some were fresh."

"Really?" the Prince sat back. Keeping the selfish boy in line was the bane of Zephyr's existence, but the Athlete never left a mark. Was Ferdinan making people mad enough to attack him? But he usually stayed hidden in his lab...

"What's happening at school?" Tenalia pressed.

"Nothing that I know of," Zephyr shrugged – pinky waving side to side. "He's unsocial and keeps to himself..."

"Hear me. I want this to stop."

"Yes, ma'am." *I'm not even back and he's causing me trouble.* "I'll look into it."

19

* * *

"Xhou?"

Already? Xhou turned and faced his guest. Jon looked nervous – as if facing the unknown. "Ah! Jon! Have a seat."

Doing as he was told, the growing giant sat across from the Science Lead. "How're you doing?"

"I'm fine." A yawn seized him. "Little tired, but fine."

"Bottling everything up isn't good."

"Do I seem like that kind?"

"Ya." Leaning forward, Jon locked onto Xhou's blue-black eyes. "Not mourning. Not allowing yourself to feel – that's why Ferdinan's the way he is."

A flame of resentment scorched across Xhou's chest, but he kept it off his face. *Ferdinan did nothing wrong.* But his heart blamed the Tinkerer. It was illogical. Impossible. But...Ferdinan shouldn't have left Rura behind! To become like...like *that...* Her burned remains filled his mind. *He couldn't have known she was there.* Even if he did, she died instantly. But... Ferdinan did impossible things – had done so since Xhou met him. Why not pull off the impossible for Rura? "As much as I respect your ally, we're nothing alike."

"You're wrong," Jon argued. "You're both more capable than you let anyone see – care more for others than you let them know. Neither of you will burden others with your needs."

"You're as sweet as Elbie." A light laugh escaped Xhou. "I'm doing what I need to. I'll fail as Nu if I turn out like him."

"Ok..." Jon frowned, but moved on. "Please tell me this 'super important' thing we need to talk about isn't Ferdinan."

Xhou laughed – a friendly smile blossoming into existence. "No. The end of this block, you'll have had your lab for a year and a half. Normally we do this after a year, but last block..."

"Don't remind me."

"You don't know what I'm talking about."

Jon shook his head. "Not really."

"*Heh*! Have I ever told you how much I love you, Jon?" Xhou chuckled. "I wish we got more Oueshians. You earned your lab a year ago. Time to take on an apprentice."

"What?"

I thought so. He was only worried about catching up to Ferdinan. "You saw that oven and stopped there, didn't you?"

"No! ...yes..." Jon shrugged. "No one's approached me to take them on."

"That's not how it works," Xhou winked. "Since things weren't set up last block, you'll be assigned an incoming Thinker next academic year. But substituting for other mentors is great practice. Regardless, there's paperwork."

"I don't think-" A chime from the mounted screen interrupted Jon.

"You're great with people. I know at least a dozen students who've praised your teaching skills in the kitchen. Mentoring a first year isn't that different. As you know, you'll work with them for two years..."

Jon's eyes jumped between Xhou and the screen.

"The message can wait." *Sorry, Jon, you aren't getting out of this. I'm already short a mentor.*

"True..." Jon hesitated. "I know I should offer my services, but..."

"But what? It's not hard. I've even done so for Elbie and he's a Tinkerer."

"I have different priorities. My family and the school insist those come first..." Jon trailed off, chocolate brown eyes impossibly distant.

"Ferdinan? How do you feel about that?" Just saying the Tinkerer's name! Xhou's chest burned. Rura's charred remains... Endless condolences... *Children shouldn't die...* But she did...and millions more a few months before her... So much death... Xhou breathed out slowly - fighting thoughts he didn't want.

Annoyance, frustration, and other emotions overwhelmed Jon and he didn't bother hiding it. "It doesn't matter. It needs to be done. And honestly...I can't stand seeing him like this."

Really....? But Jon looked surprised by that last statement too. Patiently, Xhou waited for the younger Thinker to process his thoughts and feelings.

"Between Ferdinan and classes...I don't have time or energy for another task. I can't believe you're doing so much... I apologize." Jon stood to leave. "You should get that; I know your plate's full. And I should get to class."

"Sit," Xhou commanded. "I'll check it if it'll help you focus on this meeting. But classes don't start for twenty minutes, so I have you for fifteen more."

A timid nod signaled Jon's surrender.

The sender was completely unexpected. *Prince Zephyr?* Xhou knew of the boy, but they rarely interacted. "Hmmm..."

"What?"

"Prince Zephyr messaged me..."

"What does he want?" Hearing his ally's name sparked Jon's curiosity.

"He's asking about the fire. Wants me to confirm what happened." Xhou's face scrunched a little as he pushed his sister's remains from his mind again. "He's having difficulty believing his cousin saved those two."

"Two?"

Xhou looked up and studied his perplexed charge. "You stood by me when he leapt out the window with Elbie and Yuyu."

"He leapt out with Yuyu. Oya had Elbie."

Oya? She was on my other side. "You've really rewritten that in your mind. Oya ran up with you and your brothers, remember?"

Confusion blanketed Jon, but he nodded. Concern radiated from him.

Chapter 4

Herrard should've been studying Healer Bær's notes, but it hurt seeing the same thing every morning. And living it... Every day he arrived at Isolation and changed out the Second Skin and powdered ointment Lord Ferdinan supplied. Then the Superintendent arrived. The man searched for Yuyu. Insisted her voice was there...but still couldn't communicate with her. It didn't matter how much her body healed if her mind was lost to brain damage.

If Herrard could heal it... Searching a mind was one thing, but manipulating the brain - the actual organ - was more than immoral. It was horrific. But hoping it'd heal on its own... The likelihood of this broke his heart. But statistics didn't matter. The number of people waiting for Yuyu to wake up extended beyond the islands. She was important to many people. The least being his suitemate.

Waves lapped gently at the transport. Xhou... *How much is he hurting?* First his family and country, then his future, his little sister...and now, waiting, not knowing if Yuyu would join them.

Herrard fought the urge to cry. It felt like years since he had a break. Being Kalj...he'd never really have one. But he'd worked non-stop since the plague hit. Healing the youngest students daily to stay ahead of the damage exhausted him. Then the cure... There was only the leftover internal damage... Then the miraculous treatment came... It was amazing. Finally the Healer could breathe.

That treatment - the hope it provided - energized him through the break, the countless lessons and decisions, and training for his position. *Returning to school was supposed to be my vacation...*

Tears welled up. Herrard buried his face in his hands - refusing to lower them until he regained composure. As lead student Healer, he assisted Healer Bær regularly. He cared for Elbie's hands and lungs while Bær tended to Yuyu...initially.

Now the Head Healer tended to Yuyu in the evening, and Herrard after morning training. Nutrients were pumped into her afternoons and nights so they could heal her. Exhaustion breathed out of the Healer. Light brown eyes took in the purple dawn. The sun wasn't up yet...but he wasn't sleeping. He tried. But the weight of so many responsibilities. Adding in Xhou... *I'm so tired...*

Tears welled up again and he pressed a hand to his forehead as if it'd hide him from reality. *At least Yuyu's progressing faster than expected...somehow...* But was this a good thing?

Sitting down on the deck, the Kalj rested his head in his hands and refused to look at anything until the transport docked.

Thanking the teacher, he disembarked – keeping his eyes trained on Isolation. All his years combined didn't equal the hours he spent here the last few months. If this kept up until he graduated...

Herrard shook that thought from his mind and entered. After a quick greeting to Healer Lee, he headed to Yuyu's room – grabbing a modified laser and a container of white powder on the way. He couldn't start until Nammie arrived, but setting things up was better than pacing his room. If he hadn't seen it with his own eyes, the Healer would've never believed the powdery substance could heal anything. *Lord Ferdinan creates the strangest miracles...*

Opening the door...

Yuyu's unconscious body was expected. But that strange girl with inhuman eyes and unnatural hair... *What's her name again...? Why didn't Lee tell me...* Herrard froze. Yuyu wasn't allowed visitors yet. So how had...? *Oya...that's right...Xhou said she doesn't like titles and she can be pretty mean. And Ilu...* The boy mostly teared up at the mention of her. *But...how did she get in here?*

The strange girl sat on the bed – eyes closed and one hand on Yuyu's forehead. It didn't look like Oya was doing anything.

Still, that didn't mean she was allowed in here. Putting the materials down, he tapped her shoulder. When she didn't respond, he shook her gently. *How is she sleeping like this?*

Eventually Oya blinked and looked around. Surprise filled impossible green eyes. Then that surprise deepened. The Healer could almost see her mind search for a course of action.

"I'm sorry, but you can't be here. Yuyu isn't allowed visitors."

A wild grin curled shapely lips. "I wasn't visiting."

"Then what were you doing?"

Those eyes stared hard at him before glowing with a strange light... "You're not the only one invested in her recovery."

24

"But I'm responsible for it." Her words were irritating, but Herrard smiled gently. Being tired and frustrated didn't give him the right to lash out at a callous comment. Especially one she didn't mean anything rude by. "I'm sorry, Oya, but you need to leave."

"And if I'm not visiting?"

It took everything he had not to yell...or whimper – whichever would've left him. "Even if you were a Healer, you don't have the training or knowledge to help someone in her condition."

Oya snorted – a sneer marring her face.

"Please." He covered his eyes again. He didn't know if he wanted to cry, hit her, or was fighting back a headache. He didn't know anything. He just wanted everything to freeze. Just for a moment. Just long enough for a breath. A break. Anything.

"I can't imagine your frustration. Born able to care for simple wounds and illnesses before you realized it was special. Now facing one who won't recover without your help – or maybe even with it."

Her sincerity surprised him. Tears Herrard fought against for an eternity hit hard and fast. All he could do was crouch down and hide behind his hands. *Why...?* Showing this kind of weakness wasn't acceptable for a Kalj. But he couldn't stop. And he didn't want to. He wanted to cry until he passed out. He wanted it all to stop...

Delicate hands took his. The craze and amusement from before had vanished from those impossible green eyes. There was no grin. No whimsy in her face. This was an entirely different girl.

"Not everything can be fixed, healer." Oya looked at Yuyu. "But there's still merit in trying."

She reached for his head but stopped – considering something. A sigh left her, and she took his hands once again, pulling Herrard up with her. Standing, he found himself towering over her by a head.

"Frustration. Sorrow. Fear. Helplessness. Hopelessness..." Oya placed a hand on his heart. "How do you keep them from winning?"

His jaw trembled and his throat tightened. The tears hadn't stopped while Oya spoke, and now they came faster. "I don't know. I don't know how to help her. I don't know if she'll wake up. I don't know if any of this matters or if I'm only delaying the inevitable! If I'm making this harder for everyone who loves her!"

Why was he saying all this? He needed to stop. This wasn't something he should say to anyone – for so many reasons. But his tongue kept going until he said what haunted him.

"Her body's healing too fast! Too fast for us to make sure she'll enjoy a full life. Her hands...! She's a Tinkerer. She needs her hands. They have to heal right or she'll lose the dexterity she needs. And her brain...her brain...nothing's changed! There should be something... She should be trying to wake up... She should be trying, even if we can't let her." *Stop talking...* "Even if I heal her hands perfectly, she won't wake up... I need her to wake up..."

"It's so mysterious, the land of tears." The delicate hand on his heart moved behind his back as she pulled him into a hug. He had no idea how long he stood there crying. There was little relief from Oya's ice-cold hands. Her whole body was colder than it should be. If anything, she was soaking in *his* warmth. Yet...this comfort...

When was the last time someone held him? Let him be the scared boy he was inside? Would he ever get this again? *Please don't stop. Please don't stop...*

* * *

Securing his lab door, Ferdinan headed toward the advanced sciences classrooms – the only classes he was required to attend. At the building's entrance, he stopped and breathed in deep. Time to turn off the music. If the voice proved too much, he'd turn it on again. But...he needed to try. Constantly listening to music for the rest of his life wasn't an option. If he could make it through a class, he'd build up his tolerance from there...maybe... Tapping the earpiece ended the dancing metallic notes.

His gaze drifted to a window down the hall. On the other side was a courtyard and students relaxing in the sun. Tensing, he closed his eyes and waited for a particularly bitter memory to end.

"Master Ferdinan?"

"Huh?" Looking down, Ferdinan saw his pupil leaning against the wall. "Elbie? Shouldn't you be in class?"

How are you going to hurt him, I wonder?

"*Ugh*...no..." A pale, shaky Elbie moved forward. "I'm going back to my room. I don't feel well."

"I'm sorry. Don't worry about today's session. Just let me know when you're better."

"Thank you..." Elbie nodded pathetically. Pulling a screen from his bag, the boy offered it to Ferdinan. "I'm not contagious...Veccidi made breakfast and it...didn't taste right. Here're the blueprints for...the Inductor. I highlighted all the errors...and drew it correctly."

"I'm sorry." A grimace took over Ferdinan's face at his pupil's obvious discomfort. Food poisoning was one of the few things a Healer couldn't do much about. *His hands look like they were never damaged... Yuyu...will she be the same? Why won't they tell me anything?* "I'll look this over. When you're better, we'll discuss it."

"Thank you, sir." Elbie moaned and wrapped his arms around his stomach.

"I'll take you to the dorms."

"Thank you, but...they've already sent the transport." Awkward silence fell while Elbie caught his breath and straightened – mostly. "Um...Master Ferdinan?"

"Yes?" Ferdinan knelt – putting them at eye level.

"Thank you for saving me. I thought I was going to die..." Elbie paled further and stared at his hands. "You've always done everything you could for me. Now you've saved my life. Thank you...thank you..."

Such an innocent expression...it turned Ferdinan bright red. "If not for Oya, I wouldn't have known. I'm relieved you're safe."

You? A hero? Ha!

"No! It was amazing! You found us and got us out! But..." Elbie rubbed his belly – unhappy at his sudden outburst.

"But?" Ferdinan paled at his student's agony.

"You saved us." Elbie swallowed hard – eyes filling with tears. "Xhou understands Rura couldn't be. Please don't blame yourself."

"Uh?" *Rura? Xhou's sister?*

"She died instantly..."

Numbness set in. The world stopped spinning. *Rura...? Was in the building...?*

Grating laughter filled a blurred reality. Scenery changed. Eyes stared. Air grew warm then cold. Ferdinan didn't notice he was sitting. Or the screen in front of him.

You abandoned her.

She was there...? There was another person? How did I not see her...? Time slowed, warping the sounds around him.

Enjoying the peace, murderer?

Leave me alone!

Millions weren't enough? You had to add more?

No! No one died in that fire!

You left a little girl behind. She burned to ash.

No! I didn't know –

Was there enough left to bury?

Stop! It's not true! ...it can't be true...

You experimented on Xhou's uncle 'til death.

No! Stop!

You stood by while his family died.

No! Stop it! Shut up!!

You left his sister to burn.

"STOP IT! SHUT UP!!" Ferdinan screamed. His slight weight swayed on unsteady feet. Boney fists clenched...

In the middle of the classroom.

Incompetent child. Can't keep a private conversation to yourself.

Blue crystals widened. Everyone was staring at him – faces twisted. Silence deafened the room.

Because of him.

All this sunk in, turning Ferdinan bright red.

Everything blurred as he ran.

Chapter 5

Everyone was breaking. Or already broken. Flying – beautiful carved case in hand – Oya considered how to help Herrard. The young man wasn't the only Healer treating Yuyu. But he was key. Bær might be the main Healer on the islands, but the other students looked to Herrard. *If he breaks, how will that effect Yuyu? And my friend...? But...do I have to worry about him...? Fixing the holes will alleviate the burden crushing him.*

Ultimately, accomplishing this one thing will help dozens and let Oya return to her other tasks. If only she prevented the explosion...

Regrets weren't helpful, so Oya pushed them from her mind. She'd keep studying brains and figure out how to fix that hole. But Zephyr would return soon. *I have to finish this before he gets back.* It didn't make sense, but that didn't matter. People didn't make sense. All she could do was prevent and fix as much damage as possible.

Tripping the latch on his closet window, she slipped inside. Invisible as a ninja, Oya skipped in – violin case held secure. And stopped cold. *What happened?* Ferdinan sat; head buried in stick-thin arms. The hole in his chest had eaten through and blood seeped down his back. *How do I fix this...?*

"*Not feeling well?*" She asked in her native Oŭndo. His shoulders tensed, but eventually eased. "*Do I need to get Jon?*"

"*No...*"

She slid the ornately carved box – bumping gently against his arm. "*Play for me! I miss your amazing music!*"

A boney hand swatted at something near his ear. "*I'm sorry, Oya. I'm tired. Can you please leave me alone today?*"

"*Play for me tomorrow?*" *What did I miss while with Herrard?*

"*I don't know...*" His deepening voice shook. "*Did you know?*"

Blood oozed down his back faster. The infection spread to the new opening. She didn't have to delve into his mind, it was there on the surface. He knew. He finally heard. *I wasn't there to prevent it.* "*When you lifted the beam, I saw her. She was under Yuyu–*"

Ferdinan looked up at her – face hard, fists clenched. *"Why didn't you tell me?! I would've held it longer!"*

Oya planted her bare feet. *"She was already gone."*

"I don't believe that! That can't be right! I should've gotten her!!"

"How?" Taking his arm, she embraced him. He struggled in vain until she eased him to sleep. *Tell me what happened.*

Playing with memories was easy. Opportunities to practice were plentiful here. From class to Ilu to removing herself from the fire incident...at least for those she reached in time – it'd served her well. And would again now. *I'll take it away and you'll be better.*

Reaching into his mind... All the wonder and bright bustle from before was gone. *What happened here?* Worlds weren't spinning. Thoughts and ideas stopped moving. Two dark orbs stood supreme in what was once a galactic theme park. Unified by a single thought.

"I killed her."

Cold tickled Oya's spine. But she took the first orb anyway.

"She died instantly..." Elbie's voice whispered into the eternity.

"I killed her!"

"She died instantly..."

"I killed her!!"

I won't let this spiral. She dug her nails deep into the orb. But it wouldn't break. She directed all her will into its destruction. But it held firm – growing louder! Agitating the wonder of his beaten mind. *I won't let you destroy my friend.* Oya dug deeper in and pulled. All her soul, will, and force of thought grabbed hold – securing her grip.

Resistance gave way to tearing and she flew back. *One more!*

Leaping forward, she did the same thing. Only this time it was her own voice battling with those three words. There wasn't time for this memory to form. But it had. And it was as resistant as the first.

"She was already gone." Again, she pulled with all her might.

"I killed her!" cried more furious with each tug.

Then the tear came. And with it – silence.

Panting, Oya sat staring at the two battered orbs she'd ripped from her friend's existence. She'd never tried manipulating his memories before. *Why was this so hard? How different is his brain? Is this why I don't understand Yuyu's?* The girl's was nothing like the other children she'd studied, and Elbie's brain was too distressed... She laughed. Ferdinan was always in distress.

"You think that's enough to make me forget?"

Stunned, Oya sat – completely caught off guard. That voice was Ferdinan's – but corrupted. "Who shares my friend's mind?"

A shadow materialized, sharpening into what could've been Jon, save the longer hair and crystal blue eyes. "How can I share with myself?"

This is what he'd look like if he were healthy...? "I can't call you 'Ferdinan.' You aren't him. Not truly."

Long fingers reached out and beckoned the mangled orbs to him. "As expected from one who can invade this mind. What should you call me?"

"'Eritic' would be appropriate." Slowly, Oya circled – Ferdinan's doppelganger mimicking her. *I need to get those back...*

"'Eritic'... 'Eritic'..." Another snap and the orbs vanished, "Ah, how clever. But I'm no more an imposter than the Ferdinan you know."

"I haven't seen you here before. When did you arrive?"

"I've been here for a while. Though, you're the first I've talked to directly."

"Ha!"

Her laugh startled him. "Excuse me?"

"The twitching and mumbling. He's conversing with you."

"Failing to ignore me." His grin was so warped it made Oya shutter.

"Why would he do that?" *He feels starved for attention, but too cautious to act on it.* How did Oya use that to her advantage?

"We both know truths he doesn't want to face."

"I'm good at making people face things." Her own sly grin twitched as memories of a past life danced in her head.

"Hmmm... Your offer's tempting. But I'd rather he confesses it." Raising a hand to his waist, he bowed formally then straightened with a smile.

31

"I think I have the perfect name. Please call me 'Emil.' Now, if you'll excuse me. I have things to attend to."

~

Oya stood in her friend's lab, inches from him. Dazed crystals rolled back in his head but she caught him before he hit the ground and carried the growing boy to the overstuffed sac in his closet.

He shut me out of his mind. But how...? What've you kept from me, dear friend? Unsure, Oya covered him with a blanket.

Those dark clouds were replaced by something new. Putting a hand on his head, she found herself up against black diamond – hard, unforgiving, impenetrable. *Interesting...*

She couldn't even access the latus of his brain. *Now what...?* If he found out, Jon would be coming soon. *I failed them both. I just have to be better.* Outside the sun was bright and inviting. There she waited for the growing giant to come running up the hill.

* * *

Perfect. Wonderous. Peaceful. The palace gardens' beauty after Zephyr's imprisonment was even more stunning. Sleeping in the orchard again...he'd get in trouble. But it'd be worth it.

Training and tutoring were finished. Now to do as he pleased.

A shady spot lured the Prince. Sitting, he enjoyed a fruit pilfered from the kitchen. Flesh gave way to the juicy meat. Tart overwhelmed the light sweetness of the unripe fruit. Exactly as he preferred it. Birds sang all around him. Fluffy white clouds softened the sharp blue sky.

This is nice... Warm air teased with the sweet scent of spring flowers. And his eyelids grew heavy. The hand holding his half-eaten plum slid down, resting on his lap. *I wonder...*

Pain shot from his ankle to his hip. Then a gasp and *thud.*

Rolling to his feet, Zephyr surveyed the situation – only to be embarrassed by how startled he was. A servant tripped over him and was scrambling to gather scattered squash. *Sorry for sleeping where I oughtn't...* Smiling, the Prince helped her gather the fallen goods.

"I apologize. I should've found a better place to nap." Putting a squash into the basket made her flinch. *Why's she trembling?* "Are you alright?"

Terrified eyes darted around as she backed away.

"It's ok, they're fine." Kneeling next to her - their eyes met.

Cold sweat broke out across Zephyr's golden skin.

No.

Not here.

Not in the safety of his gardens. Why was he seeing this here?! Her eyes were light brown with green flecks...but they looked exactly like Ferdinan's. *First him, then me... Now a complete stranger? What's going on?* Jumping up, he stepped back. "Who are you?!"

Trembling, the girl shrank away behind a tree.

"Who are you? Why do you look like that!?" *I'm not making any sense. I'm scaring her. But...* Red-hot fire burned inside him. "Why!? I don't need more selfish people! I don't want-"

A boulder smashed into the Prince's face - knocking him down. By the time his vision cleared, Rutoric was kneeling by the servant girl. Red marred her cheek and she cowered from the man. *What?*

Dark eyes glared at him then glanced over to the palace.

Attempting to speak was a mistake. *What's going on? Why did he attack me?* Zephyr tapped the side of his mouth before pointing at the Captain with a pinky. Rutoric repeated the gesture.

Protesting, Zephyr did as he was told. Each step was jarring, but he moved swiftly - not stopping until he was safe behind his locked door. The comfortable couch did little to ease Zephyr's fuming.

And his mind kept returning to those eyes. Blue, black, brown, they were all the same! They multiplied. Closing in. Hundreds. Thousands of selfish eyes glared from every direction! *No! Stop!*

Impossibly strong hands grabbed him. The thousands crushing him vanished...but Rutoric's expression... It was somewhere between furious and disappointed. *Why are you looking at me like that?*

The Captain's hand framed his jaw, moved forward and stopped palm up. And that expression didn't waver. It burrowed deep.

Zephyr's knuckles rapped together. "It hurts. Why hit me?"

Surprise caused Rutoric to hesitate before his hands moved.

"What are you talking about?"

Forceful expressions emphasized Rutoric's gestures.

"I know my responsibilities and my authority! But you haven't answered my question: What are you talking about?"

Rutoric grabbed his shirt – one hand gesturing sharply.

Shocked. Frozen. Zephyr fought for words. "What...?"

Releasing him, the Captain combed a hand through nonexistent shoulder length hair, slammed a fist into his palm, and pointed.

White hot scored the Prince's skin. "I've never struck a servant!"

More passion filled Rutoric's gestures.

Those words – that accusation – filled Zephyr with rage. His hands flew. "She tripped! I helped her pick up what she'd dropped! If you saw her fall, you'd have seen me help her! Not...! I'm not...!"

Fury quickened the Prince's breath. Rutoric matched his intensity. Every gesture, expression, were painfully sharp and impossible to ignore.

"I helped her! Even when all she did was cower. Even when she's selfish. I didn't hurt her!" Ice filled boiling veins. Lowering his head and hands, Zephyr confessed, "I...I yelled at her... That was wrong."

The sudden change in the Prince's demeanor surprised Rutoric. When his hands moved next, they were calm, but still firm.

Eyes down, Zephyr confessed. "I can't take more selfishness..."

* * *

"I'm sorry, Oya, I can't play right now." Being so rude to a girl... But... Screaming in class... *I've never been so terrified...* "I'm sorry."

"Don't worry about it."

"You don't know what happened!" Jon yelled.

"He found out." Her delicate hand squeezed his shoulder. "I've taken care of it."

"How?" Jon shook his head. "You can't fix that so quickly."

"*I took care of it.*" Those crazed green eyes winked at him. "Don't mention Rura and he'll be fine."

Chapter 6

The elf walked along the twilight beach like always, but her question was different this time. "Are you ready?"

"What?" The dream felt different – alive and vivid...real...

A grin spread under sapphire eyes as the elf repeated herself.

"I am." Zephyr clenched his fist at his shoulder.

"And when you see your cousin?"

I don't want to think about that. Still...those blue crystals floated before him, taunting him, egging him. He tapped his forehead, dropped his palm to face it, and shook his head. "I don't know."

"What is it?" The elf's stance screamed for him to hurry.

His hands hesitated. "My aunt told me some things."

"These things?" The elf smirked. All around them played the conversation about Family Week. "You don't believe her."

"My aunt wouldn't lie to me."

"But you can't believe your cousin would help anyone."

Golden hands flew. "He only thinks about himself."

"If she wouldn't lie, then he must be covered in scars."

"I know."

"You said you hadn't seen them." The elf stood taller.

"I haven't." He faced her genuine confusion.

"Do you know who caused them?"

Silently, he shook his head.

"You truly don't?"

"No, ma'am."

Stepping forward, she bore down. "But you've beaten him."

His hands moved more honestly than his voice could portray. "I've never scarred him. Or beat him so badly he went to a Healer."

"But you've beaten him badly enough to *need* one."

Opening his mouth to dispute the accusation, Zephyr found his tongue unable to move...until he admitted the truth. "Yes."

"You need to stop. Ferdinan aside – you'll destroy yourself."

"I don't understand." A golden finger tapped his temple.

"What kind of leader do you want to become? One who can't help a hurting child?"

"*Hurting?* He isn't hurt." Golden knuckles wrapped against each other before his hands opened and flew apart.

"Deeply." A sigh escaped her as her face fell.

Where's she getting this? But dreams are just nonsense...

"This isn't a nonsensical dream. It's not a dream at all."

A shiver ran up his spine at having his mind read. "What is it?"

"A vision. And in this vision, I'm warning you: hurt Ferdinan again and I'll kill you."

His heart jumped. She was a dream...but that threat was real.

"If you can't stop on your own, I'm willing to help you."

What...? "Why?"

The elf sighed. "'Cause he feels your life is necessary."

* * *

This isn't happening. Two months ago, they were told to vacate the village but... They thought if they stayed – took a stand and didn't budge – the Duchess's decree would turn to naught.

Now they watched their homes be demolished. Nothing stopped the machines...the felling of lives and memories... Nothing.

Like that. The Duchess stole everything.

A bus to the city was her only offer. And they couldn't refuse.

Looking at the crying infant in his arms, he bounced her for comfort. His three-year-old son held his other hand. The child, too, was crying. Crying for the loss of his room and the few memories of his mother tied to that house – that pile of splinters.

A farmer doesn't belong in the city. But there was more than himself to worry about. His eyes warmed and he looked to the sky. Everything was perfect last year. The farm thrived. They expanded their house. And they were to have twins!

Then that message came. Illness took his oldest daughter. Complications of child birth stole his wife. Then one of the twins.

He was strong. Did as much work as those with machines in the same amount of time with mules. He provided for his family. Always.

Then the Duchess took too much. A large, well-muscled body... Strong, calloused hands... They were as useless as that pile of sticks.

Tears fell as the shock eased. Sobs racked his body. Sinking down, he held his son. Apologizing. Apologizing. Apologizing. He'd die and reunite with his wife and two daughters... But there were two needing him here and now...and for a long time yet. Two to live for.

I don't know what to do, he prayed to his wife, *but I'll help them grow strong. I'll give them a good life...a happy life...so I can face you, my love. Watch over us. Watch our children grow.*

He wept – children in his arms. Minutes stretched on. Shadows shortened then lengthened again. Light ebbed away... By the time shiny shoes stopped before him, his tears had dried. And his children slept. All he had to do was look up to see the owner of those fancy shoes...the man cramming them into buses.

"Mr. Ploumount, I presume?"

Red, dejected eyes drifted up. The man wasn't what Ploumount expected. Too skinny. Barely out of childhood. *A scarcely twenty villager stuffed in fancy clothes... What did he do to deserve that?*

"Mr. Ploumount, I hear you're an excellent farmer."

Looking back down, he considered a response. "I'm not the best. But I know how to work hard."

"Any experience with minilivestock?"

"Yes, sir."

"Looking at me... I know I'm young..." the young man started. "But I'm good with people and planning. So they gave me a choice: be placed in a city job or this. I'm fed and clothed and always have a place to sleep. My family receives extra... Overall, it's better than–"

"What's your point, son?" This speech was too long, and his children would be hungry when they woke up.

"These lands will be converted for mass food production. A few hardworking people are needed to run machines and incubators." The young man shifted uneasily. "There are additional benefits plus the standard rights. Riio is providing childcare."

The man looked down at his sleeping children. Farming didn't exist in the city. And mass production... It fed the world but it wasn't farming... But he trusted Riio with his children. That was something.

Is this the closest to our dream I'll find...?

* * *

Ugh... Boney fingers physically forced blue crystals open. *My closet? When did I get here?* Every muscle ached – begging to move.

How long have I...? Pushing to unsteady feet, Ferdinan forced them to move. *Oya wanted me to play for her...* Red-hot coals filled the pit of his stomach. Tainted iron ate holes in him. *What is this?*

The heat in his gut moved to his face. *I screamed at the voice...in the middle of class...* Paling... Of all the horrible things he'd done...

Jon's voice called through the closet door. *Why can't I die? How much longer 'til they figure out I'm broken?*

How much longer, indeed?

Daggers tore through his heart. *Why does it sound stronger?*

"Ferdinan?"

Stumbling out, the skeleton leaned against the nearest counter. He felt gouged out. Shredded. Incomplete...

"Are you ok?" Jon approached cautiously.

Grating laughter blared in Ferdinan's ears and he pressed against a wall. He needed to escape. That voice screamed inside his head. *Stop! Leave me alone! Leave me alone!! Leave me alone!!!*

"Ferdinan?"

"Leave me alone!" Stinging needles bore through his shoulder. Ferdinan pushed his assailant back. "Don't touch me!"

A table stopped Jon's fall – twisting his face. "What's wrong?"

You can't resist hurting people.

Ferdinan cringed. "I'm tired... I can't... I'm tired."

Pale and shaky, Jon straitened. "Ferdinan...?"

"Please stop."

"Ferdinan, no one cares."

"*No one cares*" echoed inside him, delighting the voice.

No one cares about you. How could they?

"There's no reason to be this embarrassed. Just relax."

Focus! Please... But...he couldn't – couldn't deal with this right now... Sliding over to the window, he looked out. "Please stop."

"What's wrong?"

"Please...stop..." Ferdinan pleaded.

* * *

Screaming drums wailed in Xhou's ear. Tears streamed down his face. The picture of his dearly loved sister smiled at him.

This night was his vigil for her.

Morning sun stung swollen eyes. Night ended though the song hadn't. But that didn't matter. *I'm useless like this...but no more.*

Turning off the earpiece, Xhou placed it on the table and left the room. He returned with metal sheets and tools to work them.

Building with his hands was foreign. But...if he couldn't do this, how would he rebuild his shattered country?

Dumping everything on the table, Xhou grabbed the hammer and raised it. Every dark thought. Every pain. Every jot of anger was focused on the earpiece. Ferdinan's music consoled him. But... *My last night of weakness is over. Now I become the Nu.*

Dawn ushered in the first day of his twentieth year. He was old enough to step onto the Nu's throne – if needed. A block and a half. A block and a half to become the man his country needed.

Glaring at the earpiece, he waited for his heart to let go of the anger, the fear. Only then... Only when calm set in... The *crunch* was soft – almost inaudible next to the *slam* of metal on metal.

The hammer joined the other tools. Crushed plastic and dust were brushed into a waste basket. A few taps on the screen deleted the music from his devices.

Now for the most important task.

Xhou's blank face betrayed nothing. Not his passions. His sorrows. His nightmares.

Metallic pounding echoed through the building. It was a sound that shouldn't come from a Thinker's lab.

Grunts of frustration joined the pounding – and at times the bashing of sheet metal against a table.

The sun rose, hung high overhead, then laid back down to sleep. But...but before the stars appeared – before his first day as a man ended – he finished.

The metal box was dented and warped. Edges didn't line up. Skewed walls... And the lid didn't fit. But his bruised and blistered hands made it.

Artisans would be ashamed claiming such a defective piece. Any Tinkerer would melt it down to reuse. But the malformed box gave Xhou a spark of pride. It wasn't perfect, but *he* made it. Neither had he given up – overcome with defeat at the impossible. And if he did it once, he'd do it again.

And next time...

Next time would be better.

I'll keep improving 'til I make a box you'd love.

It might be simple. Even useless. But knowing his hands could build...

Now to build himself into the Nu his country deserved.

Picking up Rura's picture, he put it in the box and placed the lid. It didn't stop the memory of her charred remains. But that was ok. "It's not any good right now, Rura. But I'll keep trying."

I gave my last night of weakness.

Now it's time to be strong.

Chapter 7

If only I could recreate the missing pieces... But each attempt failed. Holding the repaired end in one hand, Oya searched the net. *Where do you connect to?* Collecting that woman's connections was draining. But it didn't compare to this. Putting together a hundred-billion-piece puzzle without a picture and a billion missing pieces...

Giving up wasn't an option. Neither could anyone help her. And if she did it wrong, it could end up worse than if she'd done nothing.

The information flooding her mind was overwhelming. Yuyu was nearly half her age, but the girl's brain held so much knowledge she'd never understand. *Don't focus on the information. Just the next step. This strand is A-1, so where is A-2? Where is the break...?*

...or is that part missing?

* * *

Grating music didn't stop the voice anymore. No matter how loud! It failed! *Shut up! Please! Please leave me alone!*

Warmth washed over him – pulling him back to the screen filled with the cube's contents. The voice laughed and mocked and told all the truths he couldn't bear. But...the screen...

Every time his eyes drifted. Every time he was about to scream. That warmth pulled him back. *I have to get rid of that voice!*

But how? Aimlessly, he scrolled. His muscles screamed to move. Abused ears rang from loud music. The unwrapped bar crinkled in his boney hand. *I want to die. I want this all to be over...*

Once again, warmth filled his chest and pulled him back. Three articles sat at the top of the screen. *Medicine...?* The universe fell away. *Medicine can fix a broken mind? Why was this destroyed? Why are they different?* The articles didn't cover production, but there was enough information... *Can I recreate these?*

But why? Why destroy it? How many hundreds of years were wasted in the field of medicine by the Council? That vile group was a black mark on history the world still adhered to. *I could've been stopped... I would've never become a murderer...*

But you weren't.

Shut up!!

I'll never leave you.

Yes, you will.

* * *

Small hands worked diligently until the instructor spoke. Stopping made Elbie cringe. Two minutes and he'd have finished.

Looking up, the young Tinkerer smiled at Master Nii-em. It was time for the riddle. Not getting to finish was annoying, but this was the fun part of class. Two dozen words waltzed off the woman's tongue. Each of them a different language. Giggles and moans filled the room, but they went to work decoding. First was figuring out the words, then came putting them in the right order to translate into something coherent. *Amazing how different languages work...*

Souls...the...magnificent... Elbie paused. The next word was used in different languages and had different meanings. *Son, fire, tree, or shirt...?* Until he translated the rest, he couldn't rule out any, so he wrote each option down. Or he tried.

Son. Fire. Fire. Fire... *Why is breathing so difficult?*

Elbie shook his head and swallowed his pounding heart. *Focus.* Tree. Fire... There was no explosion, but his ears rang. *Focus.* There was no explosion... But his insides shook. His skin crawled.

"Lord Elbarrat?"

Master Nii-em's soft voice banished the sensations. *Why am I panting...?* And he was covering his face. Not to hide. To protect it. Like when the lab exploded... *What was that...?*

Slowly, he lowered his hands and nodded. Herrard healed them wonderfully. They looked fine. Even if the student Healer wouldn't let him do more than write...and only for schoolwork. *My hands...*

There was no scarring. The nails were grown in. They looked normal. But they burned – stung. It hurt to move them. It hurt. But he had to keep digging.

"Lord Elbarrat?" Master Nii-em spoke quiet as a whisper.

Sweat beaded on Elbie's skin and he was panting again. It took everything to pull mismatched eyes away from his hands.

"What do you need?"

"Um..." Elbie searched. Everyone was working. His gaze returned to the screen. Son. Fire. Tree. Shirt. Fire... Then drifted back to his hands. *Yuyu's. How badly were they broken shielding her head from that beam?* His ears rang. He watched it fall. And his hands. Burnt, torn, nails pulled back. He gagged – startling the room and making the instructor move sideways. "I don't feel well..."

Smiling, she gathered his things into his bag and escorted him to the clinic on the first floor. The student Healer motioned him to the bed. He should've sat, but Elbie laid down and curled into a ball.

His hands. He didn't want to look at them, but he couldn't look away. They were whole. Nothing was wrong with them anymore. Healer Herrard grew the nails back within days. No scarring... *How badly was Yuyu hurt?* It'd been weeks. Weeks in Isolation under the constant care of Healers.

Clean air choked his lungs. His hands screamed. Pain coursed up his arms and down to his gut. Retching didn't ease his stomach. The pain. *What's happening...?*

His ears rang.

His insides shook.

His skin crawled.

* * *

Twittering birds – as Oya called them – sounded from Jon's screen. He hoped for a distraction. But it was a call request from Healer Bær instead. *How do I report what happened?* The incident in class was already taken care of. But, after...

"Healer Bær, how may I help you?"

"Jon Dinta, I trust all is well?"

I need time to figure this out... "Actually, it is."

"Good." The Healer's tone invited more detail.

"He's cooperative and hasn't been sick." After South Chūzo, Jon never wanted to hear gagging again. "And he accepted the next goal."

43

"Wonderful. I'm glad he's doing better."

"Yes, sir..." *Cooperative doesn't mean he isn't stressed or miserable...* But saying so... And after what he'd witnessed...

"And his weight?"

"He looks about the same, sir..."

Bær sat back and folded his arms.

"I'm sorry. Please grant an extension on weighing in."

"Is there a reason?" The Head Healer waited eyebrow raised.

"Well..." *I need to get him healthy...* But how? The abuse and Ferdinan not trusting him complicated things. If he pushed too hard, the gent would push back – or worse, pull away.

"Well?" Bær prompted when Jon fell silent.

Promises. Expectations. How did he fulfill them both? This problem didn't have an easy fix. Even if the gent stopped growing, and everything went well, it'd take a year for his ally to reach a healthy weight. And... *I need to earn his trust – so he'll open up about the abuse.* Getting his ally healthy was more than a physical endeavor.

"The fire... Ferdinan hasn't complained, but he's hurting. It's affecting his appetite. Can we wait a few weeks?" *Lying shouldn't be this easy...* Between Oya and Ferdinan...he was getting too good at it.

Thinking it over, Bær nodded. "Ok. His overall health is more important. Once he's feeling better, we'll reassess."

"Thank you, sir." *Now how do I find Oya?*

* * *

Nearly colorless blue crystals stayed fixed on the distilling liquid instead of acknowledging the red head climbing through the window with his violin case. It was rude, but... *What will this do?* A number of side effects were listed in the article. Fatigue being most common. But that was better than screaming at a voice only he could hear.

It's not going to work.

Ferdinan increased the music's volume then focused on the dosing suggestions. *Height or weight?* The voice pranced around inside his head – mocking him. *The larger dose... The largest.*

44

Once the water was gone, Ferdinan added the powder to the mixture and grabbed a masks and goggles for both him and Oya.

Exotic green eyes widened in surprise.

"You'll be seriously injured if you don't wear these." *I've already hurt Yuyu and Elbie, I can't hurt you too...*

Giggling, she took the offered mask and goggles. Somehow, they made her look wilder than normal. "*I'm ready!*"

He checked hers then secured his before pouring the catalyst. The reaction started immediately. This was nothing new to him but Oya watched in awe for some time. Standing near her warmed his soul. Seeing her delight and awe at such a simple thing... He smiled.

Letting her watch, he cleaned up. All his tools were stored. The tables were wiped down and the floors swept. Leaning back, he took in the sight of her. *Why did I manipulate her like that? That's why she hasn't spent much time with me... But she's here now...why?*

Forcing those thoughts away only brought his ally to mind. *Will he try dragging me to class again...?* Every day Jon tried convincing him. But how did he face Master Ludwick or his peers? And if he shouted at the voice again...? They'd finally realize he was broken...

If his mother found out... A shiver ran up his spine. *I can't let anyone know. Death's a better option.*

It'll never work.

"*Do you always come in through the window?*"

The question startled Oya, but she grinned – intrigued. "*There's more than one way into a building.*"

Amusing girl. How will you kill her?

Why isn't the music working anymore? Clenching his jaw, Ferdinan looked out the window.

Jumping up, Oya retrieved his violin case. "*Play for me?*"

No... He shook his head. Playing left him unbearably naked... He couldn't handle that right now. "*Would you walk with me?*"

"*Not run?*"

"*I'm not ready. A week or so...*"

45

Grinning, she headed to the door. "*I'd love a stroll.*"

"*I'll meet you outside after I put this away.*" His heart stopped as he waited for her to realize...accuse him of what he was about to do. But she didn't. That signature grin glowed at him before she strutted to the window and slipped out.

Measuring the larger dose... Ferdinan chewed on his lip. How unacceptable was this? Improper? But the voice's cackling laugh was all the encouragement he needed. Mixing the powder in a small bit of water, he forced down the potent chemical bitterness, stored the rest in his closet, and hurried outside.

Exotic green eyes and a gentle breeze met him. Bright sunshine warmed them. Walking next to her...losing himself in the comfort of her warmth – her undeniable presence...

You like her, hm? She'll die soon, then.

His joy vanished. *I'll ruin my country...my Family. I'll compromise my Prince's position if I don't get rid of that voice.*

You'll never escape my companionship.

After half a year... He'd impale himself to get rid of it. But that was worse. *If I were to do that...* He wanted to. Only...he hadn't suffered enough to serve any sort of justice.

Others knowing he was broken would damage his family and country, but making himself die, that'd destroy everything. It'd lose allies and treaties. His country was suffering enough. But his Prince would suffer the most... Because of him. Like always.

When've you cared about others?

Ignoring the voice was useless. Screaming in class made that obvious, but even when he was alone...

"*What is it?*" Oya cocked her head to the side and grinned at him.

"*Sorry, I was lost in thought.*" *I'm troubling her too. I need it gone now. If I double the dose...?*

Chapter 8

This can't be right. Stories told by a dozen people all agreed. Only two said anything different and even they confirmed his cousin jumped out of a burning building. Whether Ferdinan was carrying two children – or one... *He really did something heroic?*

And after...Ferdinan hid away – refusing accolades. *Why? What did he get? Is he finally thinking outside himself? Has he stopped being selfish? No. Personality staples don't change that dramatically.*

Did he do it for show? But Ferdinan was self-absorbed – the opinions of others never mattered. And he was avoiding praise... *What then? What did he have to gain? Is this some kind of joke?*

I can't think about this right now. Placing the screen on the table in his cabin, Zephyr stood and stretched. Completely confused.

* * *

I've never been so tired... The skeleton stumbled to the sac in his lab closet. Evelyn should be sleeping. *I don't deserve to play with her.* Both of his apprentices nearly died. Yuyu was still in Isolation...

You stole her future.

Anyone else would've saved her... If he'd spent time with them...invited them... Thought of them! It wouldn't have happened. But he didn't. He failed them. And they paid for his failure...

Blood-red hair somersaulted through the window. "Hi!"

Why is she suddenly being silly like this? Is she worried? Don't concern yourself over me, this is all my fault. His knees shook. "I'm sorry, I'm really tired. Tomorrow. I promise we'll play tomorrow."

Her grin grew wider. "We'll play tomorrow."

When she slipped out the window, he let sleep take him.

* * *

"You skipped dinner again." Herrard stood in the doorway only to be ignored. Again. Dinner grew cold hours ago. They should be sleeping. But... *I can't keep doing this...* Sighing, the Healer entered and put their meals on a table before approaching Xhou. Tapping the Thinker's shoulder did nothing, so he knocked away the screens.

"What?!" Blue-black eyes shot venom at him.

"When was the last time you ate?"

Xhou rubbed tired, overwhelmed eyes. "What was that?"

"Please." Shaking hands covered Herrard's face. "You don't eat. You don't sleep. I'm exhausted looking at you."

"You're exaggerating–"

"Am I?" Herrard threw his hands down. "Your mom calls me 'cause you won't talk to her except to ask for more work. Master Loucé told me you're skipping classes again – and you canceled *all* your sessions. Your friends and charges chase me down to check on you 'cause you avoid them. You're never in the suite – avoiding me! No matter how I try, you won't talk to me – or listen to my concerns. The concerns of everyone who cares about you."

"Herrard, there's–"

"No!" Flame and ice battled inside The Kalj. He was tired. So tired... "Every day, I give all I have to the little girl who's important to you. And every night I lie awake. I can't get a break. You stay buried in...whatever this nonsense is! I can't fix Yuyu! I can't help you! And I can't sleep. 'Cause all I think about is how useless I am!"

Xhou sat stunned. He didn't speak. He just waited.

Herrard looked up blinking fast. "This *isn't* good for you."

"It's important."

"More important than your health?! Your country? Family? Charges? Locking yourself in here for a theory that doesn't matter?" The Healer stared down those blue-black eyes. "I wish I could tear this from your mind so you'll stop! So you can return to life..."

"Herrard..." Xhou leaned forward, at a loss for what to do next.

"No. You're coming to the suite. We're eating dinner. And you are talking to me. Tomorrow, I'm dragging you to your session with Master Loucé. And if you skip again, I'll report to your mother."

"No! You–"

"Yes!" Herrard's free hand pointed to the door. "I see how much she needs help too. If you go home like this, you'll make her worse. You'll both spiral 'cause you're incapable of opening up."

Defiantly, Xhou stood and approached his suitemate.

Herrard hit him hard before he could argue. "You're worse than Ferdinan. Anyone can see he's suffering. But you do so with a smile."

* * *

Does this make me a monster?

But if a monster did something good did that negate them being a monster? Mad giggles left Oya as she slipped through the window and stood at Yuyu's bedside. *I have to finish tonight.* Ferdinan and Herrard were at their limits. And Zephyr was taking more time.

I've learned what I can. Eyes closed, Oya delved in to the broken net and the halted galaxy beyond. "Are you still here, young one?"

"Yes."

"I'll need you to talk to me as I work."

"I thought that distracted you."

Oya grinned. "Just say if anything changes or doesn't feel right."

"Ok."

The damage to the larger hole was more significant. But the smaller one felt more important. Between information that could be relearned or language and loved ones...she'd rather make a mistake on the former. Taking the first frayed end, Oya covered it with both hands, lifted it to her lips, and blew gently. A little warmth ebbed out of her. The end glowed and the frays smoothed. *Now where would you best connect to?*

* * *

Darkness surrounded Ferdinan. But the light and warmth and beautiful smile he desperately needed was just ahead. "Evelyn!"

Jumping into his arms, she squeezed his neck. "Big brother! You're back! I've missed you!"

"I apologize, Lady Evelyn, I've been busier than normal."

"What're we playing tonight!?"

"It's been a while since we've had a tea party." He didn't deserve her joy, but he needed it. A sincerely happy smile beamed at her.

"Yay!" Jumping down, she waved her hands. White puffy clouds formed into everything. The table, tea, cookies, and other guests.

"Are you having fun at school?" Ferdinan sat when she did.

"Oh! Yes! I made a new friend yesterday! Her name's Chicha! She loves bugs! And tag too! I'm not the only one anymore! How about you? Are you having fun with Uncle Jon and your friends?"

Hesitating, Ferdinan "sipped" his tea.

"Oh, he's having fun. I play with him every day."

Blue crystals tripled as Evelyn turned to the boy beside her.

"Jon...? No!" Evelyn beamed. "I have two big brothers now?!"

That voice... *Get away from her!!*

"You're Lady Evelyn? I've been wanting to meet you for some time."

"Really? It's nice to meet you! What's your name?"

"Please call me," the boy turned and smiled at Ferdinan, "Emil."

Ice encased Ferdinan's heart. *My second name...* He always hated it, but hearing the voice use it... Breathing proved elusive.

Moving closer, Emil opened his hand before Evelyn. A puff of blue smoke floated up, revealing a little glowing fairy as it dissipated.

Squealing, Evelyn scooped up the fairy. "What's your name!!?"

"She doesn't have one. You're welcome to name her." The charming smile Emil gave made Evelyn beam.

"Oooo, I think... Hmm...what would be a good name?"

Get away from her! The dreamscape shook. But Emil's smug smile didn't waver. That look was a challenge, betting he'd fail.

Leave us alone!! Ferdinan leapt over the table and pushed Emil back, shielding his little sister. "Evelyn, go somewhere safe."

There was a cry as black tendrils enveloped the small girl. But those shadowed arms didn't feel dangerous. Not like the one before him. "Don't ever come near her again!"

Chapter 9

Only two ends left... But standing to connect them...

"If you're who I think you are, I could use your help now." Oya grinned at the orbs and for the first time they moved into full view. Their normal soft glow brightened and rested on her. Oya gasped. Pain she hadn't noticed vanished. Energy surged. *I feel whole...*

This was cheating. But everything she did was a cheat. Grabbing both ends, she twisted them together. Blowing on them, her essence wrapped around the ends and they melted into each other.

"That's right! That's right!" Yuyu's voice and the world beyond the net moved. It was bright. Colorful. Vivid.

I did it...? Really? Those large holes were ugly. Gaps marred the net. It was the best she could do with the materials and tools she had.

"I can see again! Where are you?"

Who would she feel most comfortable with? A wicked grin curled shapely lips. *I haven't been old in a while.*

Morphing into an old woman, Oya appeared in the middle of an active galaxy of beauty and wonder. "I'm right here."

Indescribable joy filled everything! Pink eyes and tight black curls ran toward her. Yuyu hugged the old woman – refusing to let go.

Gnarled hands patted the girl's head. "You'll wake up soon, young one." *Is this enough for a monster to become human?*

* * *

Metal sheets mocked Xhou's weakness. His hands hurt. Stiffness plagued him. Joints and muscles cried out their protests. And blisters disfigured his skin – taking their time callousing. No box would be made today. But there were other things he needed to do.

It didn't take long for his mom to answer his call request.

"Hi, mama." Xhou smiled bright. *Herrard's wrong. I'll prove it.* "Am I interrupting? We haven't relaxed and talked in a while..."

The Nuwa's smile was even brighter. "I'm always happy to make time for you. How are you? I got word you'd been missing classes."

"I'm sorry. I guess I'm like you when I get drawn into a project."

"There's plenty here to get drawn into after you graduate."

"I'm sorry." Xhou opened his mouth to direct the conversation to her, but she beat him.

"What has so thoroughly consumed you?"

"I thought I'd found some information concerning the Scientist who developed the cure. I want to thank that person someday."

A soft sigh left his mom. "I understand. But if the scientist wishes to remain anonymous, we should respect that."

"I know. I was being selfish. Call it my last childish act."

"You don't become an instant adult at twenty. It's a process."

One I don't get to experience... "Thanks. How're you doing?"

Her smile turned coy. "We're working with Master Huey to get supplies and teachers for a new generation of farmers. The program should be ready by the end of winter..."

"I'll work on that. I'd like to greet Master Huey too." Xhou tried turning the conversation again. "I'm glad things look promising for our people, but how are you? The stress of carrying this alone..."

The Nuwa waved her hand. "There's plenty of chances to meet Master Huey. But make sure to call him 'Grandpa.'"

"'Grandpa?' Why's that?"

"He'd never give me a straight answer." Laughter spilled out of his mom. "Don't worry about any of this yet. I have plenty of help."

"That's good..." Blue-black eyes drifted to the three malformed boxes by the window. *No. Herrard isn't right. I have to prove it!*

Their conversation continued for an hour. But no matter how many times he asked about her, she never answered.

* * *

Tossing and turning – fire consumed Elbie. It was everywhere...

Throwing back the covers, he opened the curtains. Outside was beautiful. A full moon hung heavy – surrounded by a magnificent cloak of stars. Mismatched eyes closed. But the fire was still there.

I don't want to think about this! He stared at his hands... Burnt and bloody. Missing nails. Smoke choked his lungs. He couldn't scream! His hands begged to stop digging. It hurt so badly. *It hurts! No! They'll die!* How could he run to safety and let his sister die?

Something grabbed him, pulling him from the fire. *No! Yuyu!*

"Elbie? Are you ok?"

Heavy panting stole his words. Licking his lips, he searched. He sat on his bed, window open. It was dark, save for the moon. And the suitemate he shared a wall with hovered above. White hair framed midnight eyes. *Haoyu...* "I...a nightmare... I'm sorry I woke you."

"That's all?"

Elbie studied his hands. They were fine. Healer Herrard did a magnificent job. His nails were back within days and there wasn't a single scar. Like the explosion never happened. "Yah. I'm sorry..."

"But you're crying." Haoyu floated to sit next to Elbie – offering a stuffed fish and squeezing a stuffed dolphin. "Share it with me."

"I..." Elbie looked away. He was fine after it happened. Why was it bothering him now? What did he do wrong? How did he make this start? And how did he stop it? "I'm sorry. I don't remember..."

Nodding, Haoyu laid back – resting his head on his hands with the dolphin laying on his chest. "Think you can sleep again?"

"It's ok. I'll be ok." The Rufudar never left a person alone after a nightmare as it opened the dreamer to soul damaging attacks. Elbie was happy staying with Haoyu when the Energist had a bad dream. But he didn't hold that belief. And he wanted to be alone right now. *I have to figure this out. Why now?* It was terrifying. His heart still beat erratically. And...he wanted to be alone. "I'll fall right back to sleep. Go to bed. Water training's tomorrow; you need to be fully rested."

Haoyu smirked. "Then it's good you'll fall right back to sleep."

* * *

"Your almost back," the elf smirked. "Do you have an answer?"

"I was strolling the deck..." Zephyr looked around the twilight beach – hands settling at his sides. *Or did my dream change?*

"Your answer."

The Prince backed away at her intensity. "I don't understand."

"Why do you hate him?"

There was no escape no matter where he looked.

The elf seized his arm. "Show me where your hate began."

Struggling... Images flashed around them until the twilight beach disappeared. *Why did she bring me home?*

"Well done." A much younger Aunt Tenalia stood proud.

Excited, five-year-old hands flew in excitement. Eventually his tongue caught up. "What are you teaching me next?!"

Did I really sound like that? Hearing his early voice was odd.

"That's all your lessons today." She knelt next to the tiny golden boy. "Remember me telling you about your cousin? The one who's like you? The one who'll start school with you?"

"Yes, ma'am!"

Unquenchable curiosity curled the elf's lips. The scene continued – Tenalia explaining how, as the older of the two and future General, it was Zephyr's responsibility to care for his cousin.

Why am I recalling this?

"You were excited to meet him..." the elf leaned over.

Zephyr's hands moved...but stopped when the door opened. A slender woman entered – toddler close behind. *He looked like that?* The toddler was well-muscled with short brown hair and his skin had the beautiful glow of life. *I'm scrawny next to him. And barely taller...*

Little hands tugged at properly fitted clothing and colorless eyes darted around constantly. If not for those eyes, Zephyr wouldn't have recognized Ferdinan. A crystal blue so sharp they cut through all they landed on – filled uncertainty. *How can a two-year-old look like that?*

"What's going to happen now, Zephyr?"

"He'll bow to me, as he always does." *The Duchess, Aunt Tenalia...they look so young...*

Duchess Samultz bowed deeply to Tenalia. "My General."

"No need to stand on ceremony, Wenmeria."

The elf sniggered under her breath. "Wenmeria..."

Annoyed, Zephyr's hands emphasized her rudeness. "Without her leadership, my citizens would be starving."

"Really?" Ridiculous name or not, that impressed the elf.

Wenmeria looked down at the toddler clutching her hem and cleared her throat – making young Ferdinan tremble. But he walked to the little Prince. *He's so graceful.* Clearing her throat again caused Ferdinan to stumble five paces from young Zephyr. Head bowed, he dropped to one knee – staying perfectly still. And perfectly silent.

"Hi. My name's Zephyr." The Prince smiled – hands dancing.

The toddler shook harder.

"This is Ferdinan," the Duchess smiled warmly at young Zephyr.

Tenalia knelt beside her nephews. "Ferdinan, would you like to play with Zephyr?"

Tiny hands jumped. "Do you want to play, Fe-d-inan?"

Onyx eyes watched as the little Prince pulled his cousin up. But the Tinkerer gasped and fell backwards. "He's never-"

Tenalia rushed forward, sparking the toddler to flinch into a ball. She lifted the trembling, grimacing Ferdinan to his feet. "I finally get to see you, dear."

Blue crystals widened in terror – squirming, ready to cry...until the General released him. *He never liked being touched...*

"Those are his father's eyes... But..." Tenalia studied him. "Are you sure he's classified correctly? His musculature is a Fighter's."

An unamused smile curled her lips. "Yes. The Duke is perfectly capable of classifying a child. I'm just feeding him too well. I should reevaluate his diet before he ends up with health problems."

"Muscle is different from fat, Wenmeria."

"It is, but he's a Scientist." A sweet smile glowed on her face as she bowed to her Prince, but hardened when addressing Ferdinan. "Obey our Prince. Don't keep him waiting."

He shook. Smiling, young Zephyr took his hand again – only for him to jerk away. Their eyes met, and it seemed both would cry.

"Would you like to play, Ferdinan?" Tenalia kindly repeated. "Zephyr's excited to play with you."

"I was. I always wanted a sibling," Older Zephyr mumbled.

"There's no need speaking to him like an infant. He's a Scientist. He's capable of understanding adults and acting accordingly." The harshness in her voice eased Ferdinan's discomfort.

"Do you want to?" The little Prince tried again – hands dancing. When a tiny nod came, Zephyr pulled him into a run.

At first Ferdinan stumbled, but by the time they reached the door, his run was just as fast and graceful as the little Prince's. The elf smirked at the visibly confused present day Zephyr.

"Am I remembering this right?"

That smirk intensified. "This is straight from your mind."

They watched young Zephyr drag his little cousin around until the Duchess ended their play. When she entered, Wenmeria knelt, as she'd taught her son to do. "My Prince, it's time for dinner."

"Ok, Duchess!"

"She only let me call her 'Duchess' – I don't know why."

Young Zephyr hugged her. Five paces back, Ferdinan waited. When the little Prince turned, he was stopped short by a new look in those blue eyes. Jealousy. Intense and burning. And it didn't go away until he released her.

"Now, my Prince, there's something you need to know."

"Yes, Duchess?" The little Prince gave his full attention.

"Your cousin's starting school with you 'cause he's intelligent. But he isn't wise. He's also willful and stubborn. As his elder and the future General, your responsible to keep him in line – by force if necessary. Do whatever you feel is needed."

Confusion and uncertainty filled the little Prince's face.

A golden finger tapped his forehead then his heart and he shook his head... "I think she's told me that many times."

"Think? That's a silly thing to forget." The elf turned to him, a wide-eyed grin on her face. "What else have you forgotten?"

Chapter 10

Ferdinan's mind felt like mush as he mixed in the white powder.

Still lying to yourself?

Setting his jaw, he stirred in more. Bitterness puckered his face, but water couldn't erase the chemical's lingering taste.

Still believe you can escape me?

It doesn't matter. If it doesn't work, I'll try something else. If it does then you'll be gone. Or it'll kill me and I'll be rid of us both.

So optimistic?

"Shut up!"

The mounted screen's chime cut through the din in his head. Needing something – anything – to push the voice from his mind, Ferdinan leapt at it. A familiar – yet terrifying – face smiled at him.

"Healer Yahmo!" *Breathe. Breathe.* "How may I serve you?"

"Ferdinan, how are you?" Stress and fatigue coated the man.

"I'm as well as I can be..." This wasn't a lie. If the skeleton could be better, he didn't know how. "How can I serve you?"

"I need one radius and ulna."

"...set or variable?"

The healer's shiny dark eyes dimmed. "Variable. She's eight."

"Was she brought to you?"

"Unfortunately."

Ferdinan chewed his lip. The kinds of patients "brought" to the healer... West Chūzo's child abuse laws weren't particularly effective.

Acid burned and bile raced up his throat. Ferdinan stepped away before his face contorted and tears filled his eyes. Settling an expressionless mask in place was harder than he remembered.

"Son? Is everything alright?"

You'll fail her too.

His throat was too tight to answer. Swallowing a few times and blinking away tears...he faced the man again. "Send the specs."

"I just did. How long will it take to make them?"

Bones and a chip... Replacement bones for the young needed to mimic the child's natural growth. The chip monitored the good arm and adjusted the manmade pieces as she grew. *If I build a machine to make these, he won't have to depend on me.*

"I know it's unlikely, but..." Yahmo looked hesitantly hopeful. "Would you be available for the surgery?"

Blue crystals looked down. "School ends in nine weeks."

"I understand. I was just hoping for a sharp eye."

"Your nurses are better than I am."

"For the body. Not the hardware."

"I'm sorry." Ferdinan bowed.

"No. This was beyond your control."

"Yes, sir."

Trying to cheer trash like you, stupid man.

Yahmo's eyebrows knit together. "Umm...the boy I picked up from you... I was able to settle him into a family."

Ferdinan stood surprised. Finding someone who'd take in a child that old was a feat. But a broken child? One so far gone to have embraced the improper? "I'm glad. I hope things are better now."

"Do you want to know?"

His heart quickened again. A pained laugh shook from thin lips, reddening the skeleton's cheeks. "I don't know."

"You saved him. He wanted me to thank you. Next time you visit, he'd love to thank you personally."

"He doesn't even know me." *I didn't save him, you did.*

"Would you care in his position?"

"I've never been in his position." The healer offered more, but Ferdinan forced a hasty farewell. *I don't want to know any of it...* Boney hands rubbed tired eyes.

"*What was that about?*"

Heart pounding, Ferdinan spun. "*How long have you been here?*"

"*Long enough to see that conversation was important.*"

Now look at what you've done.

What do I do?! W...why am I panicking? She doesn't care about propriety... She's being sneaky again... "*He offered me a commission.*"

A blood-red eyebrow rose. "*You make medical things often?*"

"...yeah...I do." *Did she see me take the chemical?*

"*Jon said you've developed a number of things for medical use.*"

"I have..." If she said anything about the powder he made... But...he felt safe with her... "Is there something I can do for you?"

"*Me?*" A wicked grin popped onto her face. "*Nothing... But I thought you'd like to take this opportunity to go for a run.*"

She's so silly... "*In the middle of the day?*" Ferdinan yawned. *I want to, but I need to make those arm pieces for Yahmo.* His muscles screamed to move. *But a run sounds perfect...*

"*They're coming for you.*"

This caught his attention – interrupting another yawn. "*They?*"

"*One old man with wild hair and the tattooed boss man.*"

"Boss... *The Superintendent?*" *Sounds like Master Ludwick too...*

"*Yah, that one.*"

Ferdinan paled. The memory of shouting in class replayed in his head yet again. "*I'm not ready to face them.*"

Don't have the lies ready?

Her grin widened. "*They won't see us go out the back.*"

"You mean my closet window." *My skin's still uncomfortable...*

"*Potato, pottatto...*"

Pottatto?

* * *

"About time." Theon laughed and waved a finger. Zephyr's bag floated upward. "Welcome back. Glad you're feeling better."

"Yeah. Me too." Zephyr's golden cheeks took on a pink hue.

"Stop being weird. One awkward suitemate's enough." Theon lowered to the ground – bag still floating. "We missed you and are glad you're well. By the girls' demand, I'm stealing you now."

Zephyr's feet left the ground. This wasn't the first time Theon made him fly, but it'd been a while. "Should I scream for help?"

"Ha! That'd be a sight to see."

Golden hands swayed gracefully. "Let me drop my stuff off first."

"Nope. I've got my orders. And the girls are scarier than you."

"Only Riemalli could seriously hurt you."

"But you're soft and fuzzy next to the imagination of six girls."

"Fair..." The Prince laughed – flying in loops. *When did I last do this?* It was more fun than he remembered. As they neared the girl's dormitory an odd sound hit Zephyr's ears. "What's that noise?"

"Noise?" Theon slowed and lowered them both. "Oh. The Scientists came up with this 'music' for the Family Week show."

"Did you call this '*music?*'"

"Yah..." Theon smiled and clamped a hand on his suitemate's shoulder. "It's...I've come to enjoy it. I was surprised."

Loud drums hit along with some sort of screeching, metallic sound. "That you enjoy this?"

"Hm? No. I can't stand this one." Theon waved a dismissive hand. "I didn't know Ferdinan could sing."

"Sing... My aunt told me one song he screamed at everyone."

"Yah, that's another one I don't like."

* * *

Nammie gave him a pair of goggles and adjusted her own. Beside them sat two strange metal boxes which sanitized the Second Skin.

Herrard mixed the white powder into a clear liquid. "Ready?"

"Yes." Healer Nammie handed him the modified laser and readied to collect the Second Skin as he cut it off.

The laser worried Herrard. A mis-adjustment could seriously injure Yuyu. Slowly he breathed out. Pulling aside the blanket, he placed it at the girl's collarbone and slipped the protective plate between her neck and the Second skin. A *click* and blue light glowed from the tip. The Second Skin split where the laser sliced it and Nammie held the edges apart to keep them from sealing together.

Most of Yuyu's skin was scarred. But the damage to her face was fixed – though there was a line of skin that'd never grow hair again. Seeing this used to make him sick. Him and Nammie both.

Easing the girl onto her side allowed Nammie to get the last bit of Second Skin and place it in the sanitizing chamber.

Using a sponge, Herrard dabbed at the girl's skin. *Nammie will make an excellent Lead...* She was a year younger and easily a better Healer than himself. If she'd believe it. *I hope she'll accept the role.*

He handed the sponge to his fellow Healer and rolled Yuyu to her side for Nammie to treat the girl's back.

"Ready for the Second Skin?"

Nodding, Herrard waited for Nammie to opened the second box. Black goop. That was the only way to describe the miraculous invention. A pile of black goop. Until it touched damaged skin.

The younger Healer placed the goop on the bed, and they rolled Yuyu onto it. The goop latched onto the girl – wrapping every inch of damaged skin. And nothing more. *How did he make this...?*

"It amazes me every time I see it."

Herrard looked up and smiled. "Me too."

Nammie returned the smile. "Sure you don't want help today?"

"Thank you, but no." Sealing the metallic box, he set it to start sanitizing the Second Skin they removed. "I need you to check on Elbie. He's been begging me to remove all restrictions."

A smile and little laugh left her. "Gladly – I'll test if he's ready. That child...I'm surprised he's doing so well; I know I wouldn't be."

"True. But...pay attention to him. Remember Master Loucé's lecture? Sometimes it can take a while before any problems arise."

A light tap on the door interrupted their conversation. The Superintendent greeted them both then Nammie left.

"Mind if I start?"

A grimace of a smile twisted the Kalj's lips. If he saw the man shake his head once more... "Yes, sir. I'll put the supplies away."

Gathering goggles, laser, powder, and whatnot, Herrard made his way to storage. Slowly. If he took long enough... *I can't take it...* The comfort Oya gave made him feel better. But he couldn't handle more bad news. *Why do Xhou and Ilu think she's so mean?* Very few would put up with that kind of behavior from a stranger.

Sighing, Herrard finished storing everything and made his way back. It wasn't enough time for Superintendent Dæya to finish.

When he walked through the door, the man was crying. A man who'd earned every honor marked on beautiful dark skin stood crying over the little girl he'd been working desperately to find...

No... Sobs shook Herrard as he clenched his teeth. *No... No...*

How would he tell Nammie? The Superintendent would inform Yuyu's family. Healer Bær and Master Loucé would tell the students closest to Yuyu. But... He and Nammie and Iizrri... *No...*

"I'm sorry." The Superintendent's voice shook. "I'm sorry. I didn't mean to upset you."

He's...laughing...? "What...?"

"I found her! Her voice!" Tears strangled joyous laughter. "I found her voice!"

The room blurred. Hunching down, the Kalj buried his face in his knees. That was exactly what he needed to hear. "Thank you..."

Laughter danced around him along with joyful words and discussions of what to do next. But Herrard didn't move.

It was possible he'd never known relief until this moment.

Chapter 11

Sand rubbed under his skin – jolting the skeleton awake. *Elbie. What am I doing?* Bright red, Ferdinan looked away as a yawn took over. "Have you finished your proposal for this block's final project? I need it by the end of the week for initial approval."

"I...I can't think of anything." Mismatched eyes drifted down to gaze at his hands.

Ferdinan yawned again. "You're young...but advanced projects can be approved to be year-long. If that's your trouble."

Setting him up for failure after failing him; such a great mentor.

"I didn't know that..." Elbie looked up timidly. "But... It's... I just...nothing's coming to me..."

"Ah...I understand." Ferdinan sympathized. "Maybe seeing my past projects will help you with an idea." *I've failed him terribly...*

"Yes! Please!" Mismatched eyes brightened.

"Tomorrow then." A giant yawn seized Ferdinan and his aching muscles screamed to run. Between healing and how tired he was...

If you don't kill him before then.

"Thank you, sir!" A giant grin glowed on Elbie's face as he left.

Why isn't that voice going away? But... Blue crystals blinked. Those unwanted memories weren't bothering him anymore...

His screen chimed. *The Duchess...* His insides liquified.

* * *

Ferdinan looked honestly distressed turning down her company, but she had her own tasks, so she waved as he ran out of his lab.

A short walk down the silver roads brought her to the woman. *Time to work.* Seizing the first line, she searched connection after connection until she found where the woman's influence ended. Then she worked her way back, making each lighted string her own.

The last in this branch was an old man. Beaten down by life with only work to fulfill him... Oya studied the connections she already hijacked. *Irresponsible. How many has that kōjomä indoctrinated into her madness?* How could one person infect so many?

Sighing, she stretched. This seemed like a simple solution. Until she started. Oya studied the six newest connections she held. *Why were these six so hard to claim? Am I doing too much too quickly?* Even if she was, it didn't matter. Time was limited. *Focus. One more.*

Pinching her fingers together a needle holding a bit of her soul appeared. *I'm sorry, old man. But I can't allow this evil.* Delicate fingers jabbed the needle through the man's chest. He didn't react. Neither his mind, heart, nor body were here. Only his soul. And a soul could suffer immense agony without the person being aware.

The needle plunged deep – pushing until it passed through the man. Every connection he had fell from him – writhing, twisting into a rainbow barely the width of a hair. Taking the thread, she melded it into the one she'd pulled through the man's heart. Needle in hand, she weaved it into the others. Once, twice, thrice she knotted it. Memories and emotions she had no right to hit hard. But they always did. This was the price of claiming connections. Souls.

Everything had a price.

The woman standing behind the old man was next...but Oya was tired. And there was still Zephyr. At least Yuyu was taken care of.

A wave of the hand and the door to the silver roads opened. *I love it here.* No matter how lost she got feeling her way back was simple. *If only there was time to find the end to every road.*

* * *

Activating the chime, Xhou waited outside Jon's lab.

"Xhou?" Jon opened the door. "How're you doing?"

"Ha! Ever the one for pleasantries," Xhou smirked.

"I'm serious." Jon motioned him in.

"I'm better." Having a focus helped. *I'll find her, him, them...*

Unconvinced and worried, Jon continued, "Can I help you?"

"Yah..." Xhou scratched his neck nervously. "With everything that happened recently and Healer Bær being busy, I haven't been able to finish my end-of-year report. I was hoping you could help."

"That was due two months ago."

"Like I said."

"I don't know how helpful I can be..."

"Unusual events concerning my underlings are supposed to be recorded. Since you two were gone most of the block–" When Jon moved defensively, Xhou hurried on. "No specifics. I know we get classified requests. Just enough to justify your extended absence."

Jon relaxed and nodded. "An alumnus from a children's hospital in South Chūzo hired Ferdinan to make a medical device. I assisted."

Acid and fire burned in his chest. "What sort of device this time? He comes up with the most bizarre things." *A children's hospital in South Chūzo, why does that sound familiar?*

Jon nodded. "True. And this one was odd."

"Now you have to tell me." Leaning in, Xhou smiled.

"He called it 'Second Skin.'"

"What?" *That's being used in Yuyu's treatment... He happened to make the perfect device months before and he couldn't save my sister?* Xhou reinforced his smile as his last memory of Rura settled in his mind. Charred...lifeless... "What they're using for Yuyu?"

"Ya." Jon shook his head – studying the Science Lead closely.

"Must've been tricky to take so long," Xhou winked.

Chocolate brown eyes floated to the ceiling. "Ah...ya..."

That was an unusual gesture for the younger Thinker. *What else were you two doing?* "So the blight delayed your return?"

Jon looked away. "By the time we finished, people were scared."

"I might hunt down our elusive friend to ask how he did it."

"Good luck–" Jon cut himself off.

"Where's he been lately?" Facing Ferdinan wasn't something Xhou was ready for. Just hearing the boy's name made his heart burn, but this conversation needed to sound natural.

"He was making something an hour ago, but left when a call request from his mother came in."

"What is it?" Xhou asked at Jon's suspicious expression.

"Hm? Nothing."

"Concern's written on your face." *I lost my chance to naturally ask about the hospital's name...* Still, he had another source.

"He went to his suite to answer it. Dropped an important and time sensitive project... Said something about wanting privacy."

"Wouldn't his personal lab be more private than a room in a suite he shares with other people?"

"Zephyr isn't back yet. And Theon should be mentoring, so..."

Giving a shrug, Xhou grinned. *He doesn't know his own ally's returned?* "Who am I to begrudge a child a chat with his mother?"

* * *

How long has it been? There was no indication of time. No day or night, minutes, hours. It was just Yuyu in the middle of an active universe. Active...but not efficient. Colorful orbs of light danced, but every time they came together, they destroyed each other or missed.

Countless paths existed, but some went nowhere. And the biggest was unreachable – disconnected from the rest. *What caused this? Why hasn't the old woman returned?* Yuyu roamed, searching for materials to fix the roads. But there were none. And she didn't know how to help the orbs. So, she sat. *How long have I been here?*

If I call her...? It was silly. But she had nothing better to do.

"Hello!" *Why didn't I ask her name?* "Hello! Old woman!"

Her words floated off. Not even echoing back. Pink eyes wandered. Maybe an idea would come to her.

Wavey, pure white hair appeared, framing gold-flecked black eyes and a too young smirk. Weathered skin emphasized that grin.

"You called, young one?"

Yuyu blushed. "Sorry... It's lonely. How long have I been here?"

"Longer than I thought, but not too long."

Yuyu flinched instinctively when that gnarled hand patted hers. *She doesn't feel like anything...* Yuyu giggled. *Of course not. I'm asleep. No one's actually touching me.* "May I ask your name?"

Joints cracked as the old woman stretched. "Call me Muulam."

"Muulam...? What's that mean?"

A knowing grin deepened thick wrinkles. "It means 'one of dreams.' What does Yuyu mean?"

Did I tell her my name? But hers...it's too similar to mine...is she part of my mind? "'Dream creator.'"

"Oh?" Muulam looked genuinely surprised. "Interesting."

"Um...I'm sorry if I'm bothering you...but..."

"No, young one. I should apologize. I thought they'd wake you by now." That arthritic hand waved two chairs into existence. "Solitude isn't good for the mind – or soul."

"So...you'll stay?"

"For a while. I have others needing care." When Yuyu looked away, Muulam continued, "I'll come back every night 'til you wake."

"Thank you..."

"Well..." The old woman grinned and looked around – watching eagerly. Until two orbs approached each other and exploded. "How often does that happen?"

"About half the time. The other half they don't meet."

Standing, Muulam studied the scene. "Anything else strange?"

A little hand waved to the brick road encompassing the galaxy. "Nothing connects to it. And many smaller roads are broken."

"I see."

Muulam watched and studied. Randomly she reached out at nothing before pulling her arms in again. A colorful band of woven threads wrapped around her hand, caughting Yuyu's attention.

"What's that?"

"Excuse me?" The old woman looked back, waiting.

"Those threads around your hand."

Curiosity danced with amusement. "You can see this?"

"Yes, ma'am."

"Interesting." Instead of answering her question the woman changed topics. "Would you like to learn how to connect the roads?"

* * *

The Duchess wasn't a large woman. But her very being held power and conviction beyond what Ferdinan could withstand. Each failure she listed shriveled his soul a little more. *I'm sorry I cursed your life...* "I apologize. The supplies will arrive in two days..."

"Do you know how many were hospitalized due to this delay? How did I end up with a defect – a failure?"

"Yes, Duchess." Eyes down, Ferdinan fought back a flood. *I can't do anything right... I hurt everyone...just being alive...*

No response came. Looking up, the screen was blank.

You're a terrible son.

The skeleton went to his bathroom and filled the tub with icy water. Breath failed him. He gripped the edge with all his might.

I've no right being upset.

Pathetic.

I brought it on myself.

Disappointment.

This is all my fault.

Failure.

If I could do something good...

Useless.

If I could do something right...

Defect.

Cold bit mercilessly into his fragile skin. The voice taunted him. Sliding down, he hid his face behind boney hands. Slipping lower.

Submerging himself fully. *I can't do anything right. I'm useless. I fail at everything... I fail everyone...*

Chapter 12

"Don't argue with me." It was pointless, but Herrard was tired of Xhou's excuses every time he dragged the young man to Master Loucé. At least the Healer now had the energy for it.

Xhou still protested but followed anyway. *Good enough.* The Thinker didn't have to like it, just so long as he followed.

"Stop..." Xhou's voice called out in warning.

Startled, Herrard froze. He turned back to Xhou, then forward to where his suitemate was looking.

There weren't many sights that stopped Herrard's heart. But the skeleton was the main one. Blue crystals stood wide at the top of the hill. Lord Ferdinan might fear Healers, but the Kalj had every right to fear the Tinkerer. He knew first-hand what that boy was capable of. Neither did he want to experience that again.

All three of them stood – frozen. Terrified to move.

Until Xhou stepped forward. The skeleton scurried away a few steps then forced himself back. *Why isn't he fleeing?*

"We should take the boats..." Herrard didn't blink.

"Yah...but..." Xhou considered for a moment. "If he didn't desperately need something, he wouldn't still be standing there."

That made Herrard cringe. But he'd seen Ferdinan tear apart Healers and Psychs who'd gotten too close. The boy nearly cost him an eye once... *Samuel's wrong, he's dangerous.*

A strange sound floated down the hill.

"I can't hear you." Herrard shouted, making himself as small as possible. Anything to not spook the child. "I'm coming closer."

"No." Xhou grabbed him. "I can't handle a repeat of last time."

"If he needed something from you, he wouldn't still be here."

Gingerly, the Kalj moved forward. *Say something. Show me I'm close enough...* His heart raced... *I'm bigger and stronger now. And he's deathly thin... I can defend myself this time. But...Samuel couldn't stop him...* It took sedating the boy for Herrard to escape.

"Stop!"

The universe and all within it obeyed...

All save Xhou who shifted a confused face between his suitemate and his charge. "Was that Yi-zhé?"

Blue crystals flew around wildly. Lord Ferdinan paled, but Herrard nodded. *How does he know the royal language?* Keeping his voice deep and calm, the Healer called out. "I'm staying here."

A dry tongue licked even dryer lips to no avail. "Y-Y-Y...Y-Y..."

What am I doing? I should run away if he can't. "I'm listening. What're you trying to say?"

The skeleton paled and blushed simultaneously – entire body trembling uncontrollably. "Y-Y-Y...Yu-u-u..."

"What?"

"Y-Y...y..." Somehow Lord Ferdinan shook harder.

Though Herrard couldn't say much. He wasn't visibly shaking – but his insides... *Stay calm. Don't scare him.* "Yuyu?"

It took a moment for the Tinkerer to nod. And when he started, it seemed his body wouldn't let him stop.

Even if the boy was dangerous to him, he knew Lord Ferdinan would do anything for his apprentices. "The d-damage was extensive. She'll recover thanks to your inventions... But there's only so much we can do at a time...so it'll be a while longer."

Ferdinan's teeth clattered.

Silence held everyone in place. It took Xhou stepping between them to break the spell. "We're taking the boats."

Ferdinan crouched low – eyes darting between Herrard and Xhou. Neither did the boy move when they slowly backed away.

* * *

Zephyr turned down the dried fruit the elf offered. Again. *Is my life so entertaining?* They watched the little Prince return home after finishing his first year. The six-year-old Zephyr was now attempting a new move on the impossible to beat Captain Rutoric.

A smile tugged at his lips. *That man never let me win...*

On the ground – air knocked from his lungs – young Zephyr smiled. After a few more tries, Tenalia stepped up and let him complete the full move. Her pleased look said it was perfect.

"You have your aunt's stance, not Captain Rutoric's."

"Hmm? Aunt Tenalia oversaw my training from the start." Zephyr watched his mom enter. Three-year-old Ferdinan followed behind – head down. *Has he always walked like that?*

"Tenalia, a messenger from the capital arrived."

"Thank you, Am'ria." Tenalia apologized to the little Prince. "I'm sorry, but you don't keep the Master waiting. Or his servants."

"Yes, ma'am."

"We'll practice tomorrow. Everyone should know that move."

The little Prince's pride from that praise was tangible.

The tiny queen squeezed her son. "I need Captain Rutoric for a task. Would you play with your cousin, my darling?"

"Yes!" Young Zephyr turned to his cousin – hands flying. "Aunt Tenalia says everyone should know Hutaru. I'll teach you!"

The elf snorted. "How did the little prince become an adult?"

"What?" Zephyr didn't get an answer, so he kept watching.

Little Ferdinan nodded – shaking as normal. Time and again Zephyr showed his cousin the move, but Ferdinan was reluctant.

The elf leaned down – sapphire eyes soaking it all in. "Your cousin hasn't spoken once in the year and a half we've watched."

"It's strange he talks, we thought he'd be mute like his father."

"What?" The elf turned her full attention to him.

Golden hands danced. "I don't know how, but he suddenly started speaking a couple years ago."

"Really?" The elf considered this. "Then why not teach them a hand language like Rutoric? It worked for him."

What....? "Rutoric isn't mute." The two stared at each other while the little Prince scolded young Ferdinan to try seriously.

"He hasn't spoken yet either."

"He talks all the time." Zephyr laughed. "Hand language is as much talking as any tongue language. More so. Rutoric speaks many hand languages. The Duke - and Ferdinan 'til recently - didn't speak at all. We tried. Tongue, hands, clicks... Nothing. It was frustrating."

Movement caught their eye as young Zephyr attacked. Ferdinan hit the ground. Offering suggestions, the little Prince pulled his cousin up.

"How would a mute child figure out speech?"

Zephyr shrugged. He'd wondered that question many times.

"I'm a Fighter. A Scientist can't hurt me, so do it right. I command it," young Zephyr demanded.

This made Ferdinan tremble, but he nodded. Zephyr attacked.

Squatting low, the Tinkerer swept toward Zephyr, grabbed the attacking arm - pulling the prince off balance - while his free hand rammed Zephyr's abdomen. Ferdinan stood tall and shifted, lifting his cousin off the ground and throwing Zephyr to the floor.

Utter surprise filled the Princes' face - both of them. *When...?*

Crying, tiny Ferdinan rushed to Zephyr's side.

Laughter refused to come. By the time the little Prince found enough air to speak, a shadow fell over them and another sound echoed through the room. The little Prince's grin vanished. Pure fury cloaked the Duchess and Ferdinan knelt low - holding his cheek.

"You do *not* attack our prince." Those words were ice.

"I don't remember this," older Zephyr whispered - heart racing.

In the same breath, the Duchess's voice softened and she helped young Zephyr sit up. "Have you been hurt, my Prince?"

"N-No... Captain Rutoric's meaner." Nervousness painted those words. Two sets of onyx eyes looked from the Duchess to her son.

"Don't let him enjoy hurting those he's supposed to protect."

"I was having fun." Present-day Zephyr told the elf.

"What happened next?"

Two golden fingers came together before one dropped to his side. "I played alone that day."

The Duchess grabbed her son's hair and lifted. "Move."

"He came to my room that evening and prostrated himself." Remembering that night – watching it again – wasn't pleasant.

Young Ferdinan came to Zephyr's room ghost white and sobbing. When the little Prince insisted everything was fine – he broke down completely. Screaming wordlessly.

I wish I didn't remember this...

"What else happened?"

A golden finger bounced twice before pointing to the side.

The elf smirked. "Yes?"

He tapped his temple and shook his head. "I don't remember."

But the scenery changed to the magnificent palace gardens. The little Prince roamed aimlessly through the living maze of flowers and hedges. Until he found young Ferdinan and a pile of torn plants.

Zephyr ran up and knelt beside him. "What are you playing?"

Looking down, little hands swept the bits into a small bag.

"Are you making tea? Can you make me some?"

Ferdinan managed a shaky nod.

"Rose tea is yummy."

A small nod and Ferdinan headed to the rose garden for Zephyr to pick a flower. *Why does he look like he belongs at a funeral?* The little Prince was worried too, but nothing boosted Ferdinan's mood.

"You're sad," the elf whispered.

"I was worried. He truly looked miserable."

Soon the boys were in the kitchen where Ferdinan made two different teas. The Prince rambled for both of them before asking Ferdinan for a taste of his. This left the little Tinkerer shaking.

"Are you not feeling well?" young Zephyr offered.

Ferdinan bowed, trying to hide behind recently trimmed hair.

Worry filled the little Prince. "You should rest."

"I played alone that day too..."

Later, the little prince checked on his cousin. Ferdinan laid swallowed up in the small bed – pale and sweating profusely. On the nightstand was the tea. Grabbing it, Zephyr offered the drink to his suffering cousin. Next to the glass was the pile of plants...

Little onyx eyes doubled in size and his faced twisted.

Then everything went black.

"He didn't leave bed 'til we left for school," Zephyr's hands danced – searching for the rest. "An older Healer tried helping, but Ferdinan screamed when she got close. I've never been so scared..."

Silence drew the Prince's attention to her. "What happened? What took you from worrying about him to hating him?"

Zephyr felt heavy. Sorrow and anger oppressed him. *Why did those plants make me angry?* "I don't want to see anymore tonight."

"To think he went to such trouble producing thorns when he never should've needed them." Her ever-present smirk deepened. "And you. You shouldn't have needed them either."

"*Hello? Muulam?*" Interrupted Zephyr's response.

Both of them jumped. "Why am I hearing a girl's voice?"

"You're not the only one I tend to..." Sapphire eyes sharpened – searching the dreamscape. "Sleep little prince."

He was about to ask what she meant when she disappeared.

* * *

Exhaustion doubled after running into the Kalj, making the journey to the administration building impossibly long. But facing the glass door to the Superintendent's waiting area...

Adrenaline surged. Anxiety replaced fatigue. *If I fail...no. I can't fail this time.* Ferdinan's boney hand froze to the door's handle.

But he would. He was an incompetent coward. Facing Healer Bær when he couldn't control himself with Kalj Herrard... Even if the Kalj could do more damage to Ferdinan's country – and Jon's...

The Superintendent's office was ahead. And the skeleton froze again – searching for any distraction. *Yuyu...* They were waking her tomorrow. But...how long until she left Isolation? And... He'd never visit... *I'll message her to offer help with her course work...*

Ferdinan shook. His stomach knotted. Sharp fingers dug into his undamaged arm. One trembling breath – then another... *If I don't do this...* Breakfast leapt up his throat. He couldn't swallow. He tried. He tried... But lunged for a trash bin.

"I'll take care of that, Lord Ferdinan. They're waiting for you."

Bright red, Ferdinan looked up at Ms Radery and apologized. *I inconvenience everyone. I make everyone work harder...*

You're already failing.

Gingerly he inched over and peeked inside. The perfectly average man stood next to Master Dæya. *"Engh..."*

His heart felt like it'd explode. Quick breaths careened out of control. *This doesn't feel right...* His heart always raced around Healers – but not like this... It felt...it felt as if it'd break with the next beat. Like it was worn beyond repair. His heart...it moved faster, more recklessly. Jumping and twisting. The skeleton wanted to grab his chest – force it to slow down – but not with a Healer nearby.

I can't fail again! Not after that lecture. Facing the Duchess with bad news... *Calm down. You're making it worse.* But his heart beat more erratically. And the voice mocked him for it.

"Lord Ferdinan, please, take a seat," Dæya offered as Healer Bær shifted uncomfortably.

Ferdinan shook his head.

"It doesn't have to be here." Dæya gestured to the little lounging area between Ferdinan and the man's desk.

It was too close. "P-P-Please, I'm f-fine."

"Very well," Superintendent Dæya sighed as if a million hopes just flew out the window. "Please, your report."

Ferdinan's teeth chattered. He squeezed his screen tight and refused to look at Bær. "I-I've...over P-Prince...sch-schedule...a–"

"You've drawn up suggestions?" Dæya prompted.

"Y-yes, s-s-sir." *Calm down, calm down.* But his worn heart moved faster. Fumbling – trembling. "B-based on...what...P-Prince... already done...*ngh*...if he f-follows...follows th-th sch-schedule..."

Spots blurred his vision. Ferdinan wanted to shrink down and scream. And his heart... The fear strangled him – overwhelmed him.

"He'll need to take courses over the breaks, but he trains at home during that time," Dæya pointed out.

"H-he's-s..." Swallowing hard didn't steady his voice. "...more c-capable. Y-you just...to ap-prove."

Healer Bær looked over the schedule closely. "This is pretty heavy considering... Do you think he can handle it?"

Squeezing the screen harder, Ferdinan shut his eyes tight. "B-b-based on...p-previous st-study...y-y-yes. B-b-but..."

Scared of a man you could easily kill?

"But?" Worry pursed Dæya's lips at his student's increased terror and he motioned for his brother to move back.

Bær pressed against the window behind Dæya's desk.

"M-my sc-sc-schedule's... I w-was sh-shadow..." No more words came despite his efforts. *It'd be better for everyone if I died now.*

If only you deserved such mercy.

Teeth chattering. Stomach lurching. He needed this to end.

"You'll attend classes with him to make sure he can handle it?"

Ferdinan clutched the screen tighter and nodded. The room swayed. And his stomach... *Please, let me go...*

"Bær and I will go over this to see if any changes are needed. As it is, Prince Zephyr's expected to resume classes the beginning of the week. Thank you for your cooperation, Lord Ferdinan."

"...m...m-y...d-dut-ty..." That voice laughed gleefully.

"Dismissed."

Two steps out of the man's office, Ferdinan found himself on his knees. Ringing drowned out Ms. Radery's words. Folding himself in half and sealing his mouth, he tried not to be sick again.

Chapter 13

As expected, his cousin remained invisible. They did better separated, but that wouldn't be an option soon. *I need to know...* Though Ferdinan happily neglected details, he never lied

Zephyr and Theon returned to an empty suite after his "welcome back" party. But his cousin was still gone come morning.

I have no choice. Whether by boat or foot, the trip to Ferdinan's lab was nice. The Science's island was beautiful. And wasted on those who spent most of their time indoors. Perfect climbing trees. Flower speckled meadows. Awe inspiring panoramic views...

From the bridge, Zephyr headed to the far side of the island – where Ferdinan's lab was hidden. The farthest from everyone.

Relief filled Zephyr when he passed his ally's empty lab. *Did his family pressure him to pick this building?*

Metal pounding metal leapt down the hall. *I don't want to deal with him...* Activating the chime, Zephyr waited. And activated it two more times before his cousin's ears perked. Pale blue crystals turned. Even across the room and through the window... *Why won't he stop?* Anger boiled up, but he pushed it down until he felt empty. "Why are you so selfish? That's all I see when I look at you."

The skeleton froze – face warped in pain.

He hasn't changed... Those eyes were still the same... If not more selfish. *Why?* Zephyr studied his cousin. Ferdinan shook and was horribly pale. And thin. Much more than he remembered. The little boy from his memories filled his mind. *Why do I hate him?*

Ferdinan opened the door, but was bowed on one knee before the Prince made it inside. *Just as propriety calls for.*

"How may I serve you, my Prince?"

Zephyr studied his cousin closer, but Ferdinan looked the same as always. "Take off your shirts."

The skeleton swallowed hard.

"That's a command, not a request." Two fingers came together before throwing them forward.

"Y-Yes, my Prince." Boney fingers fumbled with the buttons of all four shirts he wore until the skeleton was shivering in the cool air.

Zephyr's stomach lurched. Scars marred Ferdinan's right side and a sheet of scar tissue wrapped around his left. "Stand."

"Yes, my Prince."

The scar wrapped skeleton rose. And rose... Though Ferdinan kept his head down, he stood over a foot taller. *When did he grow that much!?* Shaking his head, Zephyr circled, studying the frail body.

How many scars were erased by the fire? Melted skin covered most of Ferdinan's back and wrapped around his left arm - stopping as claw marks across his abdomen. And a discolored indention gouged the top back of Ferdinan's shoulder. "Why?"

"...I'm sorry, my Prince...I don't know what you mean."

Golden fingers danced. "You've been a self-absorbed, uncaring, pathetic human this entire time. So why? What did you gain?"

Ferdinan stood trembling; every muscle tense.

"What did you gain by jumping into a burning building?"

"I...I just followed my-" The skeleton froze. Guilt marred his face...and that selfishness intensified.

Unbearable heat flooded in. *What did you do?!* "Your?"

"I..." Ferdinan shook - searching for words. "I-I just did."

Pain numbed the back of Zephyr's hand as Ferdinan's head flew to the side. "Don't lie to me!"

A boney hand covered that sunken cheek. His cousin didn't say anything - but the selfishness in those eyes grew exponentially. That heat intensified. Then Zephyr was running - burning off the fury.

◊

Weak. Defenseless. Naked. He felt less than human. Shivering, Ferdinan collected his shirts. "I failed again..."

Failure.

Failure.

failure.

78

He failed again.

And he didn't understand how. *Why am I so stupid?! So blind? So useless?* His heart raced erratically. *I have to figure it out. I have to fix this. I can't fail again! I've killed so many...*

A true murderer.

Redressing, Ferdinan checked the chip was properly linked to the bones and closed the case. *They're so tiny... How could someone do that to a child? How could I use this to forget my sins?!*

Each swing of the hammer only bent the nails or hit the table. The weight of the tool...the uncooperative angle the nails shifted at. It was too much. *What did I do wrong?! How do I fix it?!*

A fiery serpent coiled around inside him.

"Why am I here? Why am I so useless!!!?" That scream left his throat, and the hammer flew from his hand – embedding itself impressively deep, high up in the cinderblock wall.

What problems will your device cause when it proves as defective as you?

Ferdinan stood too exhausted to think, but determination drove him to the chemical hidden in the back of his closet... There wasn't much. Two swallows... *How is this a month's worth?* A bony hand raised the contents to his mouth. The powder caressed his thin lips.

Jon will be the one to find me... Or Oya.

Oya could handle it...but Jon... *No, I can't do this... If I row out past my island and swim 'til I fail, there'd be no body to find...*

His arm dropped. A shaky breath escaped him and that cackling voice jumped in. He mixed a dose into a little bit of water. It was so insubstantial. *Is it enough to do anything?* ...he doubled the dose.

Think anything someone as worthless and incompetent as you makes will work?

I have to try. Ferdinan curled up on his sac – staring at his supply of nutrition bars. *Please start working...I can't do this anymore...*

* * *

Yuyu's alive... But it had nothing to do with him. The transport slowed as they neared the pier. Angry fire surrounded him. Burning rubble. Fingernails torn from seared hands. But he couldn't reach her. He was too weak. *We're going to die!*

"We're here, son."

That gentle voice ripped Elbie out of that unstoppable moment. Biting his lip got the panting under control. *Healer Herrard fixed me. My nails were back within days...* "Thank you, Master Ludwick."

"How long will you be?"

"An hour...maybe." Mismatched eyes studied his hands. *My nails were back in days. No scars...* "Depending on how she feels."

"I understand. Tell Yuyu Inoa we're happy she's awake." Master Ludwick smiled. "I have work to do, but will return here in an hour."

"Yes, sir. Thank you." Elbie waved off the transport. *I can't wait to get certified.* Depending on others for travel was annoying.

Entering Isolation, he checked in and walked down to Yuyu's room. The door was intimidating. *What do I do? I couldn't save her. I couldn't help her. I couldn't do anything... I took them there.*

Ringing filled his ears. It was so loud! There was no reason for it. His ears were fine. He was fine. *Do I deserve to see her? She nearly died 'cause I'm not good enough. But how long has she been alone?* The ringing intensified and Elbie grit his teeth against it. *Which is worse? Seeing her or not?* Dozens were begging to visit, but she chose him. *It's only 'cause Master Ferdinan can't come...* Elbie hugged himself, fighting back the memories. *That doesn't matter. She's my sister. I can't let her be trapped here alone.*

A shaky breath left him. Then another. And another. Until he was ready to signal the chime – announcing himself.

Elbie painted on a smile and opened the door. She sat at a little table near the window – reading something and massaging gloved hands. The same gloves he used to wear. There was a strip of missing hair. But her pink eyes were still bright and her smile beautiful.

"Elbie! I'm glad...!" There was an unusual pause, "...you came!"

Sitting across from her, he offered his hand. "How are you?"

"Much better now you're here." A gloved hand hovered over his.

They were both hesitant. And curious. Slowly it lowered until his hand cradled hers. Burning cold wrapped around his fingers and palm – working its way to his shoulder. It was sharp and intense. Like always. He kept his face steady – though he couldn't stop himself from flinching. Yuyu's smile twitched and discomfort danced in her eyes. But she didn't pull away.

"I was worried..."

So was I. Considering the damage to her body, it wasn't beyond reason to believe she'd feel different or that everyone else would feel different to her. "You're the same Yuyu to me too."

They sat grinning despite the pain. If this was the same, maybe everything else would return to the way it was. Taking his hand back, Elbie looked at her screen. "You're doing schoolwork already?"

Light giggles left her. "No. I've been..."

A strange look lined his sister's face. "You've been?"

Grabbing the screen, she focused on it. "I talk to my family. And read some messages."

"They must've been excited to hear from you." Melancholy hit him, but he didn't know how he could miss what he never had.

"Lots of tears!" Yuyu laughed and Elbie joined. "How are you?"

"Completely healed." Lifting both hands, he showed them to her. But fire filled his mind. "All restrictions have been lifted too."

Pink eyes stared at his hands. "I'm sorry you were hurt."

"It wasn't your fault. And...it wasn't anything like you..." Clearing his throat, Elbie hid his hands under the table so he didn't have to look at them. "How about the messages?"

"Mostly they're..." Again, her words stopped. It took focusing on the screen for her to continue. "They're from instructors. Master Ferdinan offered to help with work I can't do."

That's just like him. But... "He is the best."

"Yah..." Yuyu looked to the window and ocean beyond.

"Yuyu?" He leaned forward. "Yuyu? Are you ok?"

She turned back, but didn't speak until she focused on the screen again. "How's Master Ferdinan? I heard he was hurt too."

"I'm not sure..." *What's going on?*

This grabbed her full attention. "What do you mean?"

It wasn't fun, but he told her about how tired their mentor was – even dozing off. The strange tension between Master Ferdinan and Jon Dinta. All of what little he knew. She didn't speak much – which was unusual for her. And when she did, Yuyu continued losing what she was saying until finding a focus. "Are you sure you're ok?"

"I..." Her gaze turned razor sharp – burrowing into him. "It's all there. But when I speak...it's gone."

Elbie wasn't sure what stabbed through his heart, but it was a pain he couldn't describe. "I'll send for Healer Bær."

A gloved hand reached out for him but stopped – returning to rest on the table. "Thank you."

* * *

Ferdinan wouldn't stir, so Oya laid down facing him, the top of her head inches from his shoulder. Red marred his face. Clothing covered the rest of the damage. Delicate fingers ran through his hair, but that diamond shell was still there. *Hm... Do I have to amuse Emil to get back in?* "Good evening!"

A slight twitch and Ferdinan rolled to his side.

Sitting up, she shook him again. "*Jon'll become a mother hen if he catches you sleeping.*"

A muffled groan answered, "*Why are you nice to me?*"

Bare toes wiggled on the hard floor and her entourage of glowing orbs danced around them. "*Why wouldn't I be nice to a nice person?*"

"*I'm not nice...*" Ferdinan's skeletal body relaxed.

When Oya couldn't wake him a second time, she stood and made her way to the one who hurt her friend.

~

The golden boy slid down a cliff face. A *smooth* cliff face. No amount of desperation would manifest a handhold or perch. She made sure of it.

The elf hovered – a cruel, unforgiving smile on her lips. And her rage... The earth he clung to thrashed in agony. And when she backhanded him, unseen rings tore open his cheek.

I thought there was good in you.

82

Words flooded the sky – falling heavy and painful. Crushing his spirit. Words he feared. Words his soul writhed under. Words he hid from... She wouldn't let him store them in darkness anymore. She'd take away his escapes this night.

The sky shattered – falling as glass. Reflecting those dark hidden things. Every reflection terrified Zephyr. She magnified it. And he slid farther. Inch by inch. Until his feet ran out of solid rock.

The elf sneered and watched him struggle. When his grip failed, she looked on as he plunged into eternal nothingness.

You will learn – I don't care how.

Snap. His flailing and screaming ended with a wet *thud* on a bed of ten-thousand needles. Piercing, blood trickled out with his agony.

Another *snap* and Zephyr was stripped and bound to a table. Craze sparkled in sapphire eyes and pleasure laced her grin. A vile, serrated knife appeared in her hand – barbed and a foot long.

Starting at the fingers on his left hand, she cut, stabbed, tore, up to his heart. Then she moved to the right. And then his toes – left – right. All four were cut and sliced and carved. Blood coated both of them. Screams filled the air. Never ending. Fading only when he fought for breath. But it wasn't enough. *Now for your face.*

The line she drew across his forehead bled profusely, trickling down to fill one eye. "Maybe you didn't believe I'd kill you."

This beast attacked her friend again...after she showed mercy to it! After she started helping it! *You hurt my friend and betrayed my trust.* "One warning. One lesson. Next time you die." The vile blade sung – stopping just before touching his eye. "Do you understand?"

All Zephyr could do was cry breathlessly. Until she banished the pain. If a full night of torture didn't teach him, nothing would.

"...duty..." Fear weakened his voice. "I was fulfilling...my duty."

The elf all but growled. "You're duty? This...!? There *is* a responsibility you have, but you're failing it miserably."

"I...I don't...understand..." One last *snap* and the restraints disappeared. Torn skin became whole and the blood vanished. He stood unharmed, looking up at her. "You really will kill me."

Sapphire eyes shimmered menacingly. "Yes."

Zephyr clenched his fist below his nose and threw forward an open palm. "Is he so important?"

"Yes." Her face softened. "Even if he wasn't, *you* need to find a better way. It's better for your country to turn to chaos and upheaval than allow you to remain like this. Do you understand?"

Swallowing hard, Zephyr flinched. "I'm obeying orders."

"Whose orders? The General you'll replace?"

"No."

"The ruling monarchs – your parents?"

"No."

"How can you be order by those lower than you?"

Golden hands danced, but no words left his mouth.

"Why do you hate him?" Silence stood between them for a moment. "You'll never be an acceptable general as you are."

His hands clenched into fists. "Before..."

"Yes?"

"Before...you said you'd help me understand. Help me."

This startled the elf. *He's asking for help?* "So you don't die?"

"Yes. I want to live." Golden hands danced. "And I want to understand what's stopping me from being a strong general. And... and if understanding helps both of us, then isn't that best?"

"You truly are selfish." The elf scowled. "But it's a start."

Bowing, Zephyr asked more formally. "Please help me understand what you're teaching me."

"Starting tomorrow night."

"Tomorrow?"

"You'll be exhausted when you wake up." The elf grinned.

"Yes, ma'am."

She didn't want to deal with him anymore. But...he actually asked for help... *Don't disappoint me again.*

Chapter 14

A little hand waved – drawing Ferdinan's attention to his pupil. Red coated him. *...have I been dozing?* Covering a yawn, the skeleton looked away. "I apologize, that was rude."

Worry painted Elbie's smile.

Only you could make a child look like that.

Blue crystals fell upon his own project. "We discussed the programmable flying disk, the energy conversion cuffs, and pet robot... Would you like to see this block's final project?"

Mismatched eyes doubled at the unusual offer. "I'd love that! Are you sure?"

Rubbing his eyes, Ferdinan smiled. "If it'll help you, I'm happy to share."

His mentor's finger directed Elbie to a well-polished steel toroid about the size of a small melon. It had two sets of double holes on opposite sides and a black plug between. No buttons or screens. It looked like an odd paperweight. "What is it?"

"My heart..." Ferdinan picked it up – it wasn't as heavy as it looked, but it had some heft. "My old design wasn't as good...they're needing replacing. So...I made something better."

"Heart?" Elbie asked once Ferdinan stopped yawning.

"Sorry, engineer jargon. 'Heart' is the power source. My first design was sufficient...but inefficient, and not as durable as I'd hoped. But I've learned a good bit since then."

"How does it work?"

"Small scale fusion." Offering the toroidal to his pupil, Ferdinan rubbed his eyes, then his face. *Wake up!* It took longer and longer each day to find any kind of energy. *A couple more weeks and I'll be used to it...*

"Small scale fusion?!" Mismatched eyes marveled at the steel donut in his hands. "No need to argue a purpose for this..."

"Ah...I'm sorry... That'd make it less useful for you."

You're supposed to teach him to think when you can't?

"How? I know how fusion reactor plants work, but how did you make it so small?"

"After your ninth-year courses you'll understand enough for my explanation to make sense... I'll pick something more useful. I apologize." *I'm so stupid.*

You're incompetent.

"No! It's awesome!" Elbie stepped back to hide his concern. "I wish I already learned enough to ask you about it."

The room tilted, forcing Ferdinan to sit. Doubling the weight of his eyelids. It took a minute to get his mind moving, but he remembered a device Elbie would love. With great effort he got to his feet, then to his closet and back. Shaking his head, the skeleton laid a small rod before his apprentice.

Elbie picked up the strange piece. "What is it?"

"That's the..." After a long yawn, Ferdinan finished, "OP-72-1. It's used to open screens."

Elbie marveled over it – making Ferdinan blush.

Distract him with something shiny? You can't do better than this?

Shut up! I know I'm incompetent!

Discordant laughter echoed around his skull. It wouldn't stop. No matter how much he demanded. No matter how much he pled! No matter how much of that chemical he took.

Gritty sand crawled under his skin – making Ferdinan realize he was covering his ears, panting.

"Master Ferdinan? Master Ferdinan?" Wild, mismatched eyes looked over the skeleton as the boy repeated his name.

What am I doing? Why am I doing this!? The voice answered happily, but he couldn't keep engaging it. Not around others. Especially not around someone as young as Elbie.

Shaking his head didn't banish the sleep from his eyes or the voice from his mind. But it threatened to knock him out. Even his words felt slurred. "I apologize, what were you asking?"

Elbie frowned but answered. "Does anyone know about these? 'Cause I'd use it."

"No... No one uses them..."

Elbie reached for his bag and pulled out an old screen. Laying it on the table, he took the rod – which looked like it might've been a screwdriver at one point in its life – to the back.

"No! You'll lose everything on it!" Ferdinan jolted forward, stopping an inch from Elbie's hand. Bright red, he eased back.

"Oh...ok." Deactivating the tool, Elbie returned to studying it, though he glanced at the blushing skeleton in concern.

Chewing on his lip, Ferdinan hurried out of the room before Elbie could say anything. When he returned, he had a small stack of old screens. "These are all...*yawn*...dead."

"Really? Are you sure?" Elbie hesitated looking between the tool and his bag.

He wants to leave...why am I like this? "Yeah. The school gives me the dead screens to see if I can salvage any."

Awe filled Elbie's eyes. "You can do anything, can't you?"

Stupid child!

Why did he say that? I'm useless. I can't do anything. Even the medicine isn't working... "No. There's far more I can't do than I can. I just wanted to learn how those work...but the company's tightlipped. It took a year...to rig something to open them. I broke the first one beyond salvation...but saw how they sealed them. From there I figured out...how to open them."

"How did this get approved? The school always shipped these back to the company, right?"

"I argued scientific...curiosity and...if I learned how they worked, the school could fix them...instead of getting more."

"How many have you fixed?"

"A few dozen... To be fair..." Ferdinan yawned – his entire body shaking. *Is this medicine actually a sedative?* And the fatigue was increasing each day...but the voice wasn't going away. "...there was a backlog when I proposed the OP-72-1. Now...I just fix them...as I get them."

Turning it back on, Elbie attacked the edge of the screen. "Is this how I hold it?"

"Hm? About two inches...from the edge... They put the release in pretty deep."

Following instructions, Elbie was rewarded with a small *pop*. "Ok, now what?"

"Slide the back in...the direction of the arrow."

"Oh?" The young boy forced a smile, but it didn't extend beyond his lips. "I thought that was their logo."

Rubbing his eyes, he gave Elbie a grin. "Yeah, they were smart. Two-fold purpose."

If only you could be so useful.

Elbie was surprised to see the screen was two sheets. It really looked solid. And once the back was removed, it was no longer clear like glass. A million questions left the child about the inner workings of the device. But...even if his apprentice knew enough physics, Ferdinan drifted off before he could explain anything.

* * *

The Duchess glared at the one groveling before her as she tapped a small wrapped nutrition bar against the desk. "Why are these numbers so high?"

"The southern plantations are failing. The population's migrating to the capital thinking they'll be fed. And they were 'til so many arrived and the food supplements were delayed."

"Tornados are beyond anyone's control." Sharp eyes studied the little bar. Natural disasters were no one's fault, but they were the responsibility of her station. And they tested how well lesser nobles did their job. "Those plantations only *started* failing. They should still have more food than here in the north."

"According to hearsay, Duke Orthan squandered it on parties. But if rumors are true, a number of lower dukes and lords are doing similar things."

"Pretending they have surplus to avoid scrutiny." Grabbing a screen, paper, and pen from her desk, she pulled up the records of their various holdings. Taking from emergency rations was never preferable – even in situations they were designed for. But that's why they had them. Starting with the ones needing wares rotated soonest, she wrote down all pertinent information and handed it to the man. "Start with these. Hopefully the supply chain will be repaired before they run dry."

Swallowing hard, the man took the paper and looked over the information. It was odd having it written instead of on a screen, but he knew better than to question her. "Yes, ma'am."

"Fools. Doing nothing is worse than mass hysteria at this point." Again, she tapped the bar against her desk – considering her options. "How much land is abandoned?"

"A bit. I'll get you exact numbers."

"Good. We'll be tightening our belts again." Piercing eyes turned to the man. "Arrange for me to visit Duke Orthan and any other pertinent areas. Emelica will serve in my absence."

"And your youngest?"

Normally she kept her children with her until they started official studies. Trannie still had another year, but this wasn't the kind of business she'd take a young child to. "Unfortunately... Kananni can care for her for a few weeks."

"Yes, ma'am. When would you like to leave?"

"As soon as possible."

* * *

Chimes sounded from somewhere.

Bells...

Birds took center stage in his mind. A groan left thin lips. Boney fingers forced open blurry eyes. Everything ached...

Why am...I cold...? Ugh... His left hip, shoulder, and both knees felt like they'd been hit with something hard.

Giggles and a perfect void enveloped him. *What...?*

"You'll turn into an old man like that."

89

"Old..." *man...?* Crystal blue eyes latched on to bare, golden-brown feet. *Why won't...she wear shoes...?*

"*Jon's on his way. He's been ordered to drag you to class.*"

That emptiness attacked his cheek, scrunching his face. "*Tired...*"

Useless.

"*Let's get your blood moving, that'll wake you up!*"

Giggles filled reality and the void swallowed him up again. Was he moving?

"*Maybe a cold shower...*"

A barely functional brain grasped onto that suggestion. "Yeah..."

Oya steadied him, guiding him to the bathroom. "*Don't slip or I won't care how modest you are.*"

It took too much energy to blush.

First stop was the sink to splash cold water on his face. *What is this...?* It felt too extreme for a side effect... More likely healing, projects, teaching, and shadowing his cousin pushed him past his limit. *Zephyr's schedule...I need to...write up a report...*

Moving helped. Between this and the cold water, his eyes opened. But his feet were unsteady. Stripping down, Ferdinan took a *cold* shower. Whether it woke him or just gave him incentive to move faster was up for debate. Either way, he finished and dressed by the time Jon arrived with food.

"Are you ok?"

Ferdinan wobbled out of the closet and latched onto the nearest table. "I'm having trouble waking up."

It's your fault.

"Food should help."

Of course, you'd say that...

Jon slid a plate next to his ally before sitting down to his own. A third plate disappeared when Oya walked out of the lab. "You have to attend class today."

"I'm shadowing...my cousin..." Ferdinan blinked at the waffle piled high with fruit – not sure what to do with it.

"Zephyr's sick. You're coming to class." Jon frowned when Ferdinan turned transparent. "I don't know why they're letting you off so easy. Even you have to be falling behind after missing this much."

"I'm not..." Ferdinan mumbled. *The Duchess is keeping Master Dæya away...isn't she...?* Besides, Ferdinan already finished his course work. Everything was submitted. Class was unnecessary...

Show Jon how superior you think you are.

"Ferdinan?"

A yawn took over, right alongside a full body stretch.

"What did Oya do to you?"

Blinking fast, Ferdinan latched onto a moment of alertness.

"I ask her to help with a couple meals and you can't keep your eyes open. You've stabbed the same piece of fruit for five minutes."

"Huh?" Looking down... Dozens of puncture wounds perforated a poor piece of mango.

"Don't bother stalling. If you don't finish before it's time to leave, I'm dragging you out anyway."

"I should check...my Prince..."

"Healer Herrard's looking after him. He's fine."

Mentioning the Healer sent Ferdinan's heart racing.

"If you aren't going to eat," Jon slapped his hands against the table, "we'll leave now so Master Ludwick can tell you what you've missed. Where're those bars of yours? You can eat one of them."

Ferdinan glared at his ally. Until his eyes drifted to the floor. Stinging needles encased his shoulders. "What?!"

Jon stood back, hand on his hips "We're talking about this *now*."

"What...?" Ferdinan looked around. A long wooden box caught his attention – twisting his stomach. "I forgot about that!"

"What?" Jon watched Ferdinan struggle to cross the room.

Nails laid scattered. *Hammer...what did I...do with it...?* Not seeing it on the table, he searched below – only to fall over. His heart tore. *She's lost her arm 'cause of me!* Scooting under the table, he pressed against the wall and curled up. *Why won't I die?*

You failed her. Deprived her life of opportunities. You crippled her.

An ocean surged behind blue crystals. *I forgot...? I'm horrible!*

You're the worst.

I'm the worst...

"Ferdinan?" Jon offered a hand. "Tell me what's going on."

"It doesn't...matter."

"Obviously, it does." Jon tried again, "What did you forget?"

Why hasn't...Yahmo called...asking...about it...?

"Ferdinan?"

"That box...should've...gone out...weeks ago."

You stole her arm.

◇

Jon inspected the box. Bent nails did nothing to hold the askew lid in place. Inside were two odd metal poles and a small electrode. *He's not forgetful...* But dust attested to how long it sat there.

Where's the hammer? Ferdinan's work was precise and meticulous. Not being able to hammer a lid shut... Looking up, Jon wished for his family more than ever. Near the ceiling was a blemish he'd missed – with a handle sticking out. *What happened?*

Might as well get it ready. Rummaging for another hammer – Jon sealed the addressed box. *How do I get him out of here?* Squatting down... *He's asleep again?* Neither would the gent stir when shaken.

Another sigh and Jon stood and checked the supply boat's schedule. *It leaves in the morning...* The next didn't come for two more weeks. *I should send this; his work is usually time sensitive.*

Besides. This felt like the only thing Jon had any control over.

"Oya," Jon stepped out of the lab and looked out over the water. "If you're nearby, please watch him."

92

Chapter 15

"Please! Take her! Please!" Ilu burst into Jon's lab and grabbed the taller boy's shirt. Maniacal laughter danced behind him. "I don't understand. How do you do it?"

Between Ferdinan and her... Sighing, Jon called toward the hallway. "Please stop it, Oya."

"What fun is that?" Inhuman green eyes glowed from the open doorway. "Need a moment?"

"Please."

Nodding, she vanished. She didn't move or hide, just vanished like always.

"See! She does that every time! Then she appears out of nowhere! I can't classify her! Everything fails! None of it makes sense! How does she even do that?! No one can do that! It's not possible!!"

I have no idea... "Ilu...are you familiar with the various ancient gods?"

"Yes..." The Healer's brown eyes darkened in despair.

"Puck, Loki, Lilith, Anansi, Tanukis, Jibranate, Wamerak, Ese're'inie."

Ilu rubbed at his face. "Trickster gods throughout human history."

"I'm sure all those gods were based on people like Oya." *I can't believe I'm saying this about a girl.* "Don't take her seriously."

Ilu stood taken aback. "That's how you deal with her?"

"She's a girl...even if I forget..." Jon knew this conflicted with his earlier statement. "Women are worthy of deep love and respect. Even if we don't understand, they do what they do for our own good."

Ilu's expression turned incredulous.

"Yes, she pushes us to our limits, but she cares. She pokes and prods those who are hurting, but makes sure they're ok. Her ways aren't the most palatable, but she means well."

"How does any of this help us?" Exasperation sighed out of his island brother.

"Personally?" Sympathy wrapped around Jon's smile. "It doesn't. She's teasing you for entertainment. But...it's giving Ferdinan time to heal and recuperate."

"*Ugh...*" Ilu dropped his head in defeat.

"I'm ok with her selfishness and obnoxiousness. 'Cause she cares for him. I...things would be worse if she didn't have this obsession." A timid smile hid Jon's fatigue. "I'm sorry. Just a bit longer. When Ferdinan's healthier, she'll torture you a little less."

"Everything always goes back to him." Irritation saturated Ilu's voice – until guilt softened the Healer's expression.

Their disrupted lives... Since the day Jon was assigned to assist Ferdinan in South Chūzo, things kept getting worse...

"I don't have to feed my ally tonight...I was hoping all of us could sit down and talk. It's been a while. And there're things I need to address. And apologize for."

"You haven't done anything wrong..."

"Humor me." There was another issue wrapped up in all this. "Maybe give up on classifying Oya for a bit and focus on Marcus. I should be spending more time with him but... He's been hiding in his room...sleeping more... Can you make up for my lacking? At least 'til I can figure out what's going on with my ally?"

"...Marcus..." Ilu sighed – placing a hand against his forehead. "I've been failing on all sides..."

"No, you haven't. There's just too much happening right now." Giving Ilu a squeeze, Jon called out. "Oya, will you play with me for a while?"

Golden brown arms appeared out of thin air and wrapped tightly around them both. "I love touching moments!"

At Jon's gesture, Ilu made his escape.

"Really, Jon? Puck and Ese're'inie?"

Jon gave a wry smile – one he thought she'd appreciate. "Am I wrong?"

"Nope, they're my favorites!"

"Thank you for staying. And please stop tormenting my island brothers."

"But! They're fun to play with. Especially Tuel! I love his hair and he can outmaneuver me in the air! It's wonderful!"

All Jon could do was nod – and pity Ilu. *How do you classify a trickster god?*

* * *

"You're looking way too serious for lunchtime without food being the focus." Xhou plopped down beside the youngest Tinkerer. "Food's a serious matter."

This made Elbie giggle. "I know one person who'd disagree."

"Yah, but I'm going on a majority rule here."

"Fair enough."

"How was your visit with Yuyu? I'm jealous! I still haven't gotten to check on her!"

"It was nice. She's being released from isolation tomorrow, so you can talk to her then."

"Not letting her Lead come before she's even released? I bet it's Herrard's doing." Xhou gave a dramatic huff.

Elbie giggled then looked down at his screen, hesitating. "Um...in your opinion...is this good enough for a final project?"

Leaning over, Xhou studied the diagram with a "*Hmm.*" "I don't think that'll quite make the cut. But Tinkerers have different requirements than Thinkers. I'd run it by your mentor first." *Say his name. This won't sound natural if you don't.*

"I was afraid of that," Elbie sighed, closing out the box and pulling up a new one.

"Don't delete that. It might not work for a final project but could be great for a class one."

Mismatched eyes looked up – grinning. "Don't worry. It seemed fun, so I want to keep it."

"Your...Ferdinan would be happy to help you think of something." Reaching over, Xhou mussed the child's hair – nabbing the screen.

"Master Ferdinan already is." Elbie reached for the clear sheet the older boy held aloft.

Wiggling it back and forth, Xhou gestured that it was his hostage. "Oh?"

"Yah. We're going through his previous projects and discussing them." Elbie looked longingly at his screen. "And...he's still in class. I can't schedule extra time with him for a few days–"

"What's going on?" *But Ferdinan always makes time for apprentices...* "Wait... He's never had class at this time. The weirdo crams everything in the mornings."

"He's shadowing his cousin 'til he's fine-tuned Prince Zephyr's schedule."

What...? "Who ordered that?"

"I don't know." Mismatched eyes moved from the screen to Xhou. "I didn't think it mattered."

Xhou chuckled. "It wouldn't, would it? Sounds like the usual nonsense." *No way the school would have a student do that...*

"'Usual nonsense?'" Elbie parroted back.

"Heh? Nothing you need to worry about. North Chūzites are particularly protective of their soon to be General." Bringing the screen down but holding it out of Elbie's reach, Xhou changed topics. "When you were doing screen sessions last break, where was Ferdinan responding from? For the life of me I can't remember the name of the lab and it's driving me nuts."

Elbie froze – staring at his hands. "It was a hospital."

"Yah, but he was using their lab... It's on the tip of my tongue! What *is* that name...?" Allowing frustration to wrinkle his forehead completed the show.

Elbie shook his head, then smiled. "Yurranie Private Children's Hospital."

"Yurranie! How could I have forgotten that? He never did tell me what he was working on, guess it was classified," *Wasn't that the hospital that distributed information about the cure?*

"No...he just didn't like talking about it."

"He told you and not me? His Lead? His mentor?" A huge sigh left Xhou and he handed over the screen. "I wish I knew how to get him to like me."

"He has to trust you."

The six-year-old's blunt insight was unexpected. But Ferdinan thought and observed too deeply – of course he would pass that onto his apprentices. "I wish I knew how to make him trust me."

Giggles filled the space between them while Elbie slipped the screen into the safety of his bag. "You're too energetic for him. He always looks frazzled after talking to you."

"Ah...how's he doing? I can't be any kind of decent Lead if I don't check up on the health and wellbeing of *all* my charges." Anger's dull ache smoldered. But Ferdinan was the only Scientist he'd been ignoring. Still...he didn't want to see the skeleton.

"He's...looking rough. Maybe it's 'cause he's still healing..." Elbie trailed off for a moment – mismatched eyes returning to stare at his hands. "It must've been hard. He improved for a while... Or at least I thought he did."

"Oh?"

"He looks exhausted. Having to do this for his cousin...it's best if I don't push him too hard."

"It's not your job to worry about him – *he's* supposed to worry over *you. I'm* supposed to worry over *him.*"

"Yah... But this last year..."

Elbie cringed when Xhou hugged him – but the Lead just squeezed harder. *Don't become like Ferdinan...* "If you're worried about anything – Ferdinan or otherwise – talk to me. Us busybodies love that sort of stuff."

* * *

"Shall we try again?" The elf hovered over him.

"I've done nothing wrong!" The Prince scrambled away – heart racing. But instead of the terrifying elf who'd tortured him, she looked normal.

"If you had, I'd be killing you very slowly right now." Leaning forward, she gazed into his soul. "Why do you hate him?"

"I don't know." Zephyr tapped his forehead, dropped his palm to face it, and shook his head.

"Then let's continue." A wave of her hand and more memories played.

After the tea, Zephyr spent less time around his cousin – until they actively avoided each other. Ferdinan's malnutrition quickly became apparent, and his cousin acted like the Prince's manservant.

And whenever Zephyr became angry, everything stopped. *Why does she keep ending them?*

Color intensified. Bright and vivid as Tenalia greeted her two nephews from the boat.

The elf smirked – paying more attention than before. "You cherish this memory."

"Yes." Golden hands danced in delight. "This was when I was presented to the military. I've never had so much fun."

The young Zephyr sparred every commander of North Chūzo's various platoons. Games and feasts. Music and dancing... It was a wonderland of a party!

And in the background, hazy and almost forgotten, was Ferdinan.

Giggles left the elf. "Why did you keep turning down meats? They look delicious."

"Those..." Zephyr rolled his eyes at himself. "It doesn't agree with me."

A delicate eyebrow rose high on her brow.

"Fighters and some Athletes can't digest meat."

"Wouldn't they need it more than others?"

"Meat isn't the only source of protein." Zephyr shrugged and returned to observing.

The next day was brighter – culminating in a lavish feast – the Samultz's in the seat of honor. Everyone enjoyed it. Except Ferdinan. The underweight child stared at his hands and ignored his food.

"He refused to eat the entire week," Zephyr pressed his stomach and threw his hand to the side. "He was a bane to everyone."

Workers rushed in to clean up when the meal ended – allowing the Samultz's to adjourn to an extravagant sitting room. Stories commenced. Somewhere in the shadows, Ferdinan snuck off. It was sometime later before the General noticed.

"Where's Ferdinan?"

"Don't worry, my General, he's probably using the restroom," the Duchess answered smoothly.

"Hmmm...?" The elf fidgeted – eyes scouring the room.

"What?" Zephyr tried keeping his voice in check, but he didn't want to think about what came next.

"Is the Duke dead?" The elf asked – still searching the scene.

Tenalia looked doubtful. "Zephyr. Let's try a little test."

Present day Zephyr was taken aback. "What?"

The little Prince beamed in excitement. "Yes, ma'am?"

"I've yet to see him. And this was an important occasion." The elf returned his annoyance.

"Show me how good your tracking skills are," Tenalia grinned. "Go find your cousin."

Though the younger Zephyr frowned, he bowed to the General – tapping his palm.

"He can't handle two people." *I don't want to see.* "Even time with his family is spent one on one. A celebration's beyond him."

As the little Prince left the room, everything dimmed.

"You've tried forgetting this."

I hate this. "Let's skip this part like you did with the others."

"I haven't skipped anything."

"We've stopped abruptly a number of times."

"I didn't skip those – you did."

The hazy memory sharpened, playing reluctantly. An odd sound from the kitchen caught young Zephyr's attention. Entering, he found hidden in the shadows, Ferdinan.

Feeding.

The little Prince froze confused. But older Zephyr looked away.

"What is it?" the elf prodded.

"This is shameful."

It didn't take long before Ferdinan reached his physical limit. Partially chewed food spewed everywhere. Memory Zephyr shot out of the kitchen and into a servant – hands flying.

He called for the Duchess then returned to watch his cousin. The thin, immaculately kept woman appeared and pointed at her son. Coughing, gagging – Ferdinan shook, unable to stop dry heaving.

"Please leave, my Prince." Utter disdain glared at Ferdinan.

"But he's sick," the seven-year-old Zephyr objected – hands punctuating the point.

"He chose to do a foolish, selfish thing to himself. This is the consequence. Feel no pity for him."

Starlight eyebrows twitched. "She said that about her own son?"

Golden hands moved as harshly as his words. "The Duchess was right. He did that to himself. I watched him engorge himself. He just kept eating 'til... He was foolish and selfish! Refusing to eat 'til he made himself this hungry... It was all his fault."

"Watch your tongue before I remove it," the elf snapped. "You're the fool for not trying to understand him."

Chapter 16

I'd never know this place burned down... Pink eyes soaked in everything in the building's center lab as Yuyu rubbed aching hands. It looked exactly as it always did...only shinier – newer. It didn't seem possible. But...between the Energists, Athletes, and Scientists, getting a building like this built and stocked in a month was simple.

She checked the time. *He's late...* But Elbie was never late. When it came to punctuality, he was as anal as Master Ferdinan. *Did something happen? Is he ok?*

Gloved hands returned the screen to her bag. These were really weird. Not just the goopy material they were made from, but they didn't feel like gloves. If not for the black sheen, she'd forget they were there. If only forgetting the pain was so easy. *Would they let me continue wearing it on the rest of my body?* They stopped wrapping her in it shortly before releasing her from isolation. But Yuyu wished they hadn't. Seeing her skin... They focused on her face and hands – and she was grateful. If she looked in the mirror and saw a face twisted and melted from fire...

It took swallowing hard to stop that line of thought. Sighing, Yuyu shook her head. *He should be here by now...*

There had to be something wrong. Turning, she headed outside to find Elbie standing at the tree line – staring at the building.

Why is he just standing there? It took getting closer to realize he was shaking. Mismatched eyes glanced down at his hands before returning to the lab building. Sometimes he'd lift a foot, but it wouldn't go anywhere – ending up where it'd started.

When she waved, he didn't respond, just kept looking between his hands and the building. "Elbie!"

She called out again – hurrying up to him. Relief eased his strained expression when he noticed her.

"I'm sorry..."

Why...? Yuyu looked down. She didn't remember any of it. The three of them were running around playing while Xhou made lunch. Then she was staring at a ceiling she didn't recognize. *What was it like? How scared was he? I was told he tried pulling me out.* She loved him for that. *Could I have done the same?* "We don't..."

Every word vanished. *What was I thinking? Saying?* Looking around... *The building...it was about the building...* "We don't have to meet here if this is too difficult."

"No. It's fine. I just need to try harder..." Elbie fidgeted at his sister's disappointed look. "You wanted to talk? I told Master Ludwick I was helping you, so we have a while."

Yuyu studied her gloved hands. *Focus on the thought. Hold it in my hands...* "If we have that long...then tell me about what happened. I don't remember anything after meeting Xhou and Rura for lunch."

Elbie paled. It took her nudging him to get him talking.

"I'm sorry. My mind wandered... Guess it's too beautiful of a day to concentrate." Elbie couldn't look at her. "We took Rura to the lab and there was a chemical explosion but Master Ferdinan saved us."

"I already..." *Focus on Elbie. That's where the thought is.* "I already know that much."

"That's all that matters." Elbie gestured to the skintight black gloves. "You need to focus on healing."

It took a bit, but Yuyu fixed on Elbie – anchored every word to his presence. "Knowing won't impact my healing."

"There isn't anything more worth knowing." Elbie's eyes pleaded for her to stop. "What was it you wanted to talk about?"

Blowing out a breath, she took the screen from her bag and focused on it. "I told you about Master Ferdinan's offer to help with my schoolwork and projects 'til my hands were healed?"

A worried smile bloomed on Elbie's face.

"It was tempting. But he's struggling with so much. Adding to that burden..." Yuyu sighed. *I'm adding to Elbie's burden too...*

"I would love to help you. If you'd let me."

Yuyu wasn't sure if she should frown or smile. *Focus.* "I was going to ask you...but it looks like you're struggling too."

"No. No I'm not!" Stepping forward, Elbie brought his hands together. "I can help and I want to."

"Elbie. I love you. You're a wonderful little brother. Which is why I can't let you become like Master Ferdinan."

"I'm not. I'm fine. Everything is ok."

"You can't enter the main lab and you look exhausted. Master Ferdinan's wonderful. He's kind and always trying to help others. But he never takes care of himself. He does everything on his own..." Pink eyes drifted to the building, taking her words with her. This was exhausting. Frustrating. *Ferdinan...the screen.* "...does everything on his own – even when it's hurting him. I might not be able to help Master Ferdinan – but I won't be the reason you end up hurt."

Elbie searched frantically for words. "Please. Let me help you."

"Elbie..." Yuyu was taken aback by his desperate voice.

"Please. I want to help."

She shouldn't ignore those frantic mismatched eyes. *It'll be easier to help him if we're spending more time together.* "I'll find someone else if you keep struggling."

"I won't. I won't worry you like that." Relief danced on his lips.

"Then what will you do?"

Elbie hesitated. "What should I do?"

* * *

"Enjoy your three back-to-back breaks, slacker?" Denila teased the approaching Zephyr. "Wish I could relax like that."

"I'll trade you places next time." Both hands held out, one tapped the other, then moved the second out of the way.

"Ha!" She gave her lifelong friend and rival a hug. "It's been boring without my sparring buddy."

"I'd rather you beat me every day then live through that again." Golden hands danced in time with his words.

She gestured the Prince to sit before her. "What was wrong?"

"I don't know. It hit suddenly and left the same way."

"No. Recently. Missing class right after returning is bad."

His hands danced as his cheeks turned red. "Everyone gets sick."

"Stop it." Denila slugged Zephyr's shoulder. "I want the boy who always teased with me. But I'm glad you're better."

"Thanks..." Zephyr looked back at her and snorted. "But I'll never be able to take the samurai mermaid seriously."

Laughter doubled her over. "That's my spoiled Prince!"

She didn't send me away... After what happened with him last block, being treated the same was a relief.

"Time to make up for your vacation."

"Oh?" One hand came forward as if offering a present.

"You, me, ten miles to the main island as the fish swims." In one motion, she stripped down to her favorite swimsuit.

Zephyr sniggered and showed he came prepared.

This made her laugh. "You know me so well? Ten miles as a fish, another thirteen to the guest apartments!"

"*Pfft!* Seventeen along the beach to the guest apartments." Zephyr gave the cockiest, most self-assured, smug face he could.

"Challenge accepted!" Denila smirked. "Three. Two. ONE!"

* * *

He keeps passing out. It wasn't normal sleep; it was as if he was sedated. And the infection eating away at his chest was different. It stopped spreading, but it was growing denser, darker. And it was one of many things she didn't understand.

How did Yuyu's voice reach the dream I built for Zephyr? And why could he hear her too? How long will the golden boy run from what he was? And what was Ferdinan doing to himself?

A drowsy skeleton sat up and searched – blue crystals stopping at the tree Oya leaned on. *Can he see me?* She waved at him.

He waved back. *He saw me enter his lab through the window too. How? One more test.* She subtly motioned him over. Ferdinan smiled pathetically and forced himself to his feet. *Interesting.* But how? And would she find answers to all her questions?

"*Good evening, Oya.*"

"*Hi!*" Setting aside her concerns, she grinned. "*There was the most magnificent yellow butterfly!*"

"*Really?*" A boney hand batted at his ear as he sat down, smiling.

Emil... "*It was as big as my head! Bright yellow! And outlined in white with tiny blue dots!*"

"*How did a Tarosaba make it out this far...?*" Tired eyes unfocused and drifted far away.

Delicate fingers played with her steel chain. *Don't fall asleep.* "*Want another chance to beat me in a race? You've yet to conquer!*"

"*How generous.*" Winking, Ferdinan leapt up and dashed off.

I love it when he plays! Oya bolted after him – giggles filling the warm night air. But... Soon his feet faltered and his eyes drooped. Catching him, she laid him on a soft patch of grass. *What're you doing to yourself?*

Inhuman green eyes turned to the stars above. How many more hours would he sleep? And... A thought hit and Oya felt foolish for not thinking it sooner. *If she can reach through dreams then...*

Now to find the Fisherman.

~

"It's happened twice. That should be evidence enough." Delicate hands tugged at the rectangular steel locket hanging around her neck.

"I doubt it. But you know how to check." The Fisherman sat beside Oya atop tethered logs, eyes glued on the colorful horizon.

"I was hoping for deeper insight."

"I can't say after what you did to her brain."

"Fair enough." Not wanting to argue, she changed topics. "If black diamond were to shatter, would it damage the mind?"

"You mean the barrier he's hiding behind."

"Yes."

"The question you should ask," the Fisherman turned serious eyes to her, "is why do people fortify their surroundings?"

"To protect against attacks."

"Or to hide while they lick their wounds?"

Oya pursed her lips. "I'll agree with that."

"How long will they keep those fortifications?"

"'Til the threat's gone or they feel safe enough to leave." Frowning, Oya laid back. Her fingers tickled the water's surface.

"And if you try destroying those defenses?"

That wasn't a thought Oya appreciated. "I understand."

"But do you?"

"Yes." *There has to be something I can do...* Rolling to her side, she moved on. "You know. I thought he'd be the king of everything or the vain man. It never occurred to me he was the drunkard."

"Zephyr?"

"Yes." Sitting up, Oya asked her next question. "How does one access forgotten memories?"

"Forgotten or repressed?" A white eyebrow rose high.

That attitude Oya could do without. "I guess they'd be repressed. Things he doesn't want to know..."

"Forcing one to face such things can damage their mind."

"I won't *force* him to remember. I'll simply give him the option."

"How much do you enjoy confronting yourself? And he'll have to face more than a wall to gain access to those memories."

"I know that much."

Clearing his throat, the Fisherman warned again. "Depending on what he's locked away and how deeply it affects him, you could seriously damage this boy."

"Then he isn't fit to rule! Or be my friend's cousin."

"Oya..." Whatever the man was about to say, he changed his mind. "What progress have you made?"

Holding up her hand, she showed him the woven strands. Multiple colors interlaced – forming something between a thick thread and a thin cord. How long until she could call it a rope?

Chapter 17

The session went longer than Elbie expected. Granted – it was his fault. Saying...talking about those things... It was hard. Much harder than he expected.

Little legs moved as fast as they were able toward the older student's lab. The one he was supposed to use...he couldn't. He couldn't stand looking at it. The idea of walking inside... Shivering, he pushed the thought aside and finished his trip down the hall and into the study area. Yuyu was already there, waiting – and looking annoyed. She rubbed and massaged her hands. But her face brightened when he dashed up to her.

"Ah! Sorry I'm late, Yuyu!" Elbie grabbed two screens from his bag. "Master Loucé went over time..."

Yuyu's adorable smile grew bigger. Pink eyes focused hard on him – as if he'd disappear if she didn't. "That's ok. I'm happy you're working hard."

Blood rushed to his cheeks. *I'm glad Yuyu doesn't remember. She suffered enough.* What he'd give to remove those memories from his own mind... Putting his bag down, Elbie climbed upon the stool next to her. "Thank you...I'll keep working. And I'll let you know if I'm late again."

"It's fine. You're volunteering to help me when you don't have to. And you're working around my sessions with Healers Herrard and Nammie. Besides, I'll always wait for you." Those pink eyes glowed – making her sweet smile even more dazzling – but they never wavered from him. "Don't stop seeing Master Loucé, ok?"

Sheepishly, he nodded. But his mismatched eyes focused on his hands. His nails were back... No scars... There should be. They should be mangled. And his sister should be dead. *We both should've died...* Elbie shook his head to stop those thoughts. They hadn't died.

For some reason this didn't feel right. Like...everything since that day was just a dream. It wasn't real. Somewhere deep inside he knew it wasn't. But neither was he waking up.

"Elbie?"

"Um... How much longer 'til you get full use back?" The Healers made him wait weeks with regular treatments and therapy. It was overkill. But Yuyu was hurt so much worse.

"With weekly healing sessions..." When she looked at her hands, Yuyu's words stopped. That forced focus appeared again. "I'll have full dexterity and control by the end of block."

They're being extra cautious with her too. But then...what was a Tinkerer without hands? Not being able to build what he imagined... That was a torture he didn't want to experience – or see his sister suffer through. "Good... It'll be fun doing a final project with you."

"I'm sorry. You're catching up on work too. But Master Ferdinan's the only other Tinkerer..." Pink eyes looked away uncertainly. Neither did she speak again until they latched onto him. "Chemicals caused the explosion...but what happened after?"

Elbie's lungs constricted. *Stop asking about this. You don't want to know.* Forcing a smile, he turned his attention to the calibrator and random materials. "Lots of fire."

"Please tell me." Yuyu took the younger boy's shoulders – making both of them flinch – and forced him to look at her. "I don't like not knowing."

The longer he hesitated, the tighter her grip became – and the deeper the burning ice sunk through his skin. *Stop! You'll hurt your hands.* "A beam fell, knocking you out...fire took hold... Then, Master Ferdinan was there. I don't know how, but he lifted the beam and grabbed you... He picked me up...carried us through the building to a room with windows...and jumped out..." *Please don't ask anything more.*

"Wow... Master Ferdinan's always been amazing...but he was strong enough to do all that?" Releasing Elbie's shoulders and seeing his distress, Yuyu changed topics – lifting the heavy mood. "Before you came, the screwdriver's handle broke."

Relief sighed out of him and a true smile shaped Elbie's lips. He took the tool from her and jumped down. "Read over the assignment 'til I get back?"

"And the next two assignments." Yuyu smirked, gaze not wavering.

"It doesn't take that long!"

"Unless the printer's out of material," Yuyu nodded and shooed him away.

That was all the encouragement he needed. Though she didn't care for waiting on the printer, his sister knew how much he loved it. While Yuyu found it boring, it was fascinating to him. Like the best toy.

The printer was in the next room over. More accurately – the printers. Most were new. But a couple older models were kept for educational purposes. It was the second oldest he loved the most. Inserting the back end of the screwdriver into one of the many slots, Elbie set the parameters and tossed the broken handle into the bin to be melted down and reused. Then he watched. It wasn't fast, but watching it run row after row of the new handle was oddly hypnotic.

Every part of him watched. There was no fire. No pain. No time. Back and forth. Back and forth. It was...relaxing... Then his imagination took over. A question rose in his mind.

What else can I print? Elbie looked longingly at the half-finished job. Mismatched eyes opened wide and a grin plastered itself on his face.

"What else can I print! Haha!"

* * *

"Wake up." Jon shook his ally as Master Ludwick approached, but the skeleton wasn't stirring. This was the second time in thirty minutes. *What's wrong with him?*

"Is everything alright, Jon Dinta?" Master Ludwick leaned in, speaking softly.

"I'm not sure. He's never slept in class before..." Jon whispered. *Though he's fallen asleep while teaching recently...*

Nothing happened when Ludwick shook Ferdinan... A nod told Jon to grab the skeleton's things and follow. Ludwick lifted and carried the unconscious boy to the small clinic on the other end of the building. Watching the instructor carry those long jumble of bones was odd. Both he and Ferdinan were half a head taller than the man, making carrying the gent awkward.

In the clinic was a twelfth-year student Healer who jumped out of his skin when he saw the skeleton brought in.

"I apologize, Healer Ummer. But he needs a bed."

"Um...sir... You know I can't be here if he is."

"Yes, I know." Ludwick laid his student on the cot. "Jon Dinta, you'll stay with your ally?"

"Yes, sir." Jon studied the gent. It felt less like Ferdinan was sleeping, and more like he was sedated.

"Um...I can't help others if this room's taken over." Ummer edged toward the door – looking paler than before.

"I'll arrange for a transport – he won't be here long. 'Til then, Jon can give you whatever you need."

Frowning, Healer Ummer nodded. "Yes, sir."

Please don't wake up here. Jon frowned – worried. His ally coming to in a clinic...the chaos... "Do you have a medical disk?"

"What?" Ummer didn't take his eyes off Ferdinan. "Oh...those silver disks... Why would we keep those?"

Jon sighed, but it was a legitimate question. Then an important thought hit. *Master Ludwick is calling a transport...*

Taking the gent to his room would make it harder for Jon to keep an eye on him. *His lab...I'll take him there.*

* * *

After a night of collecting connections, Oya needed a break. Ferdinan would be more fun to play with, but this was enjoyable in its own right.

"Run! Run faster!" Oya called to the pathetic figure staggering desperately to keep up. It'd taken egging him while Marcus was at a session to get Ilu to play. If the boy's face was any brighter red he'd pass out. Even her entourage of orbs were having trouble keeping up. *One more mile it is.*

Laughing loudly, Oya sped up. An older boy stepped into her path – smirking, blue-black eyes sparkling. Instead of slowing, she activated the cuffs and flew at Xhou. That smirk faded. By the time he was running, he looked truly terrified. "You can't escape!"

Xhou screamed when his feet lifted from the ground. And intensified when she flew him high above open waters. "Take me back! I'm too heavy for you!!"

"*Bah*! Don't worry! Enjoy the flight!" Speeding up, Oya made her way to the garden island her dear friend told her about.

Xhou wasn't happy. So she brought him down gently instead of seeing how far he'd skid, but the boy still fell over.

"Are you mad!? That was terrifying!" A pale, shaky Xhou rolled over – hugging the ground.

"*Heehee.*" Once he caught his breath, she continued, "You looked like you wanted to play."

"I better work on my expressions." Coming to his knees, Xhou brushed away sand.

"Oh?" Flopping down to her seat, Oya propped her elbows on her knees, rested her head on closed fists, and leaned forward. "Then what did you want?"

"Have you seen Ferdinan?"

"Ate breakfast with him this morning," she grinned.

"Ah! Is he doing well?"

"His skin's healed."

"That's good…" Xhou scrunched his face in thought.

"As for the rest of him, you should figure that out on your own." Oya stood and turned to skip away.

◊

Not about to let a source of information escape so easily, Xhou grabbed her arm. "What do you mean?"

"I can things tell you any number of, but you can't do anything 'til you find out for yourself." Oya tried, still jumbling the words of her new language.

"I don't understand." *What are you saying?*

"You will." Breaking his grip, she seized his waist and catapulted them both toward the nearest clump of boats. Laughter and aerial acrobatics interrupted every question he attempted – until they landed. "You're little obsession."

"Yes?" Xhou listened intently – forcing his heart back down his throat.

"To know how he's doing...understand him – start with the answers you seek."

What's she talking about...? And why not give him a straight answer instead of being obnoxiously "mysterious?" *Wait... Is she confirming what I'm trying to prove?* "I know..."

"Know what?"

Finding proof... He wanted to prove the anonymous scientist was Ferdinan. He already knew the Tinkerer developed the "medicine" to fix the leftover damage. No one else could or would make something like that... But...what did Oya mean...? *Where do I look for the proof? Or does evidence not matter?*

"Xhou?" Oya interrupted the Lead's thoughts.

"Hm?"

"Do diamonds shatter?"

"What? Of course they do. Easier than you'd think."

"Thank you. I've been wondering."

A wicked smirk filled his view – then she wasn't there.

* * *

It was rude, but Elbie couldn't wait for his session with Master Loucé to end. The sessions were important – but he finally knew what he wanted to do for his final project. And his research confirmed it was possible.

Waving goodbye, he made his way to Master Ferdinan's lab. Initial schematics were drawn and ready for inspection. There were bound to be a number of problems and errors, but his mentor would help with those. The young Tinkerer couldn't wait. *I hope he likes it!*

Down the hill and into the building Elbie flew – stopping only to trigger the chime. He waited with baited breath for Ferdinan to open it – but it remained closed. Using the handle for leverage, he jumped to peek through the door's window...but it turned. *What?* Ferdinan wasn't in the habit of leaving his door unlocked. Cautiously, Elbie edged his way inside.

There he was, bent over a table. Various items lay scattered around his head. Random items... *Did he find more of his old projects to help me?* The thought made Elbie smile.

"Master Ferdinan!" The young Tinkerer approached, but his mentor didn't flinch. "Master Ferdinan?"

Elbie tugged the skeleton's sleeve, but...no reaction. *This is wrong...* He pulled harder – nearly pulling Ferdinan off the stool.

"Huh?" Blinking, Ferdinan looked around – dazed. "Elbie? I'm so sorry...I didn't hear you come in."

"Are you ok?"

"I'm fine... I didn't sleep well." Painting on a smile, Ferdinan motioned for Elbie to sit. "I found some of my earlier projects..."

"Thank you!" Elbie bounced in his chair. "But I know what I want to do!"

Crystal blue eyes drooped. "What've you come up with?"

Elbie pulled out the screen with his blueprints. "I was fixing a tool when the idea came to me! We can print anything as long as we put in the materials and the machine is calibrated to handle them!"

Sliding the screen for his mentor to see... Ferdinan was slumped over, completely out. *Why?* Rapid breaths rung tears from him. He was so excited. Finally, he knew what he wanted... And his mentor fell asleep... *What did I do wrong...? I thought it was a good idea...*

Elbie shook his head and reminded himself Ferdinan was sleeping when he walked in. But...his heart still twisted painfully. Putting the screen away...mismatched eyes focused on his hands.

~

Why did this keep happening?

What do I do? What can *I do? I'm a child and he's terrified of Healers.* There was only one person he could think of...

Elbie tapped on Jon's open door. "Can I talk to you?"

"Yes..." Jon hesitated. "You aren't here for your session?"

"Yes." His throat tightened – making that word a squeak.

"Elbie?" Jon approached.

"I'm sorry."

Kneeling, the Thinker reached out. "What happened?"

"He keeps falling asleep." A deep frown marred Elbie's young face. "I woke him up once, but..."

A sigh left the growing giant. "I'm sorry. I thought he canceled your session. Do your schoolwork; I'll care for my ally."

Nodding, Elbie hesitated. *This is my fault, isn't it?*

"What is it?"

"Um...is...is teaching me making him sick?"

Jon's brown knit. "No! Why would you think that?"

"He was never sick enough to miss sessions with Yuyu. She even finished early. But since I've been his apprentice..."

"No."

The Firmness of that word prompted Elbie to look up.

"The timing for you...it's horrendous."

Elbie's lip quivered and he bit it. "What do you mean?"

"I don't know what was happening when you started your apprenticeship, but he's had too much the last year."

Tears welled in Elbie's eyes. "I've been so demanding..."

"No!" Jon hugged him. "Teaching you is his only joy."

"Really?" A barrage of needles tore Elbie's skin. *Please let go...*

Holding the boy to arms' length, Jon faced him. "He complains about everything, except about teaching you, helping you learn. His sessions with you are the few times I see him look happy. This isn't your fault. If anything, you've helped him get this far."

Lip quivering, Elbie dried his face as best he could – relieved when the needles vanished. "Are you sure?"

"It's the one thing I'm certain about."

Chapter 18

Relaxing with Denila was always a joy, but... "I'm sorry. I can't stand it anymore – please turn it off."

"One more! I'm certain you'll like this one."

"Then why not start with it?" Zephyr rubbed at his temples. *I'm getting a headache...*

Denila shrugged. "I hoped you'd like *some* of these."

"One more." The new song started. Onyx eyes closed – bracing against alien notes. *How did the Sciences convince everyone this was music?*

It ended and Denila turned a hopeful expression to him.

"Well...it was...*closer* to music."

Exasperation sighed out of her. "Why do you hate it?"

"The notes...they're unnatural and I can feel the beat shaking my organs."

"There were some unusual instruments..."

Unable to take it anymore, the Prince tapped the little speaker – ending the ruckus. "Ummm..."

Denila's ears perked at Zephyr's hesitation. "Yes?"

"Have you ever considered a memory and realized it didn't make sense...as if parts were missing?"

Denila thought. "I guess...there's memory fragments from when I was really little... Why?"

A nervous chuckle escaped. Golden hands skipped and their alarm chimed, "I had a dream...it reminded me of something. But I can only remember fragments as well."

"Lunch time's over." Standing up, she brushed the crumbs from her lap. "Ask an adult who was there – they usually remember what you forget from childhood."

Zephyr chuckled when she gave him a wink. "Thanks."

Waving, she headed off. *That won't work though. There were never adults in those memories, just me and Ferdinan...* But what did that mean? Why were those the only disjointed memories? *Would Ferdinan remember...?*

* * *

Falling asleep in class was unacceptable. Sleeping for two days... *If Jon had called a Healer or Psych...* Missing two days' worth of medicine didn't purge it from his body – it only lowered the concentration enough to wake up. But Ferdinan would fix it. Now.

Fog hindered his brain. Boney hands ran over the many things in his lab... Tools. Inventions. Supplies. A shelf deep in his closet held medicines he'd created for various people... One of which he didn't remember until he was holding it.

Can't recall your own creations?

This was a nasty concoction... Of all the things the Council destroyed – illicit drugs were their one failure. Though they hid it pretty well. Memories of roaming an addicts' camp flooded his mind. Most people on the islands wouldn't know such places existed...

Many drugs quietly stored themselves within the human body, making them difficult to fully purge. One such drug plagued Chūzo's lower societies after years of conflict with Mundan. Official reports denied the existence of it – as propriety would demand. But he overheard his General refer to it as "chemical warfare" to his father. Chūzo's Master's response was swift and brutal. But for those affected it was a long-fought battle. Speeding up the detoxification was one of the first medical requests he took – after Lashi Samultz turned it down. Lots of research – trial and error – led to this effective drink.

Too effective... Even with careful monitoring, it killed the healthiest of addicts. But it did exactly what it was designed to do. It forcibly removed drugs – and other contaminants – from the body. Despite the danger, it was eventually used for those exposed to other harmful substances, ingested or not.

Preparing the treatment took minutes. Waiting for curfew – hours. Sending Oya away took longer still.

Alone at last, Ferdinan locked himself in the bathroom at the back of his lab's closet.

Three doses in four hours – that was all. First, he set two alarms, one for an hour from now, and the other for three hours later.

Then, he poured each dose and set them far enough apart he wouldn't knock any over. Having seen what this did – he didn't want to take any chances. Drinking would be enough of a chore after the first glass.

Sweetness choked him. Sweet, thick nastiness... But he forced down the first dose. A thinner drink would've been nicer, but his stomach could only hold so much.

Sitting down, the skeleton waited for it to take hold.

Uncomfortable warmth swallowed him. Thirst set in. But...no water...not for an hour after the last dose. Feeling hot was a rarity. The sensation was...*ugh*! Even stripping down couldn't stem the sweating.

Suffer. Suffer as much as you can. It'll never be enough.

An alarm sounded. The first hour was finally over! *Is this really a good idea?* Drooping eyes reminded him he didn't have a choice. A shaky hand grabbed the next glass. He gulped down its contents as quickly as he could.

This is supposed to be suffering? You can do better.

Ringing filled his ears. "*Ahh!*"

Fatigue grabbed hold and threw him to the ground.

Dizziness...

His heartrate skyrocketed.

Jolts of electricity pulsed through him.

Even crawling into the shower and turning on the water couldn't quench his thirst.

What have I done to people?

What sort of torture have I created?!

Panting...gasping...

Something wet slid down his upper lip. When he wiped it away, he expected blood. A laugh escaped an impossibly dry throat. *I'm dying of thirst and my nose is running? I really am wasteful!*

You haven't agonized nearly enough.

"It doesn't-" *matter.*

After returning from South Chūzo, Ferdinan was beaten within an inch of his life. He should've died. Coughing then...he thought it was the most painful thing he ever experienced. But as convulsions gripped him, he realized how naïve he was.

Helpless he laid as his body spasmed. Limbs violently moved of their own accord. Tingling took over his extremities...

"*Agh!!*"

Swallowing back screams was useless. Contracted muscles made a charley horse feel like a minor stress knot.

Weak.

Electricity. Ringing ears. Clenched muscles. Thirst. *Water... Please...*

Time stopped. *Suffer.* He needed to suffer for his sins. That voice taunted him for being unable to atone for them all.

He was going to break...

The second alarm sounded. The third drink. The last dose. *I can't do it...*

Useless child.

Ferdinan panted. Control over his body was sporadic. Eventually he grabbed the glass. The straw mocked him. It'd never reach his mouth. *What have I done to people...?*

Pathetic waste of flesh.

Pushing forward, his face stopped an inch from the glass. He fought down the screams and ignored the laughter. *I can't do it...*

Worthless child.

Numbness took hold of his hands and feet. The electric shocks intensified. Tilting his head, he drew on every ounce of self-discipline and forced himself to drink.

Blinding pain hit. Air vanished. Light exploded. Sound echoed.

Shutting his eyes did nothing.

Cool air hit sweat-drenched skin – encasing him in ice. Yet it did nothing to temper the inferno inside him. Black spots blotted out reality. They danced – making him nauseous. *Please let this kill me...*

Every muscle in his hand contracted. His legs wouldn't move. The muscles in his back clenched. And screams tore out of him.

His chest constricted.

* * *

Unnatural green eyes shone with crazed excitement. Finding a keeper for Kámua was easier than expected. And Ferdinan...he was perfectly suited to the broken histories she kept alive. Three before she came here...and Ferdinan... But six still waited anxiously.

Melancholy filled her heart. *The day I find a guardian for you, old friend... The dream will truly be over.*

Oya slipped into Yuyu's room and pulled an ancient skeleton key from her pocket. The comforting weight snuggled pleasantly against her palm. *Ogani... It'll be sad losing you... But training a guardian takes a while...* Especially since the girl wasn't from a village or camp.

I'm relieved you can sleep peacefully, young one. Hesitantly, Oya placed the key on the girl's belly. "*What do you think? She's compatible. Her mind and heart suit you perfectly.*"

Leaning back, Oya crossed her arms and grinned. But not for long. Delicate hands tugged at the steel locket around her neck – showing her frustration.

A sigh and a nod.

"*Ogani, she survived being crushed and burned nearly to death. She's more than resilient enough... but in the end the choice is yours.*"

Warmth emanated from the key. It didn't disagree with her. But it had another suggestion. Considering the future Oya was facing... She studied the cord wrapped around her hand. What was once a single silver thread was now dozens. Various shades of blue and purple and orange and red weaved around that silver thread. And she hadn't made a dent. The more she searched, the more she found...

Oya sighed. How things would turn out... *Ogani, it's still a cruel thing to ask of anyone.*

119

* * *

Why isn't it break yet? I really need my family's help...
Everything was out of control.

Whatever was happening inside his ally's head... *I need to talk to someone about this...* But the people he trusted who could help were either at home or weren't allowed near Ferdinan.

The thirteenth-year suite was empty as usual. Next was the Tinkerer's lab... *Please be here.* His ally would randomly disappear. Which was becoming more common since Oya arrived. But wherever the third hiding spot was – Jon hadn't found it.

Every step to the lab was a struggle. What should he say? A thousand thoughts came, but all of them would drive the gent away.

Why me? Shouldn't his family be the ones worrying? Is Master Dæya reporting any of this to the Samultz's? But...Ferdinan's family... Did they only worry over Zephyr's health?

Why's my family the only ones bothered by his outrageous behavior? Walking down the hall, Jon stopped in front of his ally's lab. There were no lights or movement. Just the colors of a fading dawn through the window. *Great...*

Going to his own lab, Jon considered his options.

"I'm entering anyway," he announced to the universe at large. Maybe there was a clue? But if his ally was gone, it was unlikely he'd find Oya to help look. At least he could set out breakfast.

Standing up, Jon rubbed his face.

The primal shriek of a wounded animal leaped down the hall and bashed against his ears. *What?!* Sprinting out, Jon dashed to Ferdinan's lab, searching. Laying on the bathroom floor was his ally's body – warped with pain. Unconscious face frozen in that scream. he shook the gent, but the skeleton didn't stir. Didn't bend.

What is this...? He isn't breathing...

Neither could Jon find a pulse. "No!"

No pulse...no breath... Neither would the skeleton's body relax.

"Don't do this to me!!!" It wasn't easy, but Jon found a way to manually pump his ally's heart.

Chapter 19

"Evidence aside, I'm certain Ferdinan found the cure. But...what does that ultimately mean?" Xhou mused. "Oya said find answers, not proof. I have the answer... If proof doesn't matter, then reasons?"

Leaning back, Xhou thought out loud. "Reasons? It's Ferdinan; the reasons are obvious. He can't stand watching people suffer..."

Wait... "I'm *really* dense!" Standing, he paced. "Something she could say but he had to figure out... 'To know how he's doing... understand him.' His insane behavior... He's always been extreme... but since he got back... Why hasn't anyone's said anything...?"

Guilt twisted his heart. That was *his* job as Science Lead... Caring for his charges... But... There had to be more than him looking out for the Tinkerer... And the adults. Why weren't they doing anything?

But... Refusing to eat, being unduly distraught, stressed. Ferdinan was always like that. *I've never seen him relax. And he always hides from everyone... Is that why they don't notice or don't care?* But how can they not care about how sick he is? He looks like he's dying...

The pleasant ocean view contrasted starkly with Ferdinan's recent behavior. Nightmares that woke him up screaming... Strange ticks... Yelling in class... A *beep* interrupted his thoughts.

Hoping it'd be work from home, he checked it. But it was from his suitemate. *Dinner with the girls? He's getting mean... What's he putting them up to?* But he didn't want another argument. Sending a confirmation, Xhou returned to his thoughts.

"If *I* figured out the blight and engineered a cure, how would I feel?" Hopefully giving his tongue rein would bring light to his mind. "It'd feel amazing. Thwarting some horrible person? Stopping their plans? I'd have saved humanity! Who gets to do that? I'd be a hero! I'd go to all the parties! Ha! My family would be so proud..."

A deep ache twisted his chest. *I miss my family...* "But I'd still only have my mom... I'd have failed my family. It'd kill me knowing I wasn't fast enough to save them. A hero who failed those I love..."

Blue-black eyes took in everything he'd plastered to the walls. Photos, souvenirs, awards, letters from home – this was *his* lab.

"But I'm not the hero. Ferdinan is." *What was it like? Alone in a lab. Working endlessly – exhausted beyond hope? Hearing constant reports of the death tally as the plague spread. All alone.* "How many failures 'til success? How long did it take? In the end he won..."

Picking up a screen, Xhou looked it over and put it back down. "Winning? Millions are dead. And he can't bring them back."

Are his bizarre behaviors 'cause he's blaming himself? Xhou's heart raced. *Like I blame him...* "What would Ferdinan do to come to terms with this? What would he do if he couldn't?"

Another lap around the lab... *I need to know more...* "I need to talk this over with someone I trust... No, someone Ferdinan trusts..."

* * *

"Catching up *and* keeping top marks. Is this sustainable?"

"Yes, Aunt Tenalia," Zephyr smiled. "My schedule's *painfully* light. Hopefully, I'll get my platoon back after catching up."

"We'll see how you're doing then."

"Yes, ma'am." Golden hands danced. *She doesn't want that...?* "I'll be ready for regular training over break."

Tenalia shook her head. "We'll see. I don't want you sick again."

"I don't like being still. Without my platoon, trainee, or the classes I teach, I don't have enough to do."

"Good." Her eyebrow lifted, but she grinned. "Captain Rutoric will assess you over break. If he approves, I won't object."

"Thank you!" Relief lightened his soul. "Just don't lock me in my room if he doesn't."

"Yes." Tenalia's tone betrayed nothing. Brightening, she changed topics - telling him of his mother's trip to her home country.

"She'll be extra loving..." Five golden fingers tapped his heart.

"Indeed." Tenalia looked away as the conversation lulled.

"Anyway..." Zephyr trailed off, not sure what to say.

"How about my assignment? Concerning Ferdinan?"

"I'm still looking." *No more procrastinating.* "I'll make it stop."

* * *

Morning dawned and jumped to noon. The entire time Jon sat helplessly watching his ally's agony. Never leaving Ferdinan's side... Just watching. Crying. *I can't do this... Would mom come or Ozar?*

Though his tears dried up, he still needed someone to talk to. Everything about this was improper. He couldn't burden his island family. The adults...they'd send Ferdinan home. He couldn't tell his family over a screen – it wasn't secure enough.

Are Oya and my family the only ones invested in him...? That stabbed deep. Yes, Ferdinan pushed everyone away...but how many truly tried...? *Only Oya has... Wait... Why hasn't she appeared...?*

Jon stopped himself. Oya could take care of Oya. Thinking this was rude. He knew better, but... He had too many things to deal with.

"*Ungh...*"

"Ferdinan?" The gent's eyes weren't open, but the Tinkerer's face was scrunched up tight. "Talk to me."

◇

...my throat... Ferdinan laid motionless. Though exhausted he wasn't sleepy. His muscles burned, but weren't unbearable. Aches. Twitches. Electric jolts. Every pain was magnified. The fog holding his brain hostage had dissipated. *It worked? ...but it didn't kill me...*

Water... *Ugh...*he'd never felt this thirsty before.

Stinging needles bore into his side and arm. *Jon....?* Consciousness faded in and out as his heart raced and his body moved. *Where's he taking me?*

His ally laid him on the soft sleeping sac in the back of his closet. Then a metallic disk was on his chest – blinking. *No...don't do this...* His hand twitched but wouldn't move. *Why am I so weak...?* Red and yellow lights flashed. *Oh yeah...the detox...ugh...*

Without a word, Jon left – only to return with water. The skeleton drank greedily.

"Ferdinan... Enough." Lowering the disk, but clutching it tightly, Jon continued, "This has to stop. Talk to me."

Bitter ice splashed around inside him. *Why didn't I realize he'd find me? How impaired was my mind?* "It'll stop."

Delusional child. Pathetic.

That response startled Jon. "What do we need to do?"

"Nothing. *We*...don't have to do anything."

"Then what do *I* have to do?"

There's nothing you can do... But Ferdinan had to say something to appease his ally. "What you've been doing."

"What part? Covering for you when you're sick? Lying to the adults? Shielding you so you can digress in the shadows?" Bitterness filled Jon's voice. "What part am I supposed to keep doing?"

"Feeding me."

"So...! So you can keep fighting me?" Frustration shook Jon.

What does the disk say...? "I'm sorry. This was never your burden. You were supposed to enjoy school for fourteen years and return home to be coddled for another ten..." Ferdinan rambled off the future he stole from his ally. "...get married...start your own giant family. You were supposed to have a lifetime of bliss."

Jon's jaw dropped and his eyebrows knit together. "And you?"

What does a murderer deserve?

"I was never part of the equation. Then you were trapped with me and too stubborn to choose happiness." Blue crystals drifted closed. *How long would I sleep if I gave in?* Warmth washed over him. *Oya's histories...* "You can still enjoy a paradisiacal life."

"You deserve happiness too," Jon started, but wasn't sure where to go. Open sincerity from Ferdinan rarely happened.

How naïve!

I don't deserve the happiness I have. Evelyn's unconditional love. Oya's silliness. All the people foolish enough to help him. *I've hurt them all. Ugh...I'm so tired...*

But Jon was right, this had to end.

Chapter 20

Sunlight and a familiar chime jolted Ferdinan awake. *Where am I? What time is it?*

Grabbing a screen, the skeleton checked. *Elbie's session...* He was still exhausted...but Elbie would fall further behind... *I'm a lousy teacher.*

Lousy is generous.

Blue Crystals focused on the screen – the cube's contents. *I thought this was in the closet...* Warmth washed over him, begging him to look at the three articles again. Numbers and figures blurred in and out. *Does it matter? I'll fail again...*

Please. One more try.

...What...? Cold sweat ran down Ferdinan's spine. *Why...?*

"Master Ferdinan?" A little hand tugged on his sleeve.

He's early...? And blurry. "Elbie... Where-re-we-ah?"

"Are you feeling ok?" Elbie frowned at those slurred words.

A woozy smile floated across Ferdinan's face. *I'm fine. Don't worry about me.* That blur faded in and out. Moving to focus–

Whoa... Everything turned to snow and gravity shifted. Sand rubbed under his skin as the universe swayed. And a young voice blobbed around inside his ears. *What is this...?*

"Can you hear me?"

Panic cut through Ferdinan's fading mind. The snow melted, but everything was black. *Am I blind?* "Yes... Wha's-wron'?"

Stupid child.

"That's what I asked you."

"I'm...fine." *Oh...* Realizing his eyes were closed, he forced one open. That young face burst with fear and concern. *I'm on the floor...? What's happening...?*

Ice filled his gut and shook his spine. *I've failed again.*

125

"Master Ferdinan, you're a wonderful teacher. I'm happy you're my mentor, but..." Mismatched eyes looked at his hands before clenching them into fists. A terrified yet determined expression steeled Elbie's face. "I don't know what's going on. I don't know why you're always sick. But you *need* to care for yourself. Being good at teaching or classes or fulfilling commissions doesn't matter if you keep working yourself sick."

Those words hit hard. Putting on an expressionless mask hid the pain they inflicted. *I'm worthless. A mentor shouldn't burden his mentee. How evil am I? Hurting a child? I'm the worst.* "I'm sorry, Elbie. I've misso-many lessons...already... I don' wan' ye-fallin' behin'."

Mismatched eyes glistened with barely contained tears. "I haven't. Even being sick so often, and gone so much, you've taught me everything I needed and more. I'd rather you be healthy... Please, I don't like watching you suffer..."

Every part of him ached. His body. His mind. His heart. *I keep hurting everyone... No wonder Yuyu turned down my help...* "I apologize. Sha-we cancel today's session?"

You failed him again.

"And tomorrow's."

"Yes, sir."

There was no joking or animosity in that response. No reason to be annoyed or hurt by it – but Elbie's lips quivered. "I'll see you in two days. Please rest...I'll call Jon."

"You don' need t'trouble yourself." Those words slipped off his tongue so easily. He'd said them many times, but never to one so young.

"Yes, I do."

Ferdinan watched Elbie grab his bag and head to the door. "I truly am sorry fo'troublin' you."

Turning, Elbie gave a shaky, hopeful smile. "Then take care of yourself."

Why would anyone care about you?

I don't know.

126

You're a strange kind of pathetic worrying a young child.

I didn't mean to. I was just trying...

You're completely useless.

I am.

Completely incompetent.

Yes...

Hurting small children. Good job.

"Enough!!"

That outburst toppled him. Labored breathing accompanied his pathetic attempts to grab a stool. *The screen... I can't let Jon see it...*

Inching his way up, stick-thin arms fought to prop him atop the metal surface. Boney fingers tapped at the screen.

Footsteps rushed toward him as it turned off.

"I told you to cancel your session," Jon lifted his ally and lowered his voice. "You nearly died last night. What were you thinking?"

"Don't touch me..." He jerked away from those stinging needles but couldn't break free. Neither did Jon release him. Every bone in Ferdinan's body turned to jelly – dragging them both down.

* * *

Oya needed to test if Ogani was right – but it wasn't a test she looked forward to. Calloused bare feet danced along the sand while the island residents were in class. The silence was beautiful.

Soon Û-ya'īn rushed in, splashing at her skipping feet. "*I haven't found a guardian for you, but could you give me your transfer?*"

Water that'd jumped to play sulked away. Oya wanted to chase after, but she was tired.

"*I know, old friend,*" Oya sighed. "*But I trust you. We've always been together. But I need one I can trust – one who's compatible.*"

Û-ya'īn didn't rush back but stopped retreating.

Turning, Oya faced the ocean squarely and bowed. "*There must always be a Rā-yŭmon. Help me keep the chain from breaking.*"

Slowly...sadly... Û-ya'în rolled back – washing over Oya's feet. And when it retreated again, a tiny shell laid by her toes.

"*Thank you, old friend.*" Her sigh dissipated. This task was easy. But her others... *How do I bring the little prince back?*

* * *

Why can't I remember?! More often than not those memories ended abruptly...and the fewer memories there were. Situations built to painful intensity. Nearly transparent blue crystals turned to him... Then everything stopped. *Why didn't I notice this before?*

Memories only ended this way when they were alone, so there was only one person he could ask. *This part I'm missing...is it why I hate him?* If knowing would help him become a competent leader...

The Prince held his head high. He'd made his decision. The walk to Ferdinan's lab was quick. And Jon shouldn't be there. This was between him and his cousin.

Finding the door unlocked was unsettling. But Zephyr squared his shoulders and entered. "Ferdinan?"

Something metallic hit the floor out of sight *Why does he always hide in the closet?* Inside, Ferdinan crouched – strange tool in one hand and the other gathering up small packages scattered around his feet. That skeletal face whipped around, knocking him over. Metallic disks scattered as the Tinkerer scurried into a kneel. "M-my Prince."

What's happening...? "Do you have time?"

"Yes, m'Prince. How m'I serve you?" The skeleton wobbled – not shook or trembled, wobbled.

What...? Slurring his words – struggling to stand... A golden finger circled from his head to his stomach and back. "Are you ok?"

"I...apologize." Ferdinan fought to enunciate. "I'm...just tired."

This isn't fatigue... Should I address it...or ignore it...? "At the Inudine Festival four years ago you tended me 'til you brought lunch. Then you spent the rest of the Festival in bed. Your mom said you were sick, but Aguilla said you were injured. What happened?"

"W-why, d-do you need to know that?!" Alarm shook Ferdinan.

What's going on...? "I want to know what happened."

128

"N-nothing. Nothing happened." Ferdinan shrank – panting.

Why is he upset? His hands moved, pleading. "Tell me. Please."

Shaking his head, Ferdinan insisted on "nothing."

"The block before the festival, you kept breaking curfew. Master Wemherim asked me about it – said you weren't leaving your lab. When I confronted you, what happened?"

"Nothing." Ferdinan cringed lower, melding with the ground.

A golden hand tapped at the air before all fingers flew open.

"N-nothing happened. Y-y-you confronted me, that's all."

Why is he lying? Golden fingers thrashed. "Later, you were limping, your lip and eye swollen. How did that happen?"

"I fell. That's all; nothing happened."

Why's he lying?! Just tell me! Every event Zephyr asked about was met by the same response. "Nothing happened," and Ferdinan backing away until he trapped himself in a corner.

"I fell, that's all. I fell!"

"No one's *that* clumsy." Sighing out frustration, Zephyr knelt. Trying to make eye contact sent his cousin into a panic.

"I am!"

"Tell me the truth!" Heat flared! And was quenched by the elf's promise. *Why can't I manage something as simple as talking to him?*

"Please stop!"

Zephyr tapped his temple and brought his hand down in a fist.

"I-I-I t-tripped. I knocked over the v-vase."

Golden hands flew open. "Then what?"

"I-I-I ac-c-cept-t-ted my punishment..." Those words shook violently. "I'm sorry! I didn't mean to! I'm sorry!"

◊

Shifting their dinner containers, Jon inputted his access code into the unlocked door... Ferdinan's lab was empty, but the lights were on. Judging by the untidied project, the gent was probably rummaging in the closet. *I need him to talk to me... If I was a Mind Talker, I'd delve into his thoughts regardless of the restrictions.*

"Please stop!" Ferdinan cried out from the closet.

Again? Hearing his ally yell when alone had become common. It was one of many things he needed to share with his family. In the privacy and safety of home. *What does he keep shouting at? How do I tell them?* Jon shook his head, he had to get Ferdinan home first. If mom and dad couldn't help... Long fingers laid out their meal.

"I'm sorry! I didn't mean to! I'm sorry!"

What...? A dozen strides brought Jon to the closet, a cowering Ferdinan, and Zephyr hunched down looking frustrated.

"What's wrong?" Jon surveyed the situation.

"I'm not sure..." The Prince made room for his ally to approach.

"I'm serious, Zephyr. What's going on?" Jon knelt between them, but Ferdinan pressed harder into the corner.

"I was asking about some things I couldn't remember." The Prince's hands moved like always.

Ferdinan froze. Strangled relief painted across that skeletal face. And confusion.

"I'm sorry, but he's been sick – extra stress will make him worse." *What happened? They both look at their limits...*

"Thank you for caring for him. I'll leave my cousin to you." Waiting for Jon to nod, Zephyr gave a half-bow and left.

The beating...the scars... Ferdinan was trying to get away... Once the door latched, he asked. "Did Zephyr hurt you?"

Ferdinan reddened, teeth bared. "No! He'd never do that!"

"Then what happened?"

"I fell..." Head down, Ferdinan shifted and leaned against the wall – exhaustion creeping back in as the adrenaline faded.

"I hate when you lie to me."

"Why wou'l lie?"

Chapter 21

What have I forgotten? Zephyr plopped back on his bed. Too bad he couldn't forget his aunt's command. Dealing with the recluse took more energy than it was worth. *Who'd put in the effort of finding him just to beat him?*

Pushing those thoughts away, he turned his gaze to the stars beyond the window.

Then he was staring at sapphire eyes.

"What's on your mind?"

Guess I fell asleep... Zephyr stood and bowed to the elf. "What do you mean?"

"You won't learn well if you're preoccupied."

An ominous chill ran down the Prince's spine. "My aunt's given me a task."

"The thing you promptly forgot?"

"Ha...yeah..."

"You're a lousy cousin."

"You think I don't know?" Those biting words surprised Zephyr. *Did I just say that?*

"The little prince knew what he had," the elf turned sharp eyes on Zephyr, "'Til he realized how ordinary the extraordinary is."

"What?"

"How will you reclaim that wonder? Those extraordinary, mundane parts that made you happy?"

What is she talking about? "I don't understand."

Shaking her head, the elf responded, "There's a solution...but I doubt it'd be...appreciated."

"I'd prefer to live, please."

"I can help you with your aunt's command."

Another chill coursed through his spine. "What?"

"You already know. You've just locked it away from yourself."

Locked it away? "How do I reach it?"

Circling the Prince, the elf studied him. Walking away melted the twilight beach and inky waves lapping against gray sand until they stood in nothingness.

"Where are we?"

"Where we always were." Sapphire eyes shone with an inner fire. "Truth is cruel, but blinders hinder us."

A golden finger tapped his temple and he shook his head. "I don't understand."

"It's disturbing...looking deep and drawing up what you want to forget."

"*Want* to forget?"

"Those memories ended abruptly 'cause *you* locked them away."

Golden hands flew. "I tried asking Ferdinan."

"How did that go?" The elf's face said she already knew.

"He wouldn't say anything. He only became upset."

"Understandable." Slender bare feet walked across nothing – increasing their distance.

"How is that understandable?"

"You can access those forgotten things on your own." The elf smirked at his surprise. "But can you handle it?"

"I'll do what I must." *She's manipulating me...but why?*

"That's easy to say. But the box was never meant for you. Neither was it intended to hide in."

Box? "What does that mean?"

Sweeping an arm behind her, a path of soft soil formed. "If you do this...you'll find you aren't the person you think you are. You won't be able to hide anymore."

"I know who I am."

"Are you sure?"

Zephyr's hands moved defensively. "I know who I am better than anyone else."

The elf didn't bother hiding her smirk. "Then follow the path. Find the locked door."

She won't come with me...? No. I'm asking too much already. "Thank you."

Head high, he followed the path. It grew sturdier until it was a solid road. But...he found no door...

Until he looked back...

When...? Dark wooden doors surrounded him – flush against each other. He couldn't swallow. Couldn't breathe. *I guess...I'll try the first one...*

The handle turned. But he didn't open it. It wasn't locked, so this wasn't the right door. Going around the circle, he checked door after door multiple times.

"I don't understand; they're all open!"

Nothing. Not even an echo answered him.

Returning to the path... The circle of doors vanished. *Not deep enough...?*

So he walked. Nothing. Ran. Still nothing. *Faster! Find it!*

With each beat of his heart, he pressed his legs faster. *What is this?!*

Countless nightmares crowded the emptiness beyond his vision. But he kept going. Until he collided with nothing. Pushing himself back to his feet he approached more cautiously. The road ended at a wall of nothingness. He couldn't move past. Couldn't see anything. Looking back didn't bring any doors into existence.

"Now what?"

"Are you sure you want to meet me?"

Zephyr shivered at the sound of his own voice. "Who are you?"

"Me? I'm the one who does what needs to be done."

"What kinds of things?" Ringing filled his ears and his heart beat erratically. Yet, he felt connected to the one speaking.

"Things that hurt you. Things that'd make you see what you truly are."

A dark figure stepped out from the nothingness. Chains bound him. His face was heavily shrouded, but...everything about the figure matched Zephyr. Dread and desire to run away hit. *That isn't me!*

"How will you know unless you open the door?" the chained figure answered Zephyr's unspoken words.

"There's no door..."

Even through the shroud, Zephyr could sense a cocky grin. Bound hands reached forward – offering a key. It was old. Rusted. Dented. One of the teeth were chipped.

A ball of acid burst in his chest. *I...I don't want to know...* The Prince stepped back.

"You don't have to. I'll do my job as long as you want." But the figure continued offering the key.

His lungs constricted. *I know who I am. I know who I am.* Reaching out, Zephyr took the key. *I know who I am.*

The figure vanished. In his place was a carved oak door. If not for what was carved, it would've been beautiful. But... Onyx eyes avoided the images – focusing on the lock.

Inserting the key...

Shadow and mist blew through him. An impossible weight pulled him down. Ice burned his skin and fire ravaged his insides. Clutching at his chest... *My heart's pounding too hard... I'm going to die...*

The door swung inward.

Inviting him.

Mocking him.

Warning him.

~

Have I shrunk? Zephyr tried looking around, but his body wouldn't listen. All he could see was a little boy lying in bed. His lips moved...but the voice...it was too young to be his. "Are you alright? Would you like some water?"

Little Ferdinan reached weakly for the glass.

"It's ok, everyone gets sick." Helping his cousin sit up, Zephyr took the cup of tea on the night stand and offered it. That's when he noticed the little sack of plants. The ones Ferdinan collected for his tea. It was open and its contents partly spilled, as if Ferdinan didn't have the energy to put everything back properly after making a glass.

What kind of tea does he like? Studying the plants closely... Ice filled his chest. "Don't drink that!"

A startled little face turned to Zephyr.

"The tea was made from these?" The Prince pointed to the sack, hoping he was wrong.

Ferdinan shook and looked down.

"It's poison." Not all the plants. But at least three of those were ones Rutoric warned him about.

And unexpected expression filled his little cousin's face. Not surprise. Or fear. When the Prince reached for the glass, Ferdinan clutched it tighter. Those nearly colorless blue crystals were...angry. Disappointed. They searched for a solution to something...all the while refusing to give up the tea.

"Aguilla! She knows all about plants; she can fix this!"

Clutching the cup tighter, Ferdinan shook.

What...? His heart twisted. How was helping family any trouble? *No, he always thinks that.* Zephyr rushed to the door. *Aguilla will need to know what plants...* Bringing them would be faster. And he didn't want to tell her the wrong ones by accident.

Turning back...the ice in his chest grew so cold it burned. *Stop! Why are you drinking that?! After I told you not to?!* His hands flew. "Why would you do this?!"

By the time Zephyr got the cup away, it was empty. Everything blurred! Golden hands grabbed the sick child and shook him. "I told you not to drink that! I told you it was poison! Why?!"

Ferdinan lowered his head, but not before the Prince saw tears.

Shock held Zephyr and he felt he'd cry. Grabbing his cousin, he tried pulling Ferdinan out of bed. "You need to throw that up!"

His cousin didn't budge. Perfect still and calm settled around Ferdinan despite the little Prince's bellowing.

The young Tinkerer turned his hand and grabbed Zephyr's wrist – stopping the commotion. Ferdinan's grip was strong. Too strong for a sick child. Blue crystals stared steadfastly.

It took a while for Zephyr to soak in that "No." When it hit, fire exploded – overpowering everything else. Lunging forward, he grabbed Ferdinan's shirt and shook. His cousin's head slammed repeatedly against the headboard. "WHY NOT!?!"

For the first time, Ferdinan presented the eyes that'd haunted Zephyr for over a decade.

It didn't make any sense...

Red filled his vision.

Zephyr didn't realize he'd made a fist until blood ran from Ferdinan's nose. Grabbing the sick boy, he pulled his cousin away from the headboard and pinned the Tinkerer against the bed. Another fist flew, and another. He climbed atop Ferdinan for a better position.

"Why?!! Why would you do this!?!" Small, golden hands fought between trying to speak and beating his cousin.

Eternity passed in a loop. Zephyr demanding Ferdinan throw up the drink – Ferdinan refusing – Zephyr beating him.

Fist after tiny fist hit with all the Prince's might. Until Rutoric lifted him. Even then Zephyr continued flailing.

* * *

"Um...hello?"

That was an unexpected voice. Jon turned to find Kalj Herrard standing nervously in his doorway. *What's he doing here?*

"Sorry, I...mind if I come in?"

It took a moment for his brain to move, but he gestured the young man in and offered a seat before closing and locking the door. "I apologize. How can I help you?"

Seeing the door locked put the Healer at ease. "I know you're a Thinker, but... I need a simple device."

"Why not ask Ferdinan?" nearly slipped off Jon's tongue – before remembering who he was talking to. That was the last thing the Kalj should do. "If it's simple enough... What do you need?"

Pulling a small screen from his pocket, Herrard showed him a crude drawing. "Sorry, I'm not an artist. But I need this to be small enough for a young child, and this part needs to move smoothly without much thought."

The Kalj pointed to a small circle above a washer. "Ok...how?"

Frustration creased the Healer's brow. Looking at his hand, Herrard held out two fingers while his thumb awkwardly drew a circle over them. "It needs to move like this. And it needs to be gentle on damaged hands."

"For Yuyu?" That was a simple enough guess. But what would such a device be used for? It didn't seem like it'd work for therapy. "I..."

"Am I asking too much?" Herrard's eyes darted to the door and back.

"No." Jon considered what would be needed. It was a simple design. But he didn't think it'd work well. "Does it need to look like this?"

"No. As long as it makes that motion, what it looks like doesn't matter."

A smile twitched on Jon's lips. Something he could do. Taking the screen, he sat down and drew a new design next to the first. Starting from the outside and moving in. It was still simple. Pretty much a ball bearing in a box, but it'd get the smooth motion and could also adjust for various sized hands. And it was something the machines they had could cut or print – saving time and energy.

"Will this work?"

Herrard's cheeks pinkened. The original crude drawing next to the blueprints Jon easily scribbled out were night and day. But even though Jon wasn't a Tinkerer, that didn't mean he wasn't good at improving designs. "I think it will...this...I'm amazed."

"I can program it into the printer tonight and have it ready for you tomorrow." A chuckle left Jon. "Though...the bearing, I'll need to fight the second year Scientists for the glass machine."

For a moment Herrard just stood there confused, then he burst out laughing. "I'm sorry. I was...I missed the joke for a moment."

"Is everything ok?" Jon was starting to wonder if he and his island brothers were the only ones here capable of talking openly.

"No. But it's getting there." Again, the Kalj looked nervously at the door.

Nodding, Jon moved to his work screen and started creating the schematics. "Oya's playing with him. You don't have to worry."

* * *

"Put on a mask." Ferdinan kept his eyes on the beakers while pointing to a cabinet on the far side of the room.

"*You aren't supposed to see me.*" Crossing her arms, Oya gave a little huff.

"Then don't climb in a window I'm facing." Grabbing the catalyst, he motioned to the cabinet again, then adjusted the blue mask and goggles on his face. "I'm serious. Goggles too."

Oya gave a strange look to no one beside her. Bare feet danced across the room. Mask and goggles secure, she skipped over. It was silly – almost juvenile – how fascinated she was watching the solution bubble. The two sat enjoying the chemical reaction. Oya giggled while Ferdinan looked on wearily.

It's not going to work. But I love watching you struggle.

Ignoring the voice and a deep desire to cry, Ferdinan cleaned up. Being sneaky around Oya was pointless. "I'm not up for playing today...could I offer you a story instead? You've given me so many."

"I'd rather hear you play." Her signature Cheshire grin grew.

My violin... This felt unbreachably daunting. "No. Not today."

Exotic green eyes danced. "*A story it is! One detailing how I'll defeat the earth and steal the sun!*"

A small twitch of a smile tugged the corner of his mouth. "Sounds like quite the adventure."

Chapter 22

This is new. Yuyu took in the purple-gray twilight. Sandy beaches stretched for as far as she could see and an indigo ocean lapped lazily to the side of her. A giant full moon commanded the sky – but no stars...

Ahead of her was a fire with someone huddled around it. Yuyu waved. *My hands...* The gloves she was supposed to always wear were gone. And there was no pain – no evidence they were hurt. Did Herrard finally make them whole? *Wait...am I dreaming?* It didn't feel like a dream. But then, did dreams feel like dreams while dreaming them?

"What's so fascinating, young one?"

Yuyu jumped. The fire was a stride away and an old woman sat grinning a far too youthful grin for such a weathered face. "Sorry. I realized I wasn't wearing gloves. And...I don't have to focus to talk...but..."

"Would that make you feel more comfortable?"

"No. I don't want either of those. But..." *Is it 'cause I'm dreaming?*

That grin turned Cheshire – made all the more intense with countless lines. "There's nothing here that'll hurt you."

As if to prove it, the old woman placed a gnarled hand in the heart of the fire. Yuyu cried out, but the woman didn't flinch.

"This is my world. It won't hurt me or you."

"Your world?"

"Just as that amazing galaxy of light and promise is your world. This is mine."

"Galaxy...?" Yuyu searched her mind. Somewhere in the deepest corner was a vague memory of an endless eternity repairing roads as colors floated around her. "I...I don't quite remember..."

"Would you like to?"

"I think I would."

It was impossible how quickly and easily the old woman jumped to her feet. "What might you call me?"

"Excuse me?"

"You asked my name." Gold flecked black eyes widened. "What did I tell you to call me?"

We've met? When? Taking her time, Yuyu studied the old woman. Age hadn't dimmed her rich skin - though it'd wrinkled it magnificently. Wavey hair as white as any Energist's stretched down passed her shoulders. And those eyes... Both they and her grin were far too young. As if belonging to a child. *I've never met anyone like her before.* Yet her tongue moved. "Muulam."

With that name came a universe of wonder! And too many hours of loneliness...

Muulam didn't say anything, but her expression spoke volumes. Not only had Yuyu gotten the old woman's name right - but she passed some sort of test...fulfilled an expectation she didn't know existed.

Once again, the old woman reached into the fire. Only this time when she removed her hand, there were half a dozen strange objects lying on her palm. A key, tiny shell, pebble, yellow flower, and folded paper. Those objects... They were small. Insignificant. Easily missed. Common.

But Yuyu couldn't deny their importance. *Why would she keep them in a fire? Wouldn't that damage them?* But they looked fine. Maybe that was the best place to hide them - to keep them safe.

"What are they?"

"My charges." The old woman grinned - looking longingly at the objects. "The true question is: What do these have in common, young one?"

"I don't know." Pink eyes studied the objects closer. Color, form, wholeness, use. There was no quality all of them shared. But they all *felt* similar. *They're all searching for the same thing...* But how do inanimate objects search for anything? How do they have desires? "They're alive."

"Are they?" That gnarled hand moved closer - offering them to the girl.

To hold one... Yuyu's heart quickened and a smile took over her face. "May I?"

"Only if you wish."

That's a strange way to give permission. But Yuyu really wanted to. She didn't know which to choose, but her fingers grabbed the folded piece of paper. *It's just the corner...* And it lacked color. It wasn't white or transparent. It simply lacked color. Like it should be something vibrant, but it hadn't found the right one yet.

Hello.

Yuyu squeaked at the unexpected voice. It felt like it came from the very depths of her soul. But when she looked at Muulam, the old woman just grinned and nodded. "Hello? Who are you?"

I am Umbacano. Would you like to meet me?

"Isn't that what I'm doing?" There was no sound, but Yuyu swore giggles surrounded her. "I'm Yuyu. I'd love to meet you."

Possibility filled her mind – continuing down to her soul. Possibility. Not everything that was possible in the universe. But...that moment when an idea becomes reality. When something that was only a dream a breath before proves just as deserving of existence as its creator. It was a wonderful feeling. One she'd experienced many times. One she missed while waiting for her hands to heal.

"Umbacano...what are you?" More unheard giggles danced around Yuyu. Her lungs took in every ounce of air they could hold as pink eyes turned to the giant moon overhead.

In the gray of the twilight sky etched everything. Every dream her hands desired to make reality. Every thought she'd spent hours mulling. And more flooded in. Things she'd never considered – or hadn't realized she had. Desires. *What can I do? How do I make this? What would this take?*

All her usual thoughts and dreams and imaginings. And more. "I want to remember all this! How do I keep it all?!"

What am I, little one?

Paradise. You're paradise. I want to spend my life here... "There's not a word to describe you."

This time the giggles were plain to hear. Only, they weren't the light ones echoing around her soul. These came from the old woman standing beside her. "There is. A simple word we use every day."

Yuyu turned to Muulam though she longed to keep her eyes on the sky. "What do you mean?"

"It's ok if you can't recognize its simplicity. I expect it'd be particularly difficult for a Tinkerer."

Did I tell her what I am? Considering she didn't remember meeting the woman until a moment ago...

"Maybe greeting another would help."

"But...I don't want to lose this!"

You won't.

Muulam grinned and offered her hand again.

It's ok. We can play again.

Nodding, Yuyu returned the folded paper. All that wonder vanished. Leaving an enormous void to fill with loneliness. Cold, bitter loneliness. She didn't realize she was shivering – crying – until Muulam wrapped an arm around her.

"Trust me. I understand." Pity filled gold flecked black eyes. "More so than you'll ever know."

That wasn't comforting. No one should feel like this. Still, she reached in. This time her fingers picked the yellow flower. Impossible warmth filled her. Warmth of the sun at noonday. Unlike the paper, the color of the flower intensified as the object itself denied any particular shape.

The warmth grew. Demanding respect. And promising so much more in return.

* * *

"You're mad." The middle-aged man laughed – belly rippling. Sipping on absurdly decadent wine, he offered the Duchess some again. And again, she turned it down.

"I'm serious, Orthan." The Duchess straightened every inch of her small frame. *Disgusting.* "Extravagant living at the cost of our country is unforgivable."

"'The cost of our country?' You *are* mad. Everything comes from my coffers."

"This dukedom isn't your inheritance."

"I inherited this charge fairly."

A sharp eyebrow rose high, accentuating her authority. "Being successor doesn't mean the King can't take it away."

"I work hard. It's no sin enjoying a luxury as reward. 'Til I'm told I can't run *my* lands the way *I* see fit, I'll continue."

Distain flared her nostrils. "You *are* aware of the famine afflicting our country?"

"I've heard farfetched rumors. No outside help has been offered or accepted and people are flocking to the capital's abundance."

"How did a fool take the place of a great man?"

Slamming his whine glass down nearly cracked it. "Watch your tongue in *my* estate!"

Unimpressed by the outburst, the Duchess frowned – tired of this pointless arguing. "Cousin. You got this position 'cause my brother and I were slated for other ones. I won't see an imbecile squander it. You may rule, but it's my name you're soiling."

"Your name doesn't exist here anymore." Her glare drove the man to keep talking. "Yes, *my* fields aren't doing quite as well as normal, but next season will be better."

"No, it won't. Plantation towns near the capital experienced the same thing. You'll produce less and less 'til there's nothing." A wave of her hand interrupted the man's next rebuttal – done with him. "You know... I'll let you see firsthand how well the capital is thriving."

"Paying for me to go on vacation?" the Duke laughed.

"No. I'm giving you an entirely new perspective."

"Excuse me?"

"You don't understand the importance of our station." Turning dagger eyes on him, she pinned the man in place. "First, comes our General. Second, comes our King. Third, is the people. And somewhere at the very bottom – after migratory insects and sewer mold – is us."

"Just 'cause you think so little of yourself doesn't mean the rest of us do."

"Our sole role is protecting our country. Extravagant living in lean times is an outrage. Burdening our citizens to the point that complaints reach the ears of our allies and enemies is unacceptable. If you're to play the role of 'villain,' do so with a purpose."

"My citizens love me!" Jumping to his feet, the Duke tried staring his older cousin down.

"Then you'll be comfortable joining them."

"What?"

"Duke Orthan, I hereby seize *my* family's lands for the good of North Chūzo. If you prove yourself competent among those you've driven off, you might be rewarded with another charge." All color drained from the man, but she continued, "You'll be given the same as all citizens: a ride to the city and an apartment. Once there, you'll be assessed for employment. Now...do I send you with those who've stayed? Or give you a spot among those who've fled?"

"Y-y-you can't do that!"

"They love you, right? Play for sympathy – say your big, bad, mean cousin stole your toy." Moving to the window, she looked out over the grounds. "The gardens are as magnificent as always. Good and fertile. My childhood home will come in useful with this crisis."

"You can't!"

"Calm yourself or I'll have you removed. I've chosen guards to watch you. Since it's just yourself, I expect you to pack and be ready to leave by morning."

Plump cheeks burst into flames as fury lashed off Orthan's tongue. He lunged. Rage propelled him forward faster than expected from a man his size.

Yet, the Duchess sidestepped her frothing cousin with ease. "Very well, I'll arrange for what you need to be sent. He's ready!"

Her call summoned two soldiers. They seized the man.

"Cousin."

The soldiers paused, but held the man in place.

Pulling a few small packages about the length of her palm from a bag, she placed them in Orthan's hand. "Enjoy your meals. 'Til the people have full access to real food again, we eat no better than they."

It looked like Orthan wanted to say something, but couldn't find any words before the soldiers dragged him to a waiting car. Moments later it pulled out, heading to the capital.

"You're next instruction, ma'am?" The man who'd informed her of Orthan's behavior peeked in timidly from the hallway.

"Survey the dukedom for uncontaminated soil and convert it to farming and pasture lands."

"Like up north?"

"Precisely. If the southern farms are failing..." the Duchess sighed. "Strip the estate. Send anything useful to the capital. Tear down everything and plow the land save the servant's quarters."

"Yes, ma'am. Would you like me to seek the most qualified among the locals?"

"Please." Turning, the Duchess approached the window. Orthan was easy. The man was spoiled and slothful; he never deserved what he'd been given. The others...one or two among them may still be fit to lead, but any loyal townsman would work. Luxury had no providence in hard times. Regardless of birth.

* * *

"Hello, Ferdinan." Emil stepped from the shadows, grinning.

Ferdinan froze – jaw set. "Who are you?"

"Who am I? Who else could I possibly be?"

Stick-thin arms rose unconsciously, preparing to defend. "*Who* are you?"

The voice who called itself Emil wasted away into the spitting image of Ferdinan. "The difference between us? I've done nothing worthy of punishment. I can enjoy health and happiness."

Ferdinan's throat tightened. "See. We aren't the same."

Darkness settled in heavy and cold, but Emil only smirked.

"Leave me alone. Whatever you are, leave me alone."

"What'll you do if I refuse?"

Standing taller, Ferdinan dropped his arms to his side. His skeletal face became hard – determined. Unwavering and strong. It became everything he wished he was. "I'll make you leave, even if I have to kill us both."

Emil's smirk grew and a light chuckle left him.

* * *

Cold sweat drenched the Prince and plastered his clothing to his body. But waking up didn't stop the memories. They kept playing.

One after another. And another. At the palace. On the islands. Everywhere in between. Back and forth. Back and forth. With each memory he grew older, his anger deeper, and the beatings more brutal – unrestrained.

Please! Stop! No more...!

Tightness filled him. Stretching his skin to bursting. Senses liquefied his brain. He couldn't even feel his hands clutch at his head.

All that existed was the panoramic view of dozens of beatings. Each leaving Ferdinan broken and bloody.

The memories unbearably clear.

Chapter 23

Of the other two articles, one chemical was vastly different. But so were the primary symptoms it treated. The secondary ones were what he needed... *This won't work.* Warmth blanketed him, begging him to try anyway. A different chemical... *The first one didn't do anything, so maybe....?* At least fatigue wasn't a listed side effect.

Heaving a sigh, Ferdinan picked up the container and watched the contents slosh around.

They're completely different...why waste time trying? Why? When I should swim out past my island now... His body was still recovering from the detox so he wouldn't have to swim long...

A peaceful death? After what you did to your victims.'

"You're right..." Death couldn't be peaceful. Neither could it inconvenience everyone – particularly his Prince. Warmth flooded over him as if trying to wash those thoughts away. But he wished it'd stop. Death was the least he deserved.

Blue crystals closed. One idea after another played out in his head. No one kept tabs on him over breaks... Rarely was he called home...and after the last one...why would they want him back?

Hack the boat's systems and check myself in... Then camp on his little island until it was time to check himself off. That's all. A whole month before anyone realized he wasn't there.

They'd think I ran away... I wouldn't destroy my family...country. Everyone would assume I selfishly rejected my responsibilities. That's all. Done. No one would miss him. He'd be forgotten in a few weeks. More likely a day or two – if they realized he was gone.

Stick arms wrapped around himself, providing little warmth. *That's what I'll do. It'll work...so why bother with this?*

Don't give up.

A hollow laugh left him. How broken was he for that warmth to gain a voice? He stared at the morning's dose. *I have to wait 'til break. Will this make time blur?* Not thinking sounded wonderful...

Camping with you will be interesting.

147

No.

No more.

I can't do this anymore.

Twenty million deaths. His Prince. Yuyu and Elbie. His people. His family. This was his limit. *I have to end this now. Before I destroy what's left...*

Syringe in hand, Ferdinan sucked up most of the liquid. He knew just where to inject it...

The voice laughed. Calling him weak. Mocking him for choosing an easy death over what he deserved.

Please don't!

His jaw ached. His heart raced. His hands shook.

For long seconds he stood there trying to move forward. Trying to move back. Trying... The entire time the voice mocked him.

Please.

Ferdinan sat – hand over his mouth.

Shaking, he divided the medicine into servings and took a dose.

* * *

A familiar ceiling filled his view. Reaching up, Zephyr slapped himself... The sharp pain was a huge relief. *It's over...*

He was free.

And...

He hated himself.

I'm a monster... I did those things?

No... It's just another nightmare. I'm imprisoned in the palace again. The elf. Those memories. I'm breaking. My mind's broken...

Sitting up, the world blurred. *But it's not...*

Golden hands held back the sobs choking him. *I'm a monster...*

Wait... The terrified servant girl... I hit her... Ice crawled down his spine. Dark memories flashed through his mind, suffocating him. *No! Don't think about that...* If only he could change the past.

148

What do I tell Aunt Tenalia?

Death flashed across his mind and constricted his heart. Get away... Find anywhere else! Onyx eyes searched for an escape. But...he was already in his room... If this little sanctuary wasn't safe... Of course, it wasn't. There was no escaping those memories...his actions...this horrible...thing...choking out his life one strangled breath – one muted heartbeat – at a time.

Daggers tore at his chest. *The dojos. Fight. Run. Anything...*

Swimming there was tempting, but a boat was faster. Training cries led him to an outdoor class – and the one he wanted to see. While Denila taught, he watched. *This is a mistake.* The longer he stood there, the more he yearned to join.

Tightness constricted his body. He wanted to scream. *Stay in control. You're a future General. You must stay in control!*

When the students scattered, his breath quickened.

"Do you pine to teach so deeply you'll fill the need vicariously?" Denila smirked and approached the partially hidden Prince.

Zephyr's hands moved more sharply than he intended. "Jumping in on that last round of exercises was tempting."

Stepping closer she hugged him. "Want another beating?"

He squeezed her back, waiting for his throat to loosen. "Sounds wonderful."

"Heh." Letting go, she looked him over. "You seem healthy enough. How much pounding are you up for?"

"No mercy." His smile said this was a joke, but he meant it honestly.

She chuckled. "Any particular style?"

Zephyr's hands danced in excitement. "You have to ask?"

"I love a good dagger fight."

Inside the main dojo, he grabbed his stored knife and gestured to a khanjali in the weapon rack – his second favorite. "Your choice."

"Ha! You're preferred works fine." Reaching behind her, she pulled out her kaiken. "Ready?"

Leaping back, the Prince put some space between them to deconstruct her strategy. She didn't give him the opportunity, though. Even as he retreated, she charged forward.

Time slowed.

The two of them moved in an impromptu dance. Attack. Defend. Attack. Every movement felt hindered by the tightness consuming him. Then...

That odd "music" infecting the islands floated in.

Strike after strike. Until their movements flowed with the melody weaving around them.

Then the tune changed – turning harsh and angry. *Ugh! How does a proper instrument make such a sound?!*

The grating reverberations felt like the memories he blocked out.

Uncontrollable rage formed into music. *I can't take anymore!*

Cold pierced his chest. That suffocating sensation leaked out of him. And warmth... Time returned to normal.

Looking down... His hand clutched hers. And hers held the dagger now sheathed inside him. Denila's lips moved, but all he could hear was anger kicking and screaming around him. But...

But that thing trying to burst through his skin was pacified. How poetic...it took steel pinning his lung in place to finally breathe.

* * *

It's open....? Not just unlocked, but actually *open.* Gently knocking at the open door, Elbie stuck his head inside. "Hello?"

First, it was unlocked. Now, it was wide open and Master Ferdinan wasn't there. *What's going on? Is he sick again?*

A throat cleared behind him, making Elbie jump.

"Ah! Sorry, Elbie. Can you move?"

Stepping to the side, Elbie watched Jon and Ferdinan carry in a large, heavy looking box. "What's that?"

Placing the box onto a cleared portion of floor, Ferdinan gave his pupil a worn-out smile. "A commission. I apologize; there are still more pieces to get. I didn't realize I'd taken so long."

Shiny black hair shook side to side. "No, sir. I'm early."

"Ah. Then please forgive my rudeness."

"Do you need any help?"

Jon laughed, making him jump again. "Everything's bigger than you and weighs twice what Ferdinan does..."

The skeleton gave his ally an unappreciative glare and left.

"But if you could help with the doors, that'd be great." It wasn't much of a recovery, but Jon did his best.

Smiling, Elbie nodded and followed. It was nice seeing his mentor both alert and bickering with the Dinta.

◊

Three trips later, Ferdinan sat with his pupil. But the young boy's attention was on the boxes in the corner. *Might as well use that to Elbie's advantage...* Ferdinan cleared his throat.

"Oh! I'm so sorry!" Elbie bowed in apology.

"You've accomplished more than expected while..." Ferdinan blushed, pointing to the boxes. "Let's test what you've learned."

"Huh?"

"It's a prototype for an A.R.A." Standing, Ferdinan approached the pile. *Why am I hungry? I finally overcame that...*

Elbie cocked his head to the side. "Aquatic Robot Assembly?"

"Correct. It's not working right." Ferdinan motioned Elbie over. "We need to figure out what's wrong with the assembly unit."

"We?" Elbie beamed. "I get to do outside work?!"

Getting children's hopes up...

"If you want." Ferdinan smiled awkwardly. "This is *my* commission. You're in no way expected to do anything with it."

"No! No! I *want* to!" Elbie beamed – reaching for the closest box. "I thought I'd have to wait 'til I had my own lab."

"You can't work on it by yourself. But I'll devote half your lesson to it, and...up to sixteen hours a week of your free time...if you so choose."

If Elbie was a less restrained child, he'd be jumping up and down. "Thank you! But if I can't work alone..."

"Arrange time to work on it and I'll adjust my schedule accordingly." Seeing his mentee's joy was indescribably wonderful.

"Thank you very much!"

Today's lesson is pointless... Grabbing a screen, he loaded the schematics and handed it to Elbie. "We'll go over these during your next session. Feel free to ask any questions."

"Oh...yes. Thank you!" The screen held Elbie's attention.

"Since I've lost you, you're dismissed. You prefer calm and quiet? I often get noisy intruders and my current projects are louder."

"When does this need to be done by?" Excited mismatched eyes turned to him.

"It isn't time sensitive. Whenever it gets done." Pausing, Ferdinan blushed. "This late in the block... I requested for your project to be yearlong. But I need your proposal soon."

"Yes, sir! Thank you, Master Ferdinan!" Elbie gave a quick bow and all but skipped out of the room.

I guess this hijacked his brain. Mentioning the final project was to give Elbie a chance to show the skeleton what he'd been trying for weeks to talk to him about. *I'll ask directly next time.*

"I've never seen him so excited. He told me about the A.R.A."

Ferdinan shrugged at Jon and started cleaning. *How do I get him to go away?* There was so much...but the lost histories called to him. Even if they didn't, searching them was relaxing.

"Won't waiting on Elbie be inconvenient for your employer?"

Wasteful child.

"No." Ferdinan cleared his teaching materials. "I figured out the problem and informed them. They didn't need the parts back."

"So...you have a broken assembly system taking up space?" Jon raised an eyebrow.

"No." Ferdinan smirked, "I have a teaching aid."

152

Chapter 24

Healing his wound was simple. It was a clean cut. Too bad Master Loucé's assessment wasn't. Giving the right answers was easy enough – but the three-day observation... At least he was let out of the room – was allowed to run and interact... But...

A sigh left Zephyr as he looked up through the leaves at the clear sky. *A couple more hours. That's all. It's almost over.*

Last night's memories played in his head. There were increasingly larger gaps in time between them. And now he had to watch to the bitter end. Knowing the truth about himself... This gave him more to think about than he wanted.

But he still didn't know why he hated his cousin. *He* was the monster. Not Ferdinan. *That anger...why can't I control it?* Before he realized...it'd already consumed him. Each time. For years.

No matter how hard I tried, it always ended with me beating him.

But last night, he realized something sickening - twisted. *He always looks relieved afterward.* The more savage the beating–

An "Ehem" interrupted his thoughts.

Onyx eyes shifted from the sky to his lifelong friend. The smile forming on his lips vanished when he noticed her expression. Terrified. Furious. Scared. Zephyr swallowed, but guilt stuck in his throat.

"What were you doing?!"

His hand flip-flopped from palm down to palm up and back. "Umm...what do you mean?"

Kneeling beside him, Denila slugged his shoulder. "What were you thinking?! What were you doing?!"

"What are you talking about?" Zephyr blinked away tears. That wasn't a playful punch.

"What do you mean, 'what am I talking about?!' You turned *into* my blade! It was a feint - it never should've made contact! I know you saw it! We've been sparring for how many years?! How did this even happen?!"

...I scared her... "I don't know. I didn't see it... You were fast."

She unleashed a barrage of strikes to his arm – numbing it. "Don't lie! They wouldn't have let you back here if you were unable– Something...so simple!"

I made her cry... That tightness constricted his lungs. Injuring each other in sparring was normal, but she never reacted like this. *I turned into her blade? I'd never do that.* "I'm sorry. All I remember is enjoying our fight and then that weird music changed."

"Music? You made me stab you 'cause of some music playing on the other side of the island?!"

Her lecture continued, but he didn't stop it. He just let her run her course.

* * *

Maniacal laughter filled the air. As did cries for help. Tuel didn't have to look to know what was going on. Oya developed a habit of randomly tormenting his suitemate. Turning, he saw blood-red hair chasing after Ilu's shiny black. Shaking his head, the tiny boy flew toward them. The closer he got, the redder Ilu's face appeared. *Stop running. Don't play her games.*

That was easy to think. In private, his island brother agreed, but said he never could. When she was there, he couldn't help the chaos that ensued.

Eager bare feet skidded to a stop and those eerie green eyes turned on him. A wink and the crazed girl flicked her wrists.

It wasn't until she was soaring straight for him that Tuel remembered the cuffs used at the Family Week show.

"Haha!"

The flying shadow dodged out of the way – but that didn't discourage her. Oya came around for another pass. And she was fast! Golden-brown fingers grazed his snow-white hair. Then he was standing on one of the outer islands.

"What...? What just happened?"

A mischievous grin filled his view right before plopping onto the ground and leaning back. "You're not the only one who has no one."

154

What?

"Marcus..." Oya looked at the water before circling back to him. "Marcus isn't the only one suffering. You deserve the same support."

"What're you talking about?"

"Your island family."

Why is she talking about them? She doesn't know us. "I didn't lose anyone. Marcus lost everyone. But... There's enough stress in our suite without you torturing Ilu too. Please stop."

Something he couldn't describe flashed across her alien green eyes. "You can't lose what you never had."

Fire coursed through his veins. Clenching his jaw tight kept him from saying something he'd regret.

"There once was a man who flew to close to the sun." Squatting down, Oya looked up at him.

What is she doing? Her gaze... It felt like she was looking right through him. She stayed like that for a long time. Should he move? Or... What was going on? He blinked and she was standing again, her hand just shy of touching his chest.

"You have a good heart. Keep building the life you want."

Just as Jon complained about, she vanished. No running or flying away. She just stopped being there. *Is this a dream?* It felt too real... But...how did he get here? And what did she mean?

* * *

Ferdinan grinned – feeding off his pupil's excited energy as Elbie placed the screen between them. "This is your project?"

"Yes!"

"Wonderful! Please tell me about it!"

Elbie paused, "Is your stomach hurting?"

"No..." *What am I doing?* Blushing, Ferdinan grabbed his knees to stop punching his belly. "I apologize. Tell me about your project."

The young Tinkerer studied the skeleton for a minute. Apparently satisfied, he pulled up blueprints he was exceedingly proud of. "I'm still working on it, but it'll be a 3D printer."

Ferdinan smiled. "What makes it different from what we already use?"

"It'll print at the atomic level using carbon." One gray and one green eye twinkled against Elbie's dark skin.

A strained smile stretched Ferdinan's thin lips. As fun as this idea was, that level of atom manipulation was beyond human ability... Looking over the schematics, the skeleton considered how to...

Every word left Ferdinan's mind. *I always knew he was more intelligent than me...but...this...?* It was beyond even a Tinkerer's imagination. *How much have I underestimated him? How much have I failed him by not realizing?* The weight of responsibility tripled. Was it possible for him to be the mentor Elbie needed?

Mouth dry, Ferdinan looked at those mismatched eyes. *He doesn't understand...* Of course, the young boy wouldn't. Elbie hadn't yet learned this was impossible. Awe blanketed the older Tinkerer... *All the uses... This is an entirely new field of study...* But... *It's better he doesn't know. I want to see how far he can take this...* "Interesting. What do you plan on doing with it?"

"Carbon's the basis of most things. It's inexpensive but valuable in more complex forms. So, I thought, it'd be useful to print gems."

That was among the ideas Ferdinan had as well. It'd be amazing. And horrible. "Why print gems?"

"So many bad things have happened recently," Elbie started. "So much was lost and destroyed. Gems could rebuild those broken places. All the hungry people could be fed."

His heart's in the right place. "Those are wonderful things."

Now to crush him.

Elbie nodded.

"As long as this stays on the islands, there won't be a problem." This statement drew his apprentice's attention – distracting from the boney fist pounding Ferdinan's stomach, again. "But... What will happen when people realize gems can be printed?"

"They wouldn't have to mine them or scout old ruins?" Elbie thought – then smiled brighter. "That'd get rid of dangerous jobs..."

"That's true. Jobs will be lost."

"Huh?"

Ferdinan's heart ached.

Burdening a young child.

"Printing gems... Flooding economies with enough to rebuild broken areas and feed all the hungry would make money worthless."

Elbie considered this. "But gems could replace money..."

"True. But the countries focused on gem collecting would fall. Unable to control massed-produced gems, those governments would collapse. It's gems' rarity that allows these places to supplement their people's needs." Ferdinan paused while his pupil stood speechless. "Let's put aside societal problems. What would easily created gems do to people individually?"

"Everyone could do what they wanted. Just print a gem to buy what they need, then they could focus on doing what they want."

A soft sigh left Ferdinan. *I hate this...* "Jobs will be lost. Highly prized work will become useless. What people need to survive is guaranteed by governments, but that doesn't fulfill their psychological *need* to work. Millenia ago we learned this. Even after ensuring all physical needs was deemed as basic human rights, the internal need to work remained. To grow and improve. To dream and make those dreams reality. When one is no longer able to obtain a goal or means to a goal – work – it takes away their humanity."

"I don't understand..."

Your work tormenting innocents is unparalleled.

"When people no longer work... When they no longer *can* work 'cause there's no work for them..." Tired of being ignored, his stomach started gnawing on his organs. "It leaves people feeling worthless 'cause they're unable to earn – unable to achieve. It steals their hope and drive. It takes away what makes us human.

"Progress slows or stops all together. Bitterness and resentment grow, and conflict intensifies. Those unable to find or create work will fall into despair 'cause they're not needed. Even those who choose not to work will eventually succumb to that same depression. Having lost the feeling of being needed, the joy of succeeding, of having a purpose... The few who find work will face vicious jealousy."

"I still don't understand. Why would that happen?"

The voice laughed...but it was much quieter - easier to ignore. Smiling, Ferdinan offered the best example one could give a child. "While you're here, how much you learn, what you accomplish, is up to you. If that's taken away... If you worked hard to learn and do as much or more than your peers, but every opportunity you were looking forward to disappeared, how would you feel?"

"...angry..."

"If you knew it didn't matter how much or little you did, nothing would change your chances to progress, how hard would you try?"

"I don't know...probably not very hard..."

"Similarly, if a class you needed was limited, but you worked hard, did everything you could to earn a spot, but was never able to take it, leaving your studies to stay incomplete. How would you feel?"

Mismatched eyes looked around the room as a dozen expressions crossed Elbie's face. "That'd be so frustrating..."

"And how would you feel toward the lucky few who got to complete their studies?" His apprentice's jaw moved, but no words came. "You'll not lose the food and shelter you have. The safety and care you need. But no matter how hard you try; how much you want to achieve the goals you have; it'll be out of your reach. You can live a long life like that. But...will you feel alive? Will you be happy?"

Looking down, Elbie nodded. "I understand."

Ferdinan continued apologetically. "Even the luckiest, hardest working, and most generous people will be adversely affected. With governments collapsed and money worth nothing, food would be the only thing of value. The areas supplementing with gems and other natural resources have less fertile lands. It's hard to give food, which is limited and seasonal, when your family's faced with hunger, than it is to give money that can be budgeted around."

Elbie's mismatched eyes widened.

Ha! Only you could make a child look like that!

I'm sorry I'm scaring you. Why am I so incompetent? "Then there are the cultural meanings held for various gems. Being so easily produced causes those symbols to lose their importance. Now people don't have a stable government to turn to, there's no opportunities for them to achieve their goals, access to food is questionable, and those symbols for strength and hope have lost their meaning."

"I...I didn't think it could be so horrible! I'm sorry!"

I'm terrible... Covering his eyes, Ferdinan took a deep breath. "Your idea's fun and could be wonderfully beneficial. As Tinkerers, we need to stop and think of the worst possible thing our inventions could cause. Even after so many millennia, humans are amazing at twisting good things into horrible ones. Why can't we learn..."

"So, I need to think of something else." A pale Elbie looked to his mentor for guidance.

"No." Ferdinan smiled. "I approve your idea."

"But...but why!?! I'll collapse governments and cause widespread depression and starvation!"

"*If* it left the islands before society was ready for it." Ferdinan knelt to eye level. "It's a fun and wonderful idea. Both new and fascinating. Scientific curiosity alone... I want you to bring this to life. Build a machine that can print gems. This isn't something I can promote to the world, but safe on these islands, I want you to have fun with it. And later you can advance it to do more than print gems."

"Really? But isn't it scary?"

"It's good to feel fear for our creations. It means we're maintaining the proper respect for our station. And it keeps us humble." Standing tall and smiling big, Ferdinan continued, "I trust you to approach this project with the proper respect."

"Y-yes, sir." Elbie shook, but his smile was full of confidence.

* * *

Jon turned to whoever was tapping on his open door. He expected Elbie again but was greeted by an unusually somber Xhou.

"We need to talk."

Standing, he motioned the Lead in. "About what?"

After sitting next to the younger Thinker, Xhou took a moment to breathe in deep before starting. "There's no easy way to say this... And I mean no disrespect...but...but considering your family and..."

"What?" Acid filled Jon's chest. *He's never at a loss for words...*

"Ferdinan."

Frustration forced air from his lungs. "Xhou, I'm not-"

"Please." The Lead grabbed Jon's arm. "I'm worried. And what I have to say... It's sensitive. I can't trust anyone else. But...you work with him every day. You fight, every day. And your family loves him."

What do I do? Ferdinan's complaints about Xhou's persistence weren't unfounded. *If I don't let him talk... But Ferdinan needs to come home with me...* If anything compromised that, his ally could die. The growing giant locked his door. "What is it?"

"I know he's the scientist who stopped the plague."

"Xhou, he was commissioned to make the Second Skin, not-"

Interrupting Jon, Xhou spoke more forcefully. "I *know* it was him. I'm not asking for confirmation, just setting up my concern."

This isn't good... "For the sake of argument then."

"Doing something so awe-inspiring..." Xhou sighed. "That's not how he'd see it, is it?"

Reluctantly, Jon gave the older boy a "No."

"You're the only one who's spent real time with him... I'm not wrong...suspecting...Ferdinan being sick so often..." Xhou leaned in to whisper, "Ferdinan's making himself sick to deal with...*that?*"

"Isn't that what you're doing?" Jon pushed himself to his feet. "You're obsession with this! Isn't that you not dealing with reality?"

"I won't deny that. But switching subjects doesn't change what's going on with Ferdinan." Xhou gave Jon a long hard look.

Shaking his head, the growing giant closed his eyes – piecing together his words. *If Ferdinan thought I said anything...* Everything would unravel. *Back away, Xhou.* "That makes perfect sense – *if* Ferdinan heard about the plague before the cure was announced."

Xhou tried arguing but Jon cut him off.

"I was there. Remember?" Swallowing hard, Jon set his jaw. "If he was the scientist, I would've been the first to know."

"And the first to deny it."

160

Chapter 25

Bitterness attacked his tongue. Lately Ferdinan felt...invigorated. Though Jon watching him intensely was annoying and inconvenient.

What can you do? A pathetic defect like you?

It was too soon to hope. The voice felt farther away, but it wasn't gone. What if it quieted now to punch him later? *Easy. Then I'll die.*

Grabbing another capsule, Ferdinan injected a dose' worth then reached for the next. The capsules were the ones used for his mints. *...I haven't needed them for a while...* Which meant he could modify his green tin to hold these. *How is this three months' worth...?* It didn't matter. He wouldn't need to make any more because...

Because he wasn't needed. Wasn't *wanted.* So why more?

Placing the last capsule in the tin and sealing it conjured Oya from his closet. Her grin was so bright Ferdinan smiled in return.

"*Wow!*"

"What?"

"*I haven't seen you smile like that before.*"

The deep magenta skeleton turned to the gray-black of night beyond the window. "*What would you like to do?*"

"*Run!*" Oya winked.

"*It's dangerous traveling the ocean at night.*" Ferdinan stumbled out a lame excuse – waiting for the red to drain from his face.

Oya spun – revealing the cuffs on her wrists. "*Why row when I can soar through the stars?!*"

That comment – her enthusiasm – made him smile again despite himself. *This feels strange...* The motion of a natural smile...it was completely foreign. Feeling this way was embarrassing.

What right have you to be so happy?

Ignoring the voice, Ferdinan nodded. "*You're right.*"

"*Fly with me?*"

Maybe the medicine hadn't fully kicked in yet. Maybe his body finally recovered from the torture it survived. But for the first time in months, he had energy to spare. "*I'd love to!*"

Oya laughed and tossed him a set of cuffs.

In return, Ferdinan handed a small bag to her. "*I made masks and goggles so we can go as fast as we want!*"

A toothy grin split her face. Within moments she was climbing through the window – mask, goggles, and cuffs in place. The night sky loomed overhead while she waited for him. After checking their speakers and earpieces were connected and her mask was on properly, they were off.

Oya called it a race, but it was closer to a battle. Each took turns dodging and weaving – avoiding being tagged by the other and trying not to be passed. Soon they were physically throwing each other off course. Even when he pushed her away from the outer islands... And when she tricked him back to the main one...they just kept going. Faster. Faster. *Faster!*

The goal should've been his island, but she stayed on this beach. Running. Battling. Playing here... It was too dangerous. But...

It's late. No one's awake at this time... And he needed to run. He needed to move. This felt so good his usual concerns melted away. He simply stopped caring.

Time meant nothing. They kept up the chase, running without regard to where they were. And once Oya convinced him she'd forgotten about their original goal, she bolted high! Then soared out to the horizon. *Tricky!*

Blood red hair didn't get too far ahead before he caught up and they started their battle again. Escalating until they landed on Ferdinan's island. Both were panting and laughing.

"*Now that we're here...!*" Oya dashed off, leaving Ferdinan behind in a cloud of sand.

"*Cheater!!*"

His body was light, and energy coursed through him. It'd been so long since he ran without restraint. *This feels nice.* Each step melted his aches. The crisp, cool night air... The soft call of a calm ocean... The diamonds decorating black velvet above... And just ahead – getting closer – was the only one to ever call him "friend."

Closing his eyes, he wished this would continue for eternity. And...nothing told him he didn't deserve such a treasure.

My heart's light. I can run forever. I never want this to end.

This break...he needed it.

Desperately.

Wild green eyes glanced at him before Oya leaned forward and pumped her legs faster. He'd never come so close to catching her. It surprised them both, but they didn't stop until they were exhausted.

Until he couldn't hold his eyes open any longer...

~

There was the door to Evelyn's dreams. On the other side waited warmth and color. And his little sister. But there was one problem.

"I'm ready." Lounging against the door was an ethereal Emil.

He's still here...

"Yes. You'll never be rid of me." Chuckles as insubstantial as the translucent Emil haunted the space between them. "I applaud your efforts. But in the end, you'll realize it's in vain."

"At least I tried." Turning, Ferdinan walked into the perfect darkness. He should wake and play with Oya if Evelyn was out of reach. *Her beautiful door stays locked until Emil's gone.*

All he had now was time, and he'd bide it – because in the end, if Emil wasn't gone, he'd rid the world of two nuisances.

* * *

It was too late to be called late, but too early to be called early. And yet Zephyr couldn't sleep. His chest was painfully tight. Energy threatened to burst out his skin. Yesterday barely ended...but...

Dressing, the Prince headed outside. *I have hours to run...*

A light jog was his warmup before giving his legs every ounce of speed he had. The rhythm of movement took over – freed his mind. Normally he planned his day, went over his studies, or daydreamed. But not today. He didn't want to think. He just wanted to forget...

The rhythm sped up. *Focus. The silence...* It was pleasant. *Hold onto this.* None of that "music" the Sciences introduced marred the air. No voices. No laughter. No screams.

Just the light whistle of a gentle breeze.

Step. Step. Step. Step. Step.

The diamond encrusted coal-black sky reflected off the water. It was lovely. His attention lingered on it until the split. *Ahead and up the hill? Or left through the meadow?*

The hill, it's more intense. And... It led to an unexpected find.

Giggles floated out to meet him. *Who's up at this time?* Zephyr shifted into the shadows, softening his steps. Cresting the hill brought the giggler into view. The giggler and her companion. Short spikey hair atop a lean body ran just ahead of a tall, gangly stick figure...

The girl turned – running backward – and shouted something. Chuckles from the tall one answered. Moving farther inland, Zephyr navigated shadows to get nearer.

Slowly they outpaced him despite his efforts. There was only one person with a silhouette like that. But...Ferdinan couldn't run well, let alone efficiently. *Except when I first met him...* Turning, Zephyr cut their distance, nearing the beach in time to watch them pass.

It really is him... Nothing made sense. *Who's the girl...? What's going on?* An overwhelmed mind slowed Zephyr's feet. Something tugged at his heart – urging him to keep watching. Moving faster, the Prince cut through trees to catch up again.

For miles... Not once did Ferdinan trip or slow. The girl was impressive – but his cousin was more graceful... And Fast. Too fast. The distance Zephyr ran was considerably less. Yet they kept pulling ahead. *He can't be faster than me, even with those long legs.*

Am I dreaming? Is the elf woman watching, ready to laugh at me? When the Prince thought he caught up, that strange girl soared into the sky – Ferdinan on her heels. *What...? Ok...this is a dream...*

Zephyr ran back to his room where he waited to wake up.

Chapter 26

"You're preoccupied."

Zephyr nodded to the elf and stood up. "I saw something...I'm not sure what to make of it."

"Oh?"

"I saw Ferdinan running."

"Don't children run often?"

"Not him. You've watched these memories; he's not a physically active person. He's clumsy and awkward and slow. When he sprints, it's short distances and always ends up tripping. But...what I saw was amazing. He was graceful – like he was meant to run. And he was *fast!* I couldn't keep up."

"And?" Her smirk plainly said how much she enjoyed his struggle.

"And...? He's a Scientist, not an Athlete."

"Scientists can't run?"

"Not like *that.* It's not humanly possible without the mutation..." Golden hands danced in confused agitation. "Even if it was...he's sick all the time, doesn't eat, and spends his days hiding in his lab."

Her smirk morphed into a wicked grin. "So what does it mean?"

"I was dreaming?" Zephyr's eyes pleaded for this to be truth. "I felt awake; but I had to be dreaming."

"There're realistic feeling dreams, but that doesn't sound like one." Stepping forward, the elf patted his head. "You're ignoring an important detail."

"What?"

"You already know the answer."

Zephyr stepped back, not sure what to expect.

"You know the answer. Now to recognize it." Snapping her fingers, Zephyr found himself aboard the transport home. Another snap brought a chair into existence and she sat - easing the burden of an impossible weight.

She never sits... The Elf pointed to where himself of a few months ago stood, rod in hand, wailing on his cousin's back. Zephyr averted his eyes. *Not again...*

"You'll miss it."

"What? What am I looking for?"

The elf pursed her lips. "Watch."

Reluctantly, he did as he was told. Every second of that beating burned in his chest, suffocating him. And then it was over.

"So?"

One golden hand circled from above to below the other while onyx eyes looked away. "I can't believe he didn't die."

"And what's the reason he didn't?"

"What?"

"Let's watch again!" The elf gave the creepiest grin Zephyr ever saw. "This time - a little slower."

Before he could respond, the memory played in slow motion - the elf pointing for him to observe. Disgust twisted his insides. *How can she enjoy this?!*

The rod came down again. And again. And again.

Then he saw it. The movement was subtle. "I never noticed this before?"

"Have you ever really noticed Ferdinan?" She smirked as her question slapped him in the face.

* * *

"I've already said there's no need to apologize. The bones arrived in time." Yahmo looked exasperated.

But Ferdinan couldn't stop. Each time that response brought him closer to tears.

Before the skeleton could start another rebuttal, Yahmo continued, "I'm sorry for asking too much from you."

"No, it isn't too much, I..." Ferdinan floundered. *I'm too weak. Too incompetent. Too broken.* There were so many ways to end that statement honestly, yet he couldn't say any of them.

What did it say...? Shaking his head, Ferdinan returned his attention to healer Yahmo. "Please, sir, I *need* to apologize for my incompetence. There's no excuse for being so late. *I* set the day and the need was urgent. Please accept my apology."

Earnest blue crystals bore into the man, twisting his face. They could go back and forth all day – Ferdinan apologizing and him insisting there's no reason. "Thank you."

A shaky sigh escaped the skeleton. "I promise it won't happen again."

"Thank you." Yahmo nodded sadly – worry creasing his face. "Are you ok?"

The Tinkerer froze. Mostly. A boney hand kept pounding against his stomach. *Why won't it stop demanding food? I gave it a bar ten mins ago.* The effort it took to still his fist was growing every day. "I'm fine. I'm sorry..."

"Are you sure?" Healer Yahmo sighed when Ferdinan looked away. "Miss Senia thanks you too."

"Miss Senia?" That name pushed Ferdinan's mind off track.

"The girl whose arm you saved. There's no nerve damage; she's finishing rehabilitation."

"...I'm glad..." Hearing those words allowed his mind to accept he hadn't stolen the girl's arm. The relief...he nearly started laughing. "I'm so glad!"

Such passion from the normally subdued boy made Yahmo smile. But worry never left the man's eyes.

* * *

Jon might be *good* at hacking. But Xhou learned from the best – meaning the younger Thinker only learned from the second best. The Science Lead smirked.

Too many things didn't add up. Even without the Dinta's help, he'd figure something out on his own.

First question: How close was the skeleton to everything that happened?

Even with Ferdinan being Ferdinan and always taking more responsibility than was healthy, his charge was still acting *too* intense. Meaning the boy had to be close.

Infiltrating Yurranie Private Children's Hospital's system wasn't easy. Its main data storage was self-contained and didn't directly connect to any outside systems. Most of his time was spent gaining access to the storage. Even when he did, the security protocols were intense – they put some Jon designed to shame. But this was a hobby of his. Twists and turns and non-destructive viruses scored him a copy of the Hospital's memory banks.

Now to rummage through it.

Jon wasn't lying about Ferdinan being hired to make that Second Skin thing. However, the number of entries addressing that paled in comparison to Ferdinan's other project. Those records were so heavily encrypted his programs were still working through them. But he had enough to start... More than enough.

There was so much it was overwhelming. But one folder caught his attention. It was simply labeled "Yewaru Jingue." Yewaru was a fairly common name; however, his uncle was the only Yewaru who was also a Jingue.

It was astounding how much time Ferdinan spent with Yewaru. The footage from his uncle's room...it made Xhou's heart sick. Seeing the man he most loved visiting over breaks was wonderful.

At first.

Then indescribable pain took over. Ferdinan never stopped visiting. And when his uncle slipped into a coma, the skeleton appeared and didn't leave. Days later, a horrible, painful *beep* screamed out the beloved man's passing.

Ferdinan didn't wail or lament, he simply fell to his knees clutching a screen for nearly an hour. An older man entered. After a short exchange, Xhou realized how sick Ferdinan was. The boy fell trying to stand. And when he finally made it to his feet, the best the skeleton could do was stagger away.

Tears warmed Xhou's face. Days of suffering through the footage... But for the first time he saw exactly what that virus did.

Not just to its victims, but to Ferdinan as well.

It took a while to get himself under control enough to continue. There were two other folders with different names, inter-hospital communications, and daily sessions with someone named Master Minjing.

The rest was still decoding, but it looked like Ferdinan was in regular contact with a couple other people. There also seemed to be information from Azuté's hospitals.

Keep going. But he didn't really want to. Seeing that happen to his uncle was enough. But Ferdinan didn't have the option to stop. He opened the smaller of the two folders.

The Tinkerer did the same thing for a middle-aged woman. But she was in worse condition initially and didn't live long. *If I ever sleep, I'll only have nightmares... How did he witness this day in and day out and not go mad?*

Xhou's chest constricted as Ferdinan stood vigil over the woman in her final hours. Just as he had for Yewaru.

There was still one more named folder. Evelyn Minjing. *The world's hero...but she's just a child...* Rura's charred body filled his mind. She was just a child. *No...* Xhou fought against the rising bile. *I can't watch a child go through that...* But he did wonder if she was related to the Master Minjing Ferdinan was in contact with. It'd make sense, though that family name was fairly common.

I need to stop. It was fine going no further. Accepting that Ferdinan saw horrible things... But Xhou didn't want to. He wanted to understand. Breathing in deeply, he opened the folder of inter-hospital communications and studied the files. Neither did he stop until Herrard appeared and dragged him away.

* * *

Ferdinan responded to the next message awaiting him. Before he could read through the barrage of written and audio messages following it, an older, jovial man filled the screen.

169

"It's about time, son! Where have you been the last few months? You know I don't appreciate being ignored."

"Grampa Huey!" Scratching the back of his head, Ferdinan stood and accepted the scolding. There were too many messages he neglected. The last one he read was from his mother, and that was some time ago. A cold sweat ran down his spine. *The Duchess...how many messages has she sent...?* Another lecture like that...even though he deserved it...

"I take it you still haven't read them."

Shrinking back at the man's raised eyebrow, Ferdinan looked down and nodded.

"Tornados took out everything in Urmsberg, including the factory producing those bars of yours. Anonymous is less than happy."

What...? The skeleton's threadbare heart raced – refusing to slow. *When...? How badly have I failed everyone? How do I make up the deficit?* "Please apologize for me."

"Already did. Over a month ago. Took the liberty of messaging a few contacts of my own. Demand hasn't been met, but supplies haven't stopped altogether. You disappearing without a word didn't help either." This lecture was supposed to be a series of lighthearted jabs, so when Grandpa Huey noticed tears running down Ferdinan's face, he stopped. "Hey, now, none of that!"

"I'm sorry." Ferdinan's voice broke. *Why am I so upset? He always teases...* Picking at each other was a fun pastime of theirs. Why did it feel as if his heart was ripped from his chest and smashed into the floor? "I won't fail again."

"Stop it or I'll come out of this screen and hug you."

"I'm sorry." Ferdinan managed a shaky laugh. "I don't know what came over me."

The bit of good humor in the boy's voice made Grandpa Huey smirk. "My guess would be your hormones are finally kicking in. I've been waiting six years for that to happen."

Crying – for any reason – was embarrassing. But Grandpa Huey's words were utterly humiliating, turning him from pink to cherry red.

"Ha! That's what you get for not checking your messages, son," he laughed heartily. "What did you call for?"

Blue crystals hid behind overgrown hair, Ferdinan mumbled, "My supplies are low..."

"And you don't want any of it traced back to you."

"Yes, sir."

"No, no! Don't be crying then calling me 'sir.'"

Another wave of heat shot through him. "Yes, Grandpa Huey."

"Wow...that was a bit too easy."

"I needed them a while ago." Still too red to look at the man, Ferdinan uploaded the list. "Also, I'll need materials for the bars and supplements. I'll make what I can here 'til production is back to full."

"Hmmm..." Pulling up the file, Grandpa Huey looked over it. "I'll get on this and fire up the time machine. The usual amounts from emergency orders?"

"Um...start with double. We'll see from there. Thanks...thank you, sir." He tried, but being disrespectful to someone who did so much for him was wrong.

"Closer! Keep working on it!"

With that, the box went blank. Ferdinan didn't place the next call until his skin returned to normal. *I fell so far behind...* But he'd use this newfound energy to catch up – until it gave out.

While waiting for his call to be answered, Ferdinan wrote a message to Master Fulason. He designed and finalized blueprints for a machine he didn't have the equipment to build. Now to see if he could use a favor to have Master Fulason make it.

* * *

No matter how many times Yuyu faced her reflection, it refused to show her what she wanted to see. Only a reality she couldn't accept.

The black material covering her hands stopped a few inches past her wrists. She wished it covered all of her. But both the Healers and Master Loucé insisted it was important for her to accept how her body looked now. So she faced her mirror every day. Every day melted skin greeted her. Seeing it didn't make her sick anymore, at least. Not like her hands.

No amount of rubbing them would ease the deep ache.

Nausea washed over her. Her body was beautiful next to her hands. *Please let me always wear the gloves.* Closing her eyes, she stepped forward, waiting for the sensation to pass. When it finally did, she opened them and focused on her face. *How much did it take to make my face normal again? How badly was it burned?* Aside from a strip of missing hair extending to above her ear – her face was normal. Exactly how it should be. But that strip of skin would never grow hair again. Neither would her mind search for a way to make it. She wanted to find a way. But...it wouldn't.

A light tap was followed by a muffled voice. "Yuyu. We're going to breakfast. Want to join us?"

"Yah...!" *What was...?* Picking up the strange toy Herrard gave her, Yuyu let her thumb spin the little ball baring. "Let me finish dressing!"

Anything to escape the unwelcome truth. If only for a short while.

Chapter 27

"Hmm...according to this..." Elbie shifted the diagram. "We need a piece shaped like a 'Y'... But I'm not seeing it."

"Maybe the last box?" Grinning, Ferdinan offered a box cutter.

"It didn't seem like so many pieces 'til we started."

"Like a puzzle. Pieces feel overwhelming before they're put together." Ferdinan's stomach didn't growl. It skipped straight to eating his spine. *I'll feed you after Elbie's time is up!* A strange look from his pupil told him he was punching his belly again.

Mismatched eyes disappeared as he dug deeply into the freshly opened box. Suddenly the boy stopped moving. "Huh?"

"What?" Ferdinan leaned back – failing to suppress a smile.

Elbie lifted a box wrapped in shiny green cloth. "What's this?"

Heat flooded his face and forced Ferdinan's gaze to the scattered metal pieces. The only distraction was his stomach demanding food. "Xhou would say you're silly for asking to work on your birthday."

"Thank you!" The now seven-year-old boy reached out, stopping when he noticed how awkward this was for his mentor. But he still smiled brightly. "I thought you didn't celebrate birthdays..."

"You do." Strained silence fell and Ferdinan tugged at his sleeve.

"Um...can I open it?"

"It's yours." Ferdinan's smile returned, but the red grew deeper. These sorts of things were difficult. *Will he like it? Will I disappoint him?* What was an appropriate gift for a seven-year-old? This was as difficult as Yuyu's seventh birthday. Yuyu... It felt like he'd forgotten about her. The first medicine numbed his mind. But...what excuse did he have now for not checking on her? There was none.

Elbie giggled and painstakingly unwrapped the box. The silk cloth was folded and placed neatly beside the gift. Inside was a large specialty sized screen. Mismatched eyes grew brighter. "Thank you!"

Cold sweat washed over Ferdinan as little hands turned on the screen. The installed program glowed and his pupil sucked in a sharp breath. *I was wrong... I shouldn't have done this... What was I thinking?* "I-I'm sorry...you...you've been e-eyeing that program..."

That pathetic excuse for an apology – and sentence – unleashed Elbie's tongue. "This is wonderful! Thank you! Please, teach me it!"

"Ah..." This was as much an affirmative as a sigh of relief. A rhythmic jarring shook him. Looking down, Ferdinan found he was beating his abdomen again. *I've fed you already!*

"An outside project and the best design software! This week's been amazing!" Elbie beamed at his mentor.

Bright red, Ferdinan reached behind him and grabbed the piece Elbie needed. "Here. But you can play with the program instead."

Torn, Elbie glanced from the part to his new screen. "I...I don't know! How do I choose?"

Ferdinan stood – smile dancing on his lips and fist pounding against his stomach. "I'll be here for another hour."

"Then...the machine. I'll read up on the program later." Elbie gingerly returned the screen to its box and the two went back to work.

When the hour ended, Ferdinan saw Elbie out then returned to another dose of medicine and a too long wait for lunch.

* * *

It was the strangest thing... Finding Ferdinan on the floor of his lab, hugging his legs... And the expression on the gent's face... His suitemates had that look when long, hard days lined up with a too late dinner. But...not this intense. Beside Ferdinan were half a dozen empty glass bottles. *I thought he always reused the one...*

"Are you ok?"

Ferdinan's stomach answered, turning him bright red. "I'm sorry. I'm just hungry..."

"I have lunch. You can eat sooner if you stay in your suite."

"No!" Ferdinan shook uncontrollably. "I won't eat there!"

"Ok, ok." Jon held up his hands placatingly and didn't move until the skeleton relaxed and pulled himself up to the table. Boney hands grabbed for the plate before Jon could lay it out. For days meals were eaten without delay or complaint. But this...

Jon poured their drinks before realizing Ferdinan was wolfing down *his* plate. Meat and all. *He...he never eats meat...* Part of Jon was excited – until the gagging started. But those boney fingers kept cramming in food. Snatching the plate nearly got him punched.

"Don't eat so fast!" Jon flinched when Ferdinan growled to give the food back. "You'll make yourself sick – if you don't choke."

"I'm eating your food like you want! Why take it away?!"

"Calm down." *This isn't Ferdinan...* "Eat a little slower."

The skeleton manhandled his desires and pushed himself back from the table. "I'm sorry. I shouldn't have yelled."

"What's going on?"

"Playing with Oya...takes a significant amount of energy..."

"True." Jon took the smaller plate. "Just don't eat so fast."

Instead of turning red, the gent paled and nodded.

This isn't a fight I thought I'd have with him... "I'm surprised you ate the fowl. I've never gotten you to touch it before."

Transparent blue crystals tripled in size and the gent ran to his closet. Then came retching. *Why? Meat will keep him satisfied longer...* Sighing, Jon took what was left of the cooked bird and switched it with the tempeh steak he prepared.

Running water, shuffling, clinking danced around the closet. When the skeleton returned, he was shaky and bright red. After each bite Ferdinan sat on his hands. And each time seemed to take more willpower. *Is he that hungry? How often should I bring food?*

He's eating more and his appetite increases every day. Yet...he looks skinnier. Should I tell Oya to not be as active around him? But she'll start tormenting my suitemates again... I can't let him be sent home for failing to maintain his weight... Ugh... This was another unpleasant thing he had to address.

"Ferdinan...you were supposed to weigh in a while ago. The extension passed... They want that information."

Chewing faster, Ferdinan forced himself to swallow. "I'm sorry... I'm sorry I made your life more difficult."

"It's ok." *He didn't get angry...* The relief this brought...

Ferdinan hid his eyes behind shaggy brown hair. "A week. I'm not ready now, but in a week."

"Ok." *He didn't argue...just asked for more time... But what'll happen in a week?* Still, Jon didn't want to push things.

* * *

How fast can I go? Oya tested the cuffs' limits every inch of the trip. *I've earned my play time.* The growing cord of connections she held proved it. *I'm glad my dear friend has energy again.*

An unexpected scene greeted her when she arrived. A long streak in the dirt ended where Ferdinan was huddled in a ball. Thin arms squeezed his legs so tightly they trembled.

"*Hello!*" She hovered above his grimacing face. *Is that a smile?*

"*Hello. Are you ready to play?*"

Giggles filled the air. His sudden extra energy was welcomed – though strange. Finally seeing him happy! She didn't think he could give an honest smile. And his soul was looking better. The dense mass of infection was nearly gone and the bleeding stopped. The gaping hole was still there, but it wasn't getting worse. Though...his soul... It was cloudy... *What does that to a soul?* "*Are you ready?*"

"*Yes.*" Rolling thunder emanated from his stomach. "*Let's play.*"

Though he said this, he didn't move – but he was obviously trying. "*How about a snack first? The trees on the island over are ripe.*"

"No. I don't want to eat."

"*Ok.*" She pulled him up, but he didn't get very far before jerking back into a crouch. "*I'll be back in five minutes.*"

"I don't want anything!" Teeth bared and panting, Ferdinan looked more like an animal than a boy. "Stop forcing me! I don't need another Jon!"

Lips pursed to the side, delicate fingers tugged at the chain around her neck. "Have I ever been like Jon?"

"*Ugh!!*" Boney fists pounded his abdomen. Activating his cuffs, he shot off like a rocket. "Forget it."

Chapter 28

"Wake up. Wake up." Those words were urgent, but quiet.

"Huh...?" Looking around, he first saw snow white hair. Then Haoyu's face came into focus. Sweat soaked Elbie's pajamas and he was having trouble catching his breath.

"More nightmares..." The Energist floated beside him.

"I'm sorry I keep waking you..."

Haoyu shook his head. "Will you tell me about them?"

It was the same offer every time. And every time Elbie lied – saying he couldn't remember. He didn't want to burden his island family. That was the reason he kept seeing Master Loucé even though it wasn't helping – not much. It was easy to pretend during the day. But at night. When he was alone. When he slept...

Staring at his hands, tears welled up. He was tired. Of everything. All of it. Why wasn't anything getting better? Even if he was only going to make Yuyu happy, he should be getting better, right? *What am I doing wrong?* Master Loucé helped everyone – so not improving had to be his fault. But the sessions right after the fire didn't prevent this. And the ones now weren't stopping the nightmares. *What am I doing wrong? How do I figure this out?*

"The curse will stay 'til you banish it."

This felt like a curse, but Elbie didn't believe it was... If so... Sobs strangled tears out of him and he covered his face. "I want it to stop."

Haoyu moved closer, careful not to touch him. "Want what to stop?"

"The fire... The explosion and debris. My hands hurting..." Elbie's words...thoughts...were incoherent, but he didn't know how to organize them. Or if he wanted to. "I want it to stop..."

Weight lifted from the mattress – shifting the bed slightly. Something soft was pushed into his arms, but Elbie didn't have to look to know what it was. Shaking, he accepted the stuffed fish. Haoyu was squeezing a stuffed dolphin. Being touched didn't feel nice. Even though his island brothers didn't know why, they didn't push. Instead Iilli returned from their first break with an assortment of stuffed toys. It was their way of including him. That dolphin was how Haoyu gave him a hug. Something he desperately needed.

"I'm listening."

"I keep seeing it. When I sleep. When I look at my hands. Other times I'm not sure about. I..." Elbie squeezed the fish hard. "Will I ever be safe again?"

"Yes." Silence reined for a long time.

Elbie's voice came out high and thready. "How?"

"I don't know. But Master Loucé helped Iilli. In time the same will happen for you."

Elbie squeezed the fish harder. "When? How? Nothing's working. I don't know what to do. What to say. How do I make my sessions work?"

"I don't know." The dolphin reached out and bopped the fish – making Elbie look up to Haoyu's soft smile. "But I walked with him. I'll walk with you too."

Not sure what else to say or do, Elbie dried his face and nodded. "There's nothing I can give in return..."

"You're my brother." Giving the dolphin another squeeze, Haoyu used its nose to muss Elbie's hair. "I care for my family."

* * *

A total absence of light surrounded him, but he could feel the faint warmth of Evelyn's door. It'd been so long... Hope – weak and worn – joined Ferdinan as he made his way toward it. With every step, he strained his eyes and ears searching for Emil.

If he didn't know what to look for, he'd have missed the voice's manifestation. Emil was nothing more than a dark gray impression against perfect black – and fading.

"I won't have to die to be rid of you." There was no mocking. No boasting. Just the weary finality of a wish nearly fulfilled.

"You think this'll beat me?" Emil's knowing sneer hinted that Ferdinan knew nothing and would soon regret it. "I'll enjoy watching – seeing your hope grow. I'll be waiting."

If it weren't for Emil moving, Ferdinan wouldn't see him. "You're hardly here now."

"Ha! So naïve." Emil's last words before winking out of existence sent a chill down Ferdinan's spine, "I'll see you soon."

All that existed was Ferdinan and a door of warmth and light. There was no victory here. Only an uneasy numbness deep inside his heart. "I've made her wait too long. I need to apologize."

Walking through that door... Color – bright and vivid – greeted him. Love and joy personified.

"Big brother!"

* * *

"Mom!" Jon hugged his screen then returned it to the mount.

"My child, how are you?"

Her smile was the definition of warmth. *I want to go home...* "I'm doing better..."

"But?"

That one word was a blanket. "Ferdinan... But...I..."

"What's going on?"

I want to tell you so badly... "I'm sorry. I hate this...but..."

"I'm listening." Mother smiled – encouraging her son.

"He wasn't doing well for a long time, then he was better... He had energy and actually looked happy. Even ate without complaint! Now he's moody and...reacts to things too strongly – he's insatiable..."

"That's...odd," Mother spoke when her son stopped. "What're you wanting to say?"

"He should come home with me this break."

"Does he want to?"

The room blurred and Jon shook his head. "I haven't asked. I don't want to 'cause he'll refuse."

Smiling sweetly, Mother urged her son to open up a bit more. "You think so?"

"Yes. He feels...far away. It's hard to describe... He'll refuse, but he *needs* to come home. Can you have him ordered there?"

"Tenalia knows Evelyn's begging for him." Mother reached out a hand. "I'll arrange it. But I need to know what's wrong."

Desperate eyes looked longingly at his mother. *I want to tell you so badly...* "Promise me your office for as long as I want?"

"Of course. Up to and including the entire break."

"Thank you, Mom. I love you." A worn smile was the best he could manage. They continued talking. The entire time Jon couldn't shake the feeling something would go wrong.

* * *

First thing in the morning for North Oueshi was midnight on the islands. But time meant nothing to Ferdinan. After running the long way around the main island, he stood in his lab staring out the window. The dark ink of a midnight ocean attested to how quickly he got here. He knew his running speed down to the second. *Between being sick, injured, and that medicine, I should be slower...* But he wasn't. Instead of worrying, he used the extra time cleaning up before the call.

Drying his hair, Ferdinan stood in front of his main screen. Dozens of them of varying sizes and shapes and purposes sat at their proper stations. But this one was for non-personal calls. Ferdinan sat, only to find himself pacing the room. *Why is sitting so hard?* Forcing himself into a chair only worked for minutes at best.

Master Ludwick was becoming frustrated with him. Jon – thoroughly annoyed. But Oya loved it.

A loud gurgle blared through the room. Luckily, no one was present to hear it. It was still embarrassing. Another gurgle came – traveling from his stomach to his mouth.

"*Ugh...*" The hunger was so pervasive, so intense... Wrapping stick arms around his middle, he pressed hard to stifle its complaints. A few more hours and Jon would bring breakfast. He could wait.

This sensation was terrible – but giving in...how he loathed it.

Ferdinan found himself in the back of his closet raiding the small stash of nutrition bars. Swallowing... Blinking, Ferdinan looked at the empty wrapper. *When....?* Boney hands grabbed for another... *Stop it, Ferdinan! Don't do this! Calm down! Stay in control!*

Feed your body.

Shut up! He didn't need a second voice bothering him after ridding himself of the first. With his full might, he put the bar back and returned to the main room. The screen flashed to life before he ended up back in the closet. It wasn't Master Fulason. Instead, there stood an older, elegant woman who'd come with his aunt, the Queen, when she married his uncle.

"Madam Aguilla! How may I serve you?" This woman attended his Queen and his Prince – he owed her much. *I've already reported on Zephyr's progress...so why's she calling?*

"Lord Ferdinan, you're doing well?"

"Yes, ma'am."

"And our Prince?"

"He's well and has adjusted with little difficulty. Prince Zephyr will graduate on time."

"Thank you for caring for him." Her sad smile was filled with pity for the skeleton. "I called to ask a favor."

"Of course! Anything!" *What could she need from me?*

"I've sent a number of soil samples your way. I need you to test them."

"Yes, ma'am. What for?" *Why me? Why not the Duke...Lashi?*

"Everything. I expect you'll figure out why before you're done."

"Yes, ma'am. As soon as they arrive, I'll start on them."

"Thank you. They should be there tomorrow." Pausing for a moment, she addressed the fact he'd been dancing back and forth their entire conversation. "Is there a reason you're so active? This early, I'd expect a child to be dead on his feet."

His cheeks pinkened. "No, ma'am. I start my day earlier than most."

A salted eyebrow rose in suspicion, but she didn't press for more. "I look forward to your results."

"Yes, ma'am." The box went black just as another flashed to life, not giving Ferdinan a chance to consider what Aguilla wanted. "Master Fulason!"

"Master Ferdinan, how're you?"

A pleasant warmth filled Ferdinan. The sight of the bald man caused a smile to bloom on his lips. "I'm doing well, and you?"

"Blissfully busy as always!" Leaning back in his chair, Fulason picked up a smaller screen and waved it at Ferdinan. "These're quite the interesting schematics. I'm not used to such simple work from you."

"It's not for me, so I wanted use and upkeep to be as elementary as possible. Would you be willing to service it when needed?"

"Depends on who it's for."

"A man by the name of Yahmo. He's a healer at a private hospital in West Chūzo."

Master Fulason blinked. "You? Doing work for a Healer? Never thought I'd see the day."

Blushing, Ferdinan lowered his head. "It's easier over a screen."

"What's this machine needing to do? It doesn't make much sense for use in a hospital from the blueprints."

Biting his lip, Ferdinan sucked in a breath. "That's...sensitive information. Innocents could be hurt were it leaked."

"Huh..." Looking over the schematics again, Fulason shook his head. "West Chūzo...? Don't get out there often, but if it's a personal request from you, I'd be happy to service it as needed."

"Thank you, sir. Is there any way I may serve you?"

"Hmmm... Actually, there is."

Excitement shook him and Ferdinan found himself smiling like a child in front of a mound of presents. "Yes?"

"We got a prototype we've been fighting with. Just doesn't want to work. Care for a crack at the diagrams?"

It took grabbing the back of a chair not to jump for joy. "I'd love to, sir!"

A curious expression filled the man's face, but he smiled. "I'm sending them your way."

A box flashed the arrival of the prototype's drawings. "I look forward to this, thank you! How much do I owe you for my project?"

"Nothing," the man laughed.

"No! It'll be expensive!" Taking advantage of a man who helped him countless times...he couldn't. "I need to pay!"

"Calm down." Fulason studied the boy, confused. "You've done so much for me this year; I'll deduct it from what I owe you."

"I haven't done that much..."

"Yes, you have." Smiling, the man shook his head. "I'll keep careful record. If it costs more than what I owe, I'll send a bill."

"I expect to see that invoice." Ferdinan chewed his lip, worry swimming across nearly transparent blue crystals.

"Don't I always give one?" A look Ferdinan couldn't interpret softened the man's eyes. "Anyway, my men'll be arriving soon; I better get going. Looks like you need to move around too."

"Huh?" Taking stock of where he was, Ferdinan realized he'd been pacing. Red hot fire ignited his cheeks. "I apologize!"

"For being a child?" Fulason chuckled. "I'll let you know when it's ready. I'm assuming you want it sent to this healer Yahmo?"

"Yes, sir. Thank you."

When the box went black, Ferdinan bolted for the door, but stopped before reaching it. There were more messages. How much trouble had he caused by ignoring them? Sitting down, Ferdinan found there were surprisingly few aside from Grampa Huey.

But there was one he couldn't ignore.

Swallowing, he tapped on the message from Healer Riaderick. That name shook him. Fear suffocated him. *Calm down... Breathe... It's just a message.* Inside was a congratulations and stats concerning the medication he developed to reverse the damage of the virus. *Eighty-seven percent made a full recovery.* Eighty-seven percent...

Boney hands grabbed his chest. Everything blurred.

Thirteen percent of survivors died 'cause my medicine wasn't good enough... Fists batted away tears. *Thirteen? How many is that?!*

Sludge and bile boiled inside him. The room turned red and his hands hurt from clutching so tightly. "NO!!"

Glass shattered. Metal *clanged.* Brick chipped. "NO MORE!!"

Smoldering red filled him. Bursting through his skin! He heard the destruction. Felt his arms flailing. But he couldn't see anything. It was just red. Everything was red!

Even the void restraining his arms!

A soft warmth caressed his ears. Red became black and all the intensity of a moment before melted away. Leaving him cold. Numb. A golden-brown hand lifted from his face and the perfect emptiness of her touch dissipated. *What did she do to me?*

With a giant grin, she stepped back and offered his violin case. "*Play for me!*"

Aside from disheveled, blood-red hair, nothing about Oya hinted at seeing the massive tantrum he threw. Or...he thought... *Did that really happen? Was any of it real?* All color left him as he scanned the room. Everything... If it wasn't broken, it was scattered, bent, knocked over. *But...it was only a few seconds. The red...was only...*

He stared at his hands. *I'm shaking...?* A new emotion surged.

Fear.

Not the kind that keeps people alive. Or the one which incapacitated him around Healers. But the kind that stopped people from doing something they'd regret. *I don't want to break the gift you gave me.* "*No. I can't.*"

Carefully placing the case on the table, Oya turned and offered her hand. For a long moment she studied him. "*Play with me!*"

A smile tugged thin lips. He wasn't sure if he'd laugh or cry. *Please don't cry...* Grabbing her hand he ran.

Out the door. Down the hall. Outside.

Outside where there were no limits.

Chapter 29

At the center of the purple sea was a little boat. Inside slept the Fisherman. A giant grin swam with all her might toward it. The intention was to tip the boat, but when Oya grabbed it, she found herself sitting across from him.

"You're no fun!" Her entourage of glowing orbs danced in her peripheral.

A smirk met her complaint. "I've worked with your predecessors."

Shrugging, Oya folded her arms. "The diamond barrier's gone."

"I know." In one fluid motion the Fisherman sat up and placed his hat properly on his head.

That's all you have to say? "Then you know his soul's become...cloudy."

"Yes." The Fisherman frowned.

"What is it?"

"Infection."

"That's what's wrong with his heart – not his soul."

With a shake of his head, the Fisherman leaned in, "How infected has his heart looked recently?"

"Touché," *I get it...* "How did it spread from his heart to his soul?"

"That's what infections do when left untreated."

Great. Now how do I fix this? But it didn't make sense. "For the first time since I've met him, he truly looks happy. He's actually feeling the emotions inside him."

"But is he feeling them normally?"

"...he reacts more intensely than the situation calls for...but he's a child. That happens."

That too perfect face shook in disagreement. "He tore apart his lab and couldn't stop until you pulled those emotions from him."

"That was a bit much..." But with the stress her dear friend suffered, she was surprised he didn't tantrum more often.

"What're you going to do?"

"Nothing." What could she do? "I don't want him to die. If he isn't craving death, I'm happy."

The Fishermen's lips tightened. "The infection's still there. The *problem* is still there."

"I know...but..." A wave of her hand summoned the silver roads. "I can't change that."

"So you'll ignore it?"

Hand squeezing her little cord of silver strands, Oya frowned. There wasn't much she could do until she figured out this new problem. But until then, she had other work to do. "I said I'd keep *all* my promises, didn't I?"

The Fisherman nodded sadly. But he didn't say anything more. Neither did he stop her when she stepped onto the silver roads. One road after another passed quickly. Soon she stood in the kōjomằ's mind. Seemed this woman slept as much as her friend.

On the other side of those curtains was more of what she didn't want to see. But she had to. It was her responsibility. The new set of victims wasn't surprising. But recognizing them...

Fire burned her insides.

Iitano... When did she find them?

The boy protecting his sister...

Why didn't I think... But her rounds were interrupted. She couldn't have known the position that boy held or what he knew. It was her duty to, but... Oya screamed at her uselessness – her limitations. If there was anything to break...! What was the point of being...? Clenching her jaw, she studied every inch of the scene.

Lifeless bodies filled tables and lay stacked on the ground. Empty eyes. But...not nearly as much blood as last time... *Why didn't I know she was there...?*

White fire returned – consuming her chest.

Then she was cold.

A dozen screens came into view. Veins snaked across agitated hands flicking from one to the next. Oya didn't know those symbols. They weren't Common. Neither were they her precious Oŭndo.

Curses filled the air at the sight of the kōjomǎ's reflection. That woman's face wasn't happy. But that was fine – neither was Oya.

Iitano just laid there... *She couldn't have learned about them...* Closing the curtains Oya returned to her twilight beach and reached out to every keeper and charge...all who were whole. Golden-brown hands combed through unnatural hair, turning it black with streaks of sunshine and stretching it long past her hips. They then smoothed over her face – leaving behind gold speckled black eyes.

Ragged, worn shorts replaced the exquisite slacks she'd been given. And a simple wrap tied over one shoulder covered her instead of the rich yellow blouse. She missed these simple clothes. But they weren't available on the islands. Neither was she particularly picky.

"Tanan! Yee! Mr. Charlie!" One after another she called – pulling them before her. "Kato. Shan. ...Ozar... And whoever holds Iinamǐ's transfer."

Three men.

Three women.

And a small child holding a faded picture.

Oya approached the child – kneeling down to eye level. "Are you safe right now?"

Tears flooded out. "They don't know I escaped."

* * *

It was disgusting. *How much food 'til you are satisfied?!* Boney hands barreled into his belly. His body wouldn't stop complaining! His muscles constantly screamed to move – and his stomach to be fed. How could he have too much energy *and* not enough fuel?

Ferdinan's feet ran faster. Hunger grew each day. After a month... *Stay in control. Think about something else...*

But that energy let him both catch up and get ahead. Everything was done for this block and the next. Sleep was unnecessary...and counterproductive – allowing him to finish his analysis of the soil samples Aguilla sent and report back in a matter of days...

187

The soil samples... Irritation prickled every nerve. It was definitely sabotage. And he had his suspicions who. Proving anything wouldn't be easy, but he'd find the saboteur.

The growl from his stomach was so loud and long, it felt to echo around the trees with his footsteps. *Shut up! You don't need anything!* The two-hour run with Oya was nice. She did a wonderful job distracting him. But...she left him... His heart twisted along with his stomach. *Who else did she have to play with?* Ferdinan stopped himself. It was good. She needed to find more friends. She needed better people than him...

But without her next to him... Tears blurred his vision.

This wasn't good enough. *Move! Move faster!* The moon hung low ahead. Morning's light clawed at the horizon. But the stars still shown brilliantly.

Faster! Outrun the sun!

His stomach reached out and clutched at every organ – squeezing them. Pulling the skeleton to his knees and rolling him across the ground. It didn't hurt. But it didn't feel right. "*Ugh!!*"

Balling up tightly, Ferdinan rocked himself with his toes. But his body refused to straighten. *Ahh! Fine! I'll feed you!!* His stomach didn't release him, so he fought past it. The hope was to run the rest of the way to his suite, but a mile in Ferdinan found himself on his knees again.

His stomach took over his mind. All he could think about was food. Activating the cuffs, he flew.

Only one thing existed.

A puff of cold air hit his face. Shaking, boney hands reached out.

◊

The ceiling was nothing more than a blur. Rubbing his eyes cleared his vision but left his golden hands moist. *What was that?* Something woke Zephyr, but he wasn't sure what.

A window slamming shook his nerves. Sliding over to his door, he listened. Soft *clinks* danced on the other side. *What....?*

Theon's never awake this early. Slowly he turned the handle and cracked open the door. *Ferdinan....? What's he doing?* Zephyr

188

slipped through the narrow opening for a better look at the kitchen. Boney hands clawed at the fridge's insides. *What's happening?*

Inching forward... *My Right of Ascension ceremony...* It was exactly like this that last night.

Shoving food into his face faster than he could chew – or swallow – Ferdinan indiscriminately grabbed whatever was in front of him. That day played side by side with the present.

"Ferdinan." No response came, so Zephyr moved closer. "Ferdinan. Stop."

No response. Not even a flinch. The prince might as well have been a ghost. *What do I do...?* Zephyr stood helpless as his commands were ignored. Physically restraining his cousin earned him an elbow to the ribs – cracking one in the process.

Ugh...how...? He's that strong? "Ferdinan! Stop this now!"

Gagging spurred Zephyr to lunge for the trash can and force it into his cousin's hands. Ferdinan fought – at first. Coughing. Painful retching. Zephyr watched in horror as his cousin's body rejected everything forced into it. Time froze – trapped in the nightmare. Trapped. Until Ferdinan slid to the floor gasping for air.

What do I do? Pain shot through his side when he crouched next to the skeleton. "Are you ok?"

Labored panting stole Ferdinan's attention. Exhausted animal eyes locked on with Zephyr's – freezing both of them to the spot. Those blue crystals widened – screaming silently.

Ferdinan bolted before Zephyr could react.

~

Black turned to gray. Colors filled the sky... Zephyr should be in the middle of his morning run...not returning to his suite in failure. *That didn't really happen...did it? It couldn't have.*

But opening the door... Food containers lay scattered along the kitchen floor and an unpleasant sent wafted through the air. *What do I do?* He had no idea how many times he'd asked himself this, but it was his fault. Still... *I wasn't trained for this! What do I do?!*

Zephyr's thoughts spiraled until Jon was there – surveying the scene, confused. *He's here for Ferdinan...what do I do? Say?*

"Good morning, Zephyr...what...what happened?"

"He's not here..." The Prince's mind whirled.

"What happened?"

Warm hands grabbed Zephyr's shoulder and turned him – making his rib unhappy. But the Prince couldn't escape the concern radiating at him. *Should I tell Jon?* It was disgusting and troublesome. *The Dinta's in charge of feeding him. Is Jon not giving him enough?* But last night...it looked like his cousin hadn't eaten in a month.

"Zephyr?"

Words poured from his mouth – every detail. *What am I doing? Why am I saying all this?* When had he decided to? But...the words felt like they were being pulled from him without his consent.

"He's gone. I tried finding him, but couldn't." It was a lie. But no one would believe he couldn't *catch* his cousin – broken rib or not.

The growing giant stood just as stunned as Zephyr felt. Those words were hard to believe. But the messy floor and lingering odor of vomit attested to them. "Have you informed anyone?"

"Just you." Zephyr hugged himself. *I don't know what to do.*

"Are you ok?" Worried chocolate brown eyes looked down at his much smaller ally. "You look shocked."

"It's not the first time." *Why did I say that...?*

"What?"

"At my Ascension Ceremony." *Stop talking!*

A sigh of relief escaped Jon. "Thank you, Zephyr."

But how many times did it happen and no one notice? It took a moment to realize the was Dinta rummaging around the kitchen instead of leaving. "What are you doing?"

"Your trash. I'll be passing by the disposal anyway."

Zephyr pinched his nose and threw his hand down. "It stinks. You don't have to do that."

Sticking a new liner in, Jon grabbed the half-full one. "I've been cleaning this up for almost a year now. It doesn't faze me anymore."

Chapter 30

Once again, Yuyu stood on the twilight beach. The first time there was so much to take in she didn't notice how sad it was. It was beautiful and calm. But it was also lifeless. More than that – it felt like hope died here a long time ago. But that could be her own bias after remembering how magnificent and busy her own world was.

Still...it felt sad here.

Beside Yuyu appeared Muulam and that strange fire. "Hello."

"Hello, young one."

"I was wondering if I'd dream of you again." Yuyu smiled at the old woman.

"Not hoping to dream of my charges?"

Heat pinkened Yuyu's cheeks. "Can't it be both?"

"It can." Withered arms reached out and hugged the girl before stepping back and asking, "Is it both?"

The words Yuyu meant to say stuck in her throat. Seeing the old woman again was nice. This person came from nowhere and freed her. Muulam showed her how to fix her world. Then introduced her to the most magnificent...whatever those charges were. But...it was those charges she wanted to see most. All of them were beyond what she could describe. They were wonderful. And...she wanted to experience that again. More than anything. But that was terribly rude to say. "I wanted to see you. But your charges I wanted to play with more."

"Good."

What?

"If I were to give you one to hold for me. Not to keep. Just to hold for a time. Would you accept it? Care for it? Love it?"

It sounded more like Muulam was asking about a pet than an embodiment... *That's what they are...*

"You've figured it out." Muulam's usual grin grew all the more pleased. "But would you accept it?"

191

Breath and words alike left Yuyu as her realization came together. She didn't know how long they stood there – her mind spinning – but the old woman waited patiently for an answer. "You'd give one to me?"

"For a time."

Why would she give me one? And why only for a little while? Yuyu wasn't sure which of these questions were most important, but both of them nagged at the back of her mind. "For how long?"

"'Til their keeper is found."

"Kepper?"

"That's a story for another time." A closed, gnarled hand stretched forward, but didn't open.

Do her hands hurt? Yuyu looked down at her own. She knew what they looked like, but here they were perfect. No scars. Full dexterity. No pain... "I don't think I could choose between them."

"Then it's a good thing I've already chosen for you." That aged hand opened revealing a shell – but not the one from last time. It was tiny. Browns and golds wrapped around the cream spiral.

That shell...the last time she picked it up... The world was so alive. Much more so than she ever realized. "Why Û-ya'īn?"

"I love all the charges. Having a favorite proves I'm a terrible guardian." Muulam gently stroked the shell. "But Û-ya'īn has been with me since the beginning. There's no one I trust more."

Blood pounded in Yuyu's ears. *Then that's the last one you should give me!* But those words wouldn't leave her tongue. "Then why not another?"

"'Cause there's no one I trust more to test and guide the Jinku."

"Jin...ku?" Even as Yuyu repeated the word, she knew who Muulam was referring too. But she didn't know what it meant or the job it entailed. "But...why?"

"You haven't passed yet." Once again, the old woman stretched out her hand to Yuyu. "Will you hold it for a time?"

"Thank you." Gently, reverently, Yuyu picked up the shell and looked at Muulam's grinning face.

"Water's good for the heart. It's the best present."

Everything faded. But not to black. It was the darkness of closing your eyes in a bright room. So Yuyu opened them.

Sunlight shone in from her window – bathing her in light. Black gloves covered her hands. And...

In her palm was a tiny spiral shell wrapped in browns and golds.

* * *

A screen shattered against the wall. Simply for being the bearer of bad news. At least Ferdinan now had something to think about other than...

Shuddering, the skeleton pushed the memory from his mind. Troubling his Prince like that was unforgivable – inexcusable. Becoming more of a burden...unallowable.

His belly growled and lurched. It's demands for food doubled him over. As punishment for its insolence, Ferdinan punched it a few times then headed out. Pain didn't stop the hunger, but it was a more pleasant sensation.

Fists clenched, jaw tight, Ferdinan made his way up the steps of the administration building. It took immense force to control his breathing. Ringing ears only irritated him more. He needed something to break! To tear apart! Something other than the Superintendent...

This summons was imbecilic... *What does my attendance matter? All my work's done!*

Another growl screamed out when he reached the reception area's door. Fire consumed his chest. He wanted to yell at his belly but clenched his jaw. Releasing the knob, Ferdinan delivered as hard of a blow as he dared. *Shut up! I fed you a bar already!*

Punishment dealt, he opened the door. Surprised eyes met him. Ms. Radery looked somewhere between horrified and concerned. But Ferdinan didn't care. He wanted this over with so he could go back to... *It doesn't matter what I do, does it...?*

"Lord Ferdinan, are you ok?"

Ferdinan turned to find Dæya looking at him as if he'd gone mad. Frozen, he took stock of himself. A rhythmic jarring pounded against his growling stomach. And when Dæya's eyebrows knitted together, red coated the room. The man was a threat. One he wanted to destroy. "You summoned me before breakfast."

Worry and uncertainty filled the man's being. "I wanted to talk to you before class; you still had time to eat."

"No time was mentioned, so I decided to get this over with." Punch. Punch. Punch.

"What food would you like?"

Ferdinan shrugged.

"*Part of you knows*" danced across Dæya's face, but he motioned the skeleton to his office. "Ms. Radery?"

"Right away, sir."

* * *

"Why is this happening again?" Zephyr hid his face in his knees. *This is a dream. It's a nightmare. Wake up! None of this happened. Wake up! It's just my overactive imagination. Wake up! Wake up and laugh for being shaken by a ridiculous dream!*

The creak of the door's hinge announced a visitor.

"Are you all right?" Denila sat beside her huddled friend.

"I'm fine." The Prince's response was muffled – but he didn't want her seeing his red, swollen eyes or unforgivable weakness.

"Theon let me in... You haven't been to class this week. I'm worried. So is everyone else."

"I'm fine." Zephyr's thumb drew a line down from his shoulder twice.

"You don't look fine. And you sound... Is your schedule too much? Do you need a break?" Her warm arm slipped over his shoulders and squeezed him.

"My schedule's fine. I just don't feel well."

"In what way?"

That question...he wanted to scream. "My stomach." *I disgust myself. I've no right being a leader...living freely. I'm vile. A blight...to my family...to everyone.*

194

* * *

The skeletal boy stopped and stared out the window, pounding on his stomach.

"Lord Ferdinan, do you understand why I called you here?" Dæya motioned to the lounging area instead of his desk.

"You were forthright in mentioning my attendance." Ferdinan sat for about two seconds before he was on his feet pacing.

What's going on with him? "Please have a seat."

"I've been sitting too long," Ferdinan snapped.

"I need you to sit an–"

"I don't want to sit!!!"

That scream terrified the Superintendent. Though just a boy, the last time Ferdinan lost control... But this was different.

"I haven't been in class! I don't *actually* need to be there, do I?!"

Dæya had seen Ferdinan so terrified the boy's heart would stop and so completely withdrawn it was like talking to a statue. But this was new. And it wasn't hunger. It looked like Ferdinan would fly apart – like there was nothing left keeping him together. Allowing a few minutes of silence, Dæya calmed his racing heart. *How do I get him to talk to me?* Nothing had worked in over a decade. "I'd like to discuss this with you, but I need you to calm yourself."

Thin lips trembled. Ferdinan twitched – fists shaking. "I'm listening, but I don't want to sit."

"I see you're upset, but I don't understand why," If he didn't address this, they wouldn't get anywhere. "Can we start here?"

Hard breaths became rhythmic. Ferdinan grabbed his upper arm and clenched it tight – boney fingers digging in deep. "I can't do everything."

Those words were nothing more than an exhale...and probably the most honest thing the boy ever said to him. "Please explain."

"That's all you ever want! Explanations!" That skeletal face twisted with pain and rage barely contained. "I can't do everything!

195

You want me to waste time in classes I don't need to be in! You want me to not push myself so I can heal! You want me to reach these goals *you* set...!! You want me to take on projects and be a perfect student! I have other things I'm required to do!! I have demands I'm expected to meet! There are other people who need me to work!! There are things far more important than this useless place!!!"

Helplessly, Dæya watched the boy pace, knocking furniture out of the way. Throwing anything his hands grabbed. Beating his stomach when there was nothing else to hit.

With each word, Ferdinan's voice got louder and more unstable. Those crystal blue eyes clouded over. *What will he do...?* Speaking only made Ferdinan angrier. *Will I be able to stop him if he hurts himself...or me? Should I let him burn out?* Shifting slightly, Dæya readied himself to physically restrain his student if needed.

"I work hard! I've done everything I've been asked! I've been a good student! I've done all I'm capable of!!!" Boney hands clutched overgrown hair, pressing hard against his skull. Muffled screams escaped clenched teeth. "I can't do everything!!!"

Cringing – doubled over – Ferdinan cradled his head. Silence hung heavy while Dæya sat trying to figure out how to respond without upsetting the boy further. "I'm sorry, Ferdinan. I'm sorry."

Covering his face couldn't hold back the sobs. The boy crumpled to the floor. Whatever fueled that tirade was gone.

But Dæya held his breath. He needed to check on the boy, but he didn't want to make things worse. *My apology...is that what he needed? Or...did he need to feel heard?* If only he could scan Ferdinan. To understand what haunted his student. How to help.

"I'm sorry. I should've listened sooner."

Sobs came faster. When Ferdinan spoke, his voice was high and strained. "Please don't report this to the Duchess..."

That whispered plea strangled Dæya's heart. *It always comes back to her...* Questioning parents wasn't his place, but that woman... *I wish I could accept the Queen Mother's claim of him.*

More words squeaked out, "I was wrong. I'll be better."

Chapter 31

Aside from the utter humiliation, Ferdinan felt better. *Will he really not tell the Duchess...? If he does...* The thought made him shudder. But he couldn't do anything about it now.

So, he ran.

It was just him and this abandoned island. Unlike his island, this one had more intense terrain. Running to his heart's content. No prying eyes. No limits. Just the freedom of movement...

He'd failed horribly this week. But he didn't care. Neither did he care that he didn't care.

Right now. In this moment. He was so alive he could live forever. Right now. He could fix everything he'd done wrong. Right now. He was so powerful nothing could hurt him.

Just like the rage in Dæya's office... He slipped into this feeling and let go of all his reservations. Here there was no one to hurt or disappoint. No danger. Nothing. Just a perfect feeling to fold himself up in.

An invincible smile... Everything down to his soul relaxed.

This is nice. No voice. Even that second one was gone. *Have I ever felt this good? This week was bad. But right now... This is all I need. Like this...*

Evelyn... Her name floating through his head made him smile. *Emil's gone! I can see her tonight!*

His feet sped up as if running faster would make night come sooner. The ocean filled his view. This was a great spot. The hill continued up, flattening out nicely for lounging. The grass was soft, perfect for a nap. But Ferdinan kept going. That view was best seen from the edge.

Bright, vibrant colors took on a surreal tint. His foot rounded the sharp edge and he pushed off with all his might. Smiling, he looked down at the jagged rocks below him. They lined the cliff face before meeting up with sand and ocean. Details of those rocks grew sharper – more focused with each heartbeat. *Yes. This is right.*

* * *

Denila trying to cheer him up was well-intentioned, but more painful than helpful. He was relieved when she had to teach. Though that relief quickly turned into brooding. Pieces scattered around his brain – but they didn't line up. "What don't I know?"

Locking his door, Zephyr laid down on the floor – considering. Memories flooded his mind, but they weren't useful. *The elf knows...she keeps pointing me to it.* A bitter laugh escaped his lips. *How much pain do I need to suffer for a straight answer?* Having his skin carved again didn't sound so bad.

Closing his eyes, he waited, but she never came. Neither did her twilight beach appear. *Why isn't this working? ...she said...she said it wasn't a dream.* If his time with her were visions then he should have some control.

Closing his eyes again, he considered how one searched for the heart of a vision. This thought he held tightly as his body relaxed and his mind slipped away.

* * *

"I'm afraid I turned you into more of a monster."

Xhou pulled his gaze from the screen to face Herrard. "Excuse me?"

"You go to class. Keep your sessions with Master Loucé. Eat every dinner with me and lay quietly in bed at night." Herrard didn't let his gaze waver from Xhou. "But you still don't talk to me. You still wear that fake smile. You still lie to yourself."

"You worry too much. I'm fine. I've gained back the weight I lost, caught up on everything I fell behind on. I'm doing everything I always did."

That's the problem. "Yah. *Everything* you always did."

"Herrard. What do I have to do to convince you?"

A long moment passed. Sitting, the Kalj looked at the future Nu squarely. "I want to listen. I want to help with whatever I can."

"Thank you. You've always been a great brother. But there's nothing to worry about." Xhou altered his smile to reflect his gratitude. "I didn't mean to worry you...hurt you. I didn't realize I was 'til you dragged me out of my lab. But I've worked hard and overcome that. I'm ok. Truly. And should I need help again, I'll seek it before hurting someone enough they confront me."

Pain twisted Herrard's face and heart. Many kinds of pain. The pain of failure. Of watching another suffer. Of seeing a bitter ending where there doesn't need to be one. The pain of helplessness. "I know you better than my own siblings. There isn't a memory I have that doesn't include you – my island brother. I love you. I'm worried about you. And I hate how incompetent I am to help you. I hope... Please stop running away from your heart before it's too late."

Two. Three times Xhou tried responding. But sat there at a loss.

"Whether here or after graduation, I'll always listen when you decide to talk." Standing, Herrard squeezed Xhou's shoulder. Then he left the suite. There wasn't anything more he could do. And...the Healer had others to care for...not to mention himself.

* * *

Why did he do that?! Oya couldn't catch him, but she knocked him out of the rocks' path – a little too aggressively. But if she moved any slower, she wouldn't have made it. If not for Û-ya'īn catching him...

Soaring down, she landed as her old friend gently laid Ferdinan on the sand. *He could've died...* "*Why did you do that!?*"

He was unconscious, so there was no answer. But she screamed anyway.

"*Do you know what I'm doing for you?! Do you know...!*" Dropping to her seat, she pounded the ground. But with the adrenaline wearing off... *I shouldn't have taken so long...* The thin rope of connections glowed in the evening dark. She didn't even have a chance to add to their number because she was seeing to Iitano's successor. If one more thing went wrong...

Another scream left her. For the first time Oya was forced to acknowledge that running from fire to fire was as useful as counting the stars.

Grabbing his head, she delved in – dragging him to her twilight beach. There was one form of hers he'd seen. Morphing into it, she approached. *He was having fun running...so why? What possessed him?*

In the distance he sat. A too thin boy bleeding profusely from his gut. *He looked like he was ready to laugh!* Then something burst from his stomach. *You were smiling at the rocks that'd impale you, why? What happened to you?*

Nearly transparent blue crystals opened wide - staring out over a world of purple-gray. Until he saw her. Panic took hold and he scrambled to his feet, but she didn't let him get far. The massive body of an ancient dragon wrapped around him - imprisoning him.

"You remember me?" The dragon's voice was gruff and hard. She wanted to rip his head off for doing such a stupid thing. When Ferdinan froze, she calmed her voice, and shifted to a more useful shape. Long, starlight hair swayed at her knees - framing sapphire eyes.

Ferdinan turned to her, face as lifeless as carved stone. "You aren't a dragon?"

"I'm what I need to be. Right now, a dragon is less useful."

"There are elves in the afterlife?"

"You aren't dead. Though you have a friend who might kill you when you wake up." *I won't let you keep your hidden plans!* But for as angry as she was, it was her choice - the rites. It was her choice and she wouldn't regret it.

"But I was alone..."

The very sight of him was pain. His cloudy soul was turned from white to green. That hole in his chest was larger. Now a new hole was torn from his stomach... *The blood is black...* Now it was the elf's turn to freeze. "That wound will kill you."

Looking himself over, Ferdinan shrugged and shook his head. "I'm not injured."

"You still can't see..."

"See what?"

I can't do this alone. If she could do anything at all. Closing her eyes, she reached out in every direction for his presence. When she found the man, she dragged him here as well. A comet landed in a flash of brilliant light. That light filled the entirety of the dream scape.

"What did you do to me?!"

"Fisherman?" Ferdinan rubbed at his eyes.

"Ferdinan?" The irritation from a moment before disappeared at the sight of the boy.

"He needs healing."

Moving closer, the Fisherman assessed the boy's stomach.

Ferdinan stepped back. "What are you doing?"

"You don't feel anything?" Shocked, the Fisherman studied the boy closer.

"There's nothing to feel."

"This wound is different...I *might* be able to repair it."

"There's nothing wrong with me."

"Ferdinan," the elf stepped between them. "You'll die. Painfully. Belly wounds don't kill you quickly. It's a terrible way to go."

"I understand." Ferdinan turned from them to the sea. "I hit the rocks and was impaled through the stomach."

Don't be stubborn. "It needs to be healed."

"No, thank you."

"Ferdinan, this is serious." The Fisherman stepped closer.

"I don't want to be healed."

"Why not?" the elf argued.

"This works. That island is rarely visited. I'll be washed away by the tide and disappear. I can't cause any more trouble. Jon will finally be free. I'll no longer burden my cousin. And Oya...she can make friends... Finally..." Ferdinan laughed up at the bright moon in the starless sky. "This works. I even enjoyed a month without that voice."

"What voice?"

This was a question the Fisherman wanted to ask, but didn't have the chance. *I didn't notice you?*

Behind them stood a boy – eyes scarred shut, deep slashes gouged from shoulder to hip, and mangled hands discolored from infection. "How did you get here?"

◊

An infinity of intersecting silver roads filled an empty abyss. Narrow roads. *If I step off, will I fall forever?* He didn't want to find out. *Now what do I do?*

The countless roads left Zephyr feeling like a rat in a maze. *Think. Tracking's a basic skill I learned before starting school.* But...how to use it in the world of dreams and visions?

A childish idea hit him. It was along the lines of "Open Sesame" and would probably be just as useful. *Stupid...think of something better!* But nothing came...

Staying here won't help... Rolling his eyes, Zephyr called out, "Guide me to the elf woman!"

Instead of an echo, a powerful presence hit him. A presence just as happy letting him live as killing him, depending on his choices. And the discomforting feeling her grin always filled him with. Disappointment and sorrow followed – the kind she emanated when he didn't understand. Zephyr held onto those sensations and followed.

One road branched into dozens more, but he took the one which felt most like her.

Twilight appeared. Then her beach. Two figures stood silhouetted against the background. Then something fell from the sky, turning dusk to noon day. Closer he edged until he could hear them.

"...Jon will finally be free... And I'll no longer burden my cousin. This works well. I even enjoyed a month without that voice."

"What voice?" Zephyr blurted before he realized he'd spoken. Why did his training vanish when the elf was nearby?

"How did you get here?" Though confused, respect twinkled in the elf's sapphire eyes.

What's going on....? "What are you doing with my cousin?"

"My Prince?"

202

Zephyr stepped closer... *What is this...?*

The Prince stood – eyes glued on Ferdinan. *What happened to him?* The longer he looked the more his insides revolted. Dropping to his knees, the prince retched. *No! I did horrible things to him, but never this!*

A sunken hole consumed the majority of Ferdinan's chest, centered over his heart. Darkened cracks splayed all around his head. Scars Zephyr hadn't seen when Ferdinan removed his shirts covered him. Most gruesome of all was Ferdinan's stomach. It looked like someone had lit a small bomb in it. Thick, blackened blood oozed out and something dark and fuzzy clung to the edges of the wound.

Gaining control of himself, Zephyr turned to the elf. "What is this? I never did this!"

The elf stepped between them. "What do you see?"

"What is that?!" Zephyr's hands shouted more passionately than his tongue.

"His soul." An older man in a fishing hat answered – steadying Zephyr. "You both have festering wounds. I can clean them."

Both? "If you can fix him then do so." Golden hands demanded.

"He refused."

Zephyr pushed past the elf to grab his cousin. "Why? How can you stand being like this?"

Ferdinan didn't flinch. He didn't kneel or show the propriety expected of him. He simply turned to the two adults. "You're manipulating me with a hallucination? My Prince would never act like this. There's no reason for him to concern himself with me. Neither will I change my mind."

"This is your cousin." Gentleness filled her words.

"My Prince would be happy to be rid of me." Ferdinan looked at him with...*pity.* "He wouldn't spout nonsense."

He thinks I'm a dream...? Or is this my own elaborate story? Releasing Ferdinan, Zephyr stepped back. *Does he honestly believe I'd be happy if he died? Or...is this the elf tormenting me?* "I want you to be healed."

"We all want things we'll never get." Ferdinan sighed as if the world was too much, and he no longer cared.

Zephyr's hands flew – punctuating every word. "I command you to accept healing!"

"Only my Prince can command such a thing." Turning away, Ferdinan approached the Fisherman. "Thank you for your offer, but I've wasted enough of your time."

"That wound won't kill you right away. I'll wait should you change your mind."

"Fisherman... Do as you wish. It'll be over soon enough. Everyone can be happy again." Sidestepping, Ferdinan approached the elf and bowed to her. "It's been a pleasure meeting you. Dreaming about something other than the dead... Thank you. If you don't mind, it's been a while since I've played with Lady Evelyn. That was rude of me. I should visit her."

Before the elf could respond, Ferdinan stepped through a door that wasn't there.

"This isn't real." Zephyr asked after a long silence – hands pleading.

Sapphire eyes turned on him. "You'll know how real it is soon enough."

Holding out his hands between him and the man Ferdinan called "Fisherman," he asked another question, "Why does he look like that?"

The man sighed and adjusted the floppy hat. "This dream wasn't made for you."

What?

"That matters?" The elf looked over Zephyr.

"Yes."

"Zephyr." She stepped back – cautious. "What do I look like?"

"A beautiful elf. Like always."

Chapter 32

All Jon's attempts at getting more information failed. *Why is he suddenly hungry all the time?* Even as Jon left, the gent's stomach continued growling. *He focuses on medical technology and medicine...did he...?*

No. The gent would never do something like *that... I need to clear my head.*

Sunshine enveloped Jon when he stepped outside. Its warmth accompanied him on his walk to the main island. Save for about a month each year – sun could always be counted on here. Though the rainy season was the best time for sleeping.

This was paradise... If only it was closer to home. Given the choice, Jon would leave this for home any day. Being smooshed by his seven older brothers... The aroma of dad's cooking... Mom laughing along at their fun...

His heart yearned for home so bitterly it twisted his stomach. Now wasn't the time for homesickness, so he forced those thoughts away.

Cresting the hill, Jon saw one of his island brothers below. Ilu looked exhausted. Red hair flared into existence, making his suitemate scream. Jon both smiled and sighed. *I told him to focus on Marcus. Is this what being a parent feels like...?*

Picking up his pace, he stopped behind Oya. While she teased Ilu, he reached around and covered her eyes.

"Oooo! Don't tell me! Based on how big your hands are you must be pretty tall..." Oya babbled excitedly and leaned against his stomach. "You're not all that broad though, and your hands are too meaty to be Ferdinan..."

Pity and gratitude mixed with apology on Ilu's face.

A nod invited the Healer to escape. "It's not that hard, Oya."

"You took all the fun out of it!" Grabbing his hands, she turned and looked up – berating him with an animated pout.

"Sorry. I haven't forgotten you. Would you play with me?"

Those green eyes glowed. "Yay! But only a short while."

Times like this she seemed like a much younger child. *Is this an act? Or is it truly how she is?* "I'll gladly take that much."

A maniacal chuckle burst out of her. "What game today?"

Those words *sounded* playful...but Jon wasn't sure how to interpret them. "First... There's something strange with Ferdinan."

"He sprouting a tail or something?"

Moving down the hill put them closer to eye level, but unless he knelt... *I don't like this... I want to stay small.* But he couldn't change that. So he told her about the skeleton's recent meals.

Her impishness faded. "He's eating like a boy his age?"

"No, he's eating like a half-starved beast."

"Well, he's been more than half-starved for how long?"

"Why would that matter now?" Jon clasped his hands. "Do you know why? I've never seen him like this and I don't know how to help. Bringing more food more often isn't working."

"We're playing often and for longer – maybe that's why?"

"May I ask what you two play?"

Oya laughed. "You may always ask."

Jon sighed. *Even simple politeness...* "What're you doing that's leaving him so ravenous?"

"We play tag and roam all around. He's showing me the smaller islands."

You must be doing more than that. Is his body simply realizing a lifetime of hunger? "How often do you play?"

"Whenever he doesn't have class...or needs a work break."

"What? That's all?"

Oya walked on tip toes a few steps then spun. "Yes."

She's tired of questions. Patting her head, Jon lifted her to his shoulders. "How's the view up there?"

"Wow!!! Is this what it's like for Ozar and Samuel!!?"

"Possibly," Jon grinned. "Wait 'til you meet Jingjing; he makes those two look short."

"I have to meet your giants!!"

He expected Oya to run him ragged, but not a half hour passed before she disappeared.

* * *

It works... No voice. No Emil. He was free. Evelyn was safe.

But... Ferdinan didn't realize the bar was gone until the empty wrapper brushed his lips. *Disgusting...I already ate it?* Pushing that thought aside, his mind returned to the larger issue. Being free of that voice was wonderful...but the cost...

Screaming at the Superintendent...jumping off the cliff... He didn't want to die in that moment...but...he didn't try stopping himself... Everything was too intense. And he didn't realize... Not until scattered materials and torn fabric littered his closet after that strange dream. Neither had he slept since.

He had too much energy to sleep. Not moving was painful. Impossible. And because he couldn't stop moving – couldn't stop eating – he was getting bigger. Nothing fit. Nothing felt right.

Neither was the mirror kind in confirming this. ...a muscle wrapped skeleton. *How did this happen? How much weight have I gained?* Ferdinan felt sick – being this out of control...

Will a lower dose still be effective? Or did he convert the numbers wrong? And he based the dose on his height and not his weight. *Am I taking too much?* Lowering the dose could fix the problems. Or... It could allow the voice to come back.

But it didn't matter. Jon would be pestering him soon – making him weigh in. The skeleton avoided it long past the extension he asked for. Turning back to the mirror, Ferdinan took in his gaunt face. It made him seem skinnier. But the Duchess would know. She'd never be fooled so easily.

"Stay in control. Exercise self-restraint. I have to... I hope I can..."

With the first shirt on and buttoned, Ferdinan reached for the second, only to find his arms and shoulders restrained. His shirts shrunk as his muscles grew. Panic and bile rose in his throat. And heat. Red. *Stupid shirt! Move!!*

"Ferdinan?"

Jon's call stopped him from thrusting his arms forward and forcing the shirt to release him. Eyes closed. Deep breath. He stepped out of his closet feeling fully naked with only one shirt.

"Ready?" Jon forced a smile, but neither boy was looking forward to this.

"Yeah." Swallowing back strangling bitterness, Ferdinan stepped up on the scale after Jon turned it on. *I don't want to know. I don't want to know. I don't want to know.* The Duchess's ire beat down – flooding him with daggers and ice.

"...no way."

"What?" Jon's disbelief dragged Ferdinan's eyes to the readout. *Twelve pounds...* The ice burned. *If I get called home...*

"That's not possible." Scrutinous eyes examined his ally's face. "Turn out your pockets."

"Excuse me?" Ferdinan wanted nothing more than to tear Jon apart for this humiliation.

"There's no way. You've obviously lost weight! Did you rig it?"

"Why would I do that?!"

Not appreciating being yelled at, Jon pulled Ferdinan off and stepped up himself. A frown marred his face. "Turn out your pockets. I know that wasn't right."

Fire flushed sunken cheeks. Shaking hands seized stick arms to keep from beating the one accusing him of lying – cheating.

"I can't report obviously wrong numbers to the Superintendent."

Jon let out a gasp. One boney hand clutched at his tailored shirt; the other was raised to pulverize his face. Every muscle in the skeleton's body shook – trying desperately to stop. Thin lips wavered between bearing white teeth and trembling.

I'm scaring him... Good! No! Stop! Teeth clenched, Ferdinan forced his fingers to loosen. "If you don't believe me... Fine."

Tearing his hand away, Ferdinan redirected his rage at the restrictive clothing. Unceremoniously he stripped and stepped back on the scale.

Both boys looked. And both were surprised to see a weight only a few ounces less.

Jon fumbled over an apology while Ferdinan grabbed his arms to keep from attacking the cruel, unforgiving machine.

Calm down. Being this upset is unreasonable. "Do you believe it now, or do we need to find another one?"

Frozen, Jon studied the grotesque skeleton. What little body fat Ferdinan once had was completely gone. But his muscle mass had exploded. Particularly in his legs, shoulders, chest, and arms. The sight was unreal. "What've you been doing?"

Running, swimming, and playing with Oya – which usually led to more running and swimming and a whole lot of fighting. This was his life. Grabbing his tattered clothing, Ferdinan dressed for the second time – his ally gawking, judging. *What right does he have critiquing me?!* "Are we done?"

"You need new clothes." Jon's statement surprised them both.

"...maybe during break."

"That shirt... Can you even bring your arms up in front of you?"

Hoping to prove his ally wrong only proved Jon right. "There's only two weeks 'til break. Are we done now?"

"No." Jon pointed to where he'd marked their heights.

And he did so again. Inch for inch they were the same. And both had grown. Seeing this frustrated his ally, but Ferdinan didn't care. *Go away.*

* * *

The gruesome vision of Ferdinan on the twilight beach haunted him. Zephyr laid back on his bed. All of this was cruel. And all of it was his fault. But...being shown over and over how much of a monster he was...what he'd done to his cousin's soul. It ravished his heart and tore at his insides. *Why?* The tightness in his chest was unbearable again – but nothing eased it. *What do I do? Why me? If it'd been someone else...anyone else...*

He curled into a ball. And again asked himself, "What do I do?"

The only response he got was a *beep*. He didn't want to talk to anyone. But others were already worried about him. And the message was a call from his aunt. No need making things worse. Smoothing his hair and straightening his clothes, he answered.

Aunt Tenalia beamed at him. The usual pleasantries gave way to heavier topics. "That's wonderful! How's your cousin?"

"The last time I saw him...he was eating more than me."

"Good!" Tenalia's smile filled with relief. "And his abuser?"

Zephyr's chest somehow tightened more as his hands danced. "I've found them."

"Who?"

"It's taken care of." Zephyr looked away.

"That's not what I asked."

"I know. But...I promise, it's taken care of. The abuse has stopped. Permanently."

"I'm sorry, but I need a name. You were told to find the person. I'll do what needs to be done to fix things from there."

"I know." *Even if I told her, she wouldn't believe me. Why didn't she see?* "If they hurt him again, I'll tell you their name."

* * *

"What's wrong?"

Looking up, Jon smiled at the sincerest person he knew on these islands. "It's that obvious?"

"I felt your concern and doubt from the main classrooms." Sitting down next to his suitemate, Gongie continued, "I know you want to talk. I'm happy to listen."

Heaving a deep sigh, Jon squeezed his island brother tight. "I can't tell you how much I love you, Gongie. Thank you."

Soaking in Jon's relief, the Psych gave a chuckle. "I haven't done anything yet."

"But you're willing despite knowing who it's about."

"It doesn't matter the subject; I can always listen."

"Every time I think I understand him the rules change." Jon was about to say more than he should. But he trusted Gongie as much as his family. And the Psych might be able to offer insight or something. "After constant exhaustion, he...got really sick. When I confronted him, he agreed it needed to stop. It was amazing hearing this... And I wasn't expecting a miracle...but even that happened. He became cooperative and happy. Joking for fun... Smiling a *real* smile! He had energy and an appetite. I was thrilled! Finally, he was getting better!"

Gongie frowned sympathetically. "But he wasn't."

"I really think he was... 'Til he went too far the other way. Seeing Ferdinan go from an emotionless statue to a normal person was amazing. But now he overreacts to everything. Like the intensity of his emotions are beyond his control. He can't sit or stand still. No matter how much food I bring, he's still hungry. And I have to take it away from him when I think he's reached his limit or he'll eat 'til he throws up. And it's happened with Zephyr too." Jon stopped to take a deep breath. "His emotions don't make sense. This morning Ferdinan was beaming when Oya arrived. I could almost hear the world sing around him. Laying out the food – he was on the verge of tears. Before I could ask what was wrong, he was attacking the plate like a ravenous beast."

Silently Gongie sat – giving Jon time to ask his question.

"This isn't normal, is it? I don't know what to do. It seems he doesn't know either."

"That doesn't sound normal."

This simple, straightforward answer was what Jon needed. Yes. Something was wrong – it wasn't just him. If only the gent could tell him what was going on inside Ferdinan's head.

"As a Telepath, I can't help hearing and feeling things from those around me. But I can't pry on purpose – especially with Ferdinan." Gongie stopped Jon's wishful thought there. "All the Psychs are reminded regularly to avoid him. I'm sorry, but that's all the help I can offer."

Disappointment and despair deflated Jon. "I know. But I guess I was hoping anyway... Mostly, I needed to say all that...I know you'll keep this between us... I'm sorry for burdening you..."

Gongie smiled and hugged the growing giant. "Watching you suffer alone is a worse burden."

* * *

It was impressive. Not only did Zephyr figure out how to traverse dreams on his own, but he invaded hers with little difficulty. Both of these were unexpected. But him seeing Ferdinan the way she did – that was impressive.

Luckily, Zephyr's eyes were only partly opened. *Neither of us are ready for him to see fully.* If he'd seen her...or himself...

Crazed green eyes turned to her friend. She couldn't beat him in a footrace anymore... But they still ran. She still tried. The only reason they were neck in neck was because he was keeping pace with her.

This was troubling, but not as much as her thoughts. *Traversing dreams and seeing the soul...*

Is he compatible with both? Or is my control of the dreamlands waning?

Oya leaned forward – willing her feet to move faster. *Have I ever felt this tired?*

Her entourage of orbs pressed in on her, offering what energy they could. *Thank you. This needs to be done.* Turning her most obnoxious grin to her dear friend, Oya slapped his arm and bolted for the boy's dormitory. Next, she grabbed ahold of Zephyr's mind and dragged him to the window. *How do I get them to tame each other?*

"Why did you stop?" Ferdinan panted – offering a hand to her.

"Haha!" Slapping it, she stepped forward. Every ounce of her power went into that punch. *What'll you do when you see his abilities, Zephyr?*

Oya bolted – drawing both her friend and her project after her. *It's good to have had a friend, even if...*

◊

What's he doing? Zephyr dashed down the three flights of stairs and out into the pitch-black night. A half-moon and a million stars gave just enough light to make out the terrain and the direction they

212

went, but a mad dash wasn't enough to catch up. That was fine. He was good at tracking. *How far away did they get?* Catching them consumed his mind. Why it was important...he didn't know. But it was.

Prints in soft soil. Damaged brush. He followed. Disturbing laughter rang out from the clearing ahead. Rewarding his efforts and bringing mixed feelings.

The girl with short hair and Ferdinan... "*You'll know how real it is soon enough.*" The elf's words surfaced. *Why does he still look like that? I'm dreaming...I have to be...*

But he couldn't look away. The two traded running for a fight. And it was grand to see. Fast and agile. Just like the fights he'd watched his mother, aunt, and Rutoric battle out. Zephyr's heart quickened, trying to match their speed. *I don't know her. She's not a Fighter...but she should be...* And Ferdinan... Ferdinan was *better* than her.

One round after another ended with the girl knocked down. Wild laughter stopped the match. Words he didn't know left her, then she ran off. But his cousin stood looking content to wait. For a moment. The skeleton fidgeted then roamed from plant to plant – studying them.

I should leave. But when his feet moved, they approached instead of slipping away.

"Oya?" Ferdinan turned.

Just her name...? "You two must be close for you to drop her title."

Shame and disgrace reddened Ferdinan's cheeks and moistened his eyes. The skeleton dropped to one knee – head down. "I'm sorry, my Prince."

"For finally making a friend?" Zephyr couldn't look away from the battered child. Knowing what he'd done to his cousin's body...and soul... *I did that to him.* Every beating he gave, every relationship he sabotaged, every burden he laid on his cousin...they were all there... The vice on his chest turned again. He'd scream...but it'd drive his cousin into a panic. It took a moment for his throat to loosen. "Why are you two out so long past curfew?"

Ferdinan stiffened and trembled in silence.

Zephyr's desire to know grew stronger. All his life he'd trained to become General...yet none of those lessons aided him now. He was helpless. And weak. And when his tongue moved it said too much. "I saw you... A couple times running and just now fighting."

The skeleton's pale skin turned translucent. His trembling intensified.

"You're a Dual." He hated saying it. Hated admitting its truth. But Zephyr saw Ferdinan move in ways a Scientist never could. And he'd seen firsthand for years how competent a Tinkerer his cousin was.

Nearly non-existent lips moved and blue crystals darted around. "No. I'm not."

"How does no one know?" A Dual...after only how many years? A bittersweet thought occurred to him. *He truly can be General. The position can go to someone better than me.*

"No!"

What's he objecting to? Zephyr's hands spoke as he did. "Ferdinan, I *saw* you. Normal people can't move like that. Even untrained, that fighting was as good as actual Fighters. And your speed! It's a Fighter's! You're a Dual."

"No!! Don't think that!" Ferdinan screamed. Those crystals darted around again, looking for an escape. Then Ferdinan bolted.

The speed his cousin left at... Athletes might be faster runners than Fighters, but Ferdinan's legs were significantly longer. No wonder he kept falling behind. Even if Zephyr could catch up...did he want to? Standing there in the starlit night, the Prince considered everything. *Why does he hide this? Why does my knowing scare him? What does this mean? He couldn't have hidden this on his own...not as a child... So...who wants this kept secret?*

An answer came to him, but he didn't like it.

Chapter 33

An amused smile filled his face. "You really love entering through windows, don't you?"

"*No fair!*" Oya stretched and wild green eyes fell on the little bar in his hand. She didn't ask permission, just looked over his shelves and grabbed one from his stash. "*Ugh... This is disgusting...*"

"*Those aren't made for a general palate. They suit my tastes.*"

Oya gave him a strange look and finished the bar, face scrunched up at it's bitterness. "*I'm bored, come play with me.*"

"One moment." *Done...* Ferdinan deleted the list. His funds, creations, and research would automatically send to those he chose once he was officially listed as "deceased." He couldn't keep himself in control and he refused to live with Emil again.

Oya played with her steel chain. "*You're taking too long!*"

"*Race to my island?! See if you can beat me this time!*" There's nothing Oya needs from me, so one more play day. One more day of fun... "*We can build a fire and I'll play every song I know for you.*"

A playful smirk split her face. "*Catch me if you can!*"

They leapt out the window – securing goggles and masks.

Bright oranges and reds filled the horizon as they flew spirals around each other – laughing and playing. Farther and farther out across the empty ocean and back again. They spun and weaved around every island! Colors faded – giving way to a sea of stars.

The moment Oya's bare feet touch the sand, she was off. He caught up to her easily. Then passed. An adrenaline filled cry left her and she leaned forward, but she couldn't catch him.

Is she slower or am I faster? Turning, he attacked. *What does this chemical do?* Even awkwardly tight clothing didn't give her an advantage. He bested her easily. Fighting. Running. He won...

But he wanted to keep fighting. Keep running. Keep feeling that impossible void whenever she touched him. He wanted to... But he wore out her until she couldn't breathe. *Time for the fire then...*

Beautiful, exotic green eyes watched him carry logs and brush. They brightened with the fire. And glistened when he struck the first note on his violin – her gift to him. She clapped and laughed. And when she recovered from their battle, she danced.

How did she do this? Being around people was uncomfortable. But not her. He never looked forward to seeing anyone before her. Never waited. Hoped. Wanted...

His heart ached and melancholy filled the notes. That wasn't true. There was one before her. One he failed. Destroyed... Pushing those memories aside, he pulled all the joy and energy that was Oya into the song. He wouldn't ruin anymore of this night for her. Song after song. She grinned. And cheered. And jumped with delight.

She's beautiful...

* * *

"Getting farms up and running will be harder than we expected." An older man with snow white hair gave his concluding topic. "There aren't enough people able to do the kind of work necessary."

"Did any of our farmers survive?" It took weeks of pestering, but Xhou's mom finally let him help Mr. Litigi with this. When it came to development of social initiatives, the man was invaluable. No one matched Mr. Litigi's insight.

"No, sir. There wasn't a farmer left to bring in the last harvest."

"How about people from other countries? Help relocating, training, and land could be provided to anyone willing to come."

"It's not a bad idea. I doubt there'd be enough to get our country self-sufficient. But a start. I'll pass along the suggestion to the Nuwa."

"I'll keep considering other options." Xhou's mind turned to rumors that – if true – could provide stability for two countries and form an alliance that'd never been achieved before. "Mr. Litigi."

"Yes, sir?"

"The famine in North Chūzo... Have we confirmed that?"

"Unofficially."

Unofficially? How bad are things if they're isolating? North Chūzo was ruled by a strange, twisted pride which clashed with many nations. But their people always came first. "Duchess Samultz is head of the primary branch family... If we reach out to her, request farmers in exchange for a percentage of food... Fewer mouths and more food while appearing generous should be an appealing offer to her."

"The Duchess isn't an easy woman to deal with. But considering her priorities..." The older man fell silent – thinking. "It's a good idea. I'll draw up an offer and discuss it with the Nuwa."

"Let me know if there's anything I can do."

"Thank you, sir. Enjoy your studies." Mr. Litigi bowed and closed out the screen.

With that done for now, it was time for his other project.

There were so many files from that children's hospital to sift through. Most of which should never get out. Saving the pilfered data to an external storage unit, Xhou went to work. *As payment for all he did for my country, I'll make sure he maintains his anonymity.*

When it came to security protocols and hacking, Xhou's mom was the best. But viruses... Not one of Xhou's had been discovered. None of them were bad. And developing them wasn't something he'd ever teach. But the security they provided was invaluable. Especially considering the rough decades ahead for his country.

"Do what you do best." Tapping the screen, Xhou unleashed a targeted program that'd self-destruct once everything concerning Ferdinan's time there was destroyed. Then he sat back and watched.

If something went wrong, he could stop it. There was important information stored in hospital systems. Destroying the wrong files could hurt or kill innocent people... Blue-black eyes turned to the external storage with his copy of the data. Should he get rid of this too? But it was truly isolated...unlike the hospital's.

As long as the information existed anywhere, it could hurt his charge. But he couldn't... It'd be like denying Ferdinan's suffering.

As Xhou mused, something occurred to him. The thought of Ferdinan didn't make him angry. There was no blame or burning in his chest. But...after seeing all that... He wouldn't deny the truths he knew. The Tinkerer wouldn't...couldn't leave someone behind. Ferdinan would die trying to reach them.

I expected him to do – to give – more? I really am selfish.

217

* * *

What's a 'Dual?' Oya flicked at the water. *Is this another issue I need to address?* "That wound on his belly...I watched it burst from the inside out. What happened?"

"There's nowhere for an infection to drain." The Fisherman sighed. "It grew 'til it broke through the confines of his soul."

What do I do about that? "Is that why he ran off that cliff smiling? He didn't even think about it."

"Repressing things you can't handle..." The Fisherman turned a stern eye. "Do you understand my warning about Zephyr now?"

My dear lamplighter, how long 'til you can no longer keep up with your turning world? I warned Zephyr, yet didn't see it myself... "But Zephyr's infection hasn't done nearly as much damage."

"Hasn't it?" The Fisherman frowned. "You've seen his hands."

Twisted, tortured hands darkened from infection – wasting to nothing... "I understand Ferdinan's wounds; his heart, mind, belly. I understand Zephyr's eyes and stomach. But why his hands?"

"How important are hands to someone like Zephyr?"

"I see." Standing, Oya opened the way to the silver roads. Iitano's successor was safe for now. As was her dear friend. Yuyu was good for a while. Now to check on Zephyr then return to collecting connections. *I won't let another sanctuary fall.* "Fisherman..."

"Yes?"

Turning, Oya looked the man in the eyes. "Considering how I...look...what'll happened to the Mwã-tonô when I'm finished?"

"The same that always happens to the Mwã-tonôs and Tonô."

Slowly, Oya nodded. Sorrow dimmed inhuman green eyes. "Make sure it's a blissfully happy life. Tonō's earned it."

* * *

When Ferdinan's stomach grumbled again, Jon offered him more. Eating in his suite was odd – but no one would look for him here. And... Like Oya, Jon didn't need anything from him. But he troubled his ally nearly as much as his cousin. So he'd give Jon this. An easy meal without complaint or resistance or inconvenience.

Edging a toe against the bag by his chair, Ferdinan felt resistance from the container inside it. It was one of many things he put on the list for Grandpa Huey to send. No one else knew he had it.

Smiling, he thanked Jon. *Leave now so I can cancel my session with Elbie.* Everything was done. Or...it would be once his ally left.

The room blurred and Ferdinan's face contorted. *Why...?* Dropping the fork, he left the kitchen and hid in his bedroom. Feeling too happy or excited was fine, but this...

"Ferdinan? Are you ok?"

I loathe that question! Stop asking me! "I'm fine..." Ferdinan's voice came out high and his body convulsed as he fought back sobs.

"Why're you crying?"

What have I done? Ferdinan brushed away tears and turned to the window. Cold numbed him. *I've killed so many...* Even now. Even now he was still hurting people. He'd wait for break, but how many more would he hurt? What if he changed his mind...?

And swimming until he drowned...he wouldn't suffer nearly enough to pay for his sins. He knew how grievous they were. And his death needed to match the pain he caused. *Jon was right. This has to stop. I should've stopped it then. I was foolish thinking...*

Turning, he bowed deeply, "I'm sorry for troubling you."

* * *

"You're back?" Golden hands scolded her. "You disappear after letting me see...*that*, then don't return 'til I know it's real?!"

"Did you learn something important?"

Zephyr turned his anger and bitterness toward the full moon.

"What's a Dual?"

The thin string holding back the flood snapped. Everything bubbled up. Hate. Anger. Frustration. Weakness – like acid fizzing and expanding, burning him from his soul up.

The elf sat beside him. "Speak."

"I've been handed everything... Been gifted in so many ways! And I don't deserve any of it! I haven't earned anything!!" Drawing

219

his legs to his chest, Zephyr buried his head in his knees. "What kind of person can do that? What kind of person? Then lock it away like it didn't exist! And blame him for all of it...! A General serves and protects! But all I did was tear him down. Every day!"

"So you'll sit and cry? Don't Generals' power come from action? Don't they protect by doing? No matter how difficult? Or beyond them?" The elf raised a hand and waved it. Two dressing mirrors appeared side by side. "This isn't a volcano you can rake out."

What does that mean? Why does she keep saying strange things? But that wasn't important. His hands accentuated the frustration filling him. "How do I fix this?"

"Fix yourself."

A gentle expression greeted him when he looked up. "How...?"

"Face those two mirrors."

"It'll fix me?"

"It'll give you the truth you've been avoiding."

"I can't... Every time I-" A nail pierced his tongue and hands.

"Pain warns you something's wrong. What's it telling you? The pain that's always been with you?"

Tears blurred the twilight beach. *No...I don't want to know how much worse I am... How ugly of a monster I truly am...*

"What kind of man will you become?"

"Please don't make me..."

Sand shifted as the elf stood. "Giving you a chance was foolish."

The farther away she moved, the faster his heart raced. Abandoned. Again. *No! Please!* "Don't leave me!"

"Why should I stay?" Her question sounded like a challenge.

"Y-you...you said you'd help me..." Zephyr shifted to his knees and leaned forward, bowing to her. "I don't want to be that monster."

"Then don't."

Trembling. Heart pounding. The Prince searched for any resolve left in him. *I don't want to see anymore...* Pushing himself to his feet... *I don't want to know how terrible I am.* One unsteady, halted step at a time, he approached the mirrors. *I don't want to see who I am...* Onyx eyes closed and refused to open.

His own voice called out from in front of him – mocking him. "What are you waiting for? What are you scared of?"

"You." A golden fist bobbed then pointed toward the voice.

"But you created me... Or maybe I created you..."

What a terrifying thought. *Do it!* Zephyr forced his eyes open. In each mirror was a different figure. One was the veiled, chained figure who gave him the key for the locked door. The other was one with a mask over his face. *What...?* "Who are you?"

"I'm the one who is seen." The masked reflection answered.

And the chained reflection added, "I'm the one who is hidden."

"Then who am I?"

They brought their hands together before pointing at him.

"Becoming what?"

"Becoming us." Again, they brought their hands together, only they pointed at each other.

"I refuse. I hate you!" Zephyr growled. Every fiber of his being hated them. The two in front of him. And the one in front of them. "Stop bothering me!"

The reflections laughed. "We can't. We *are* you. You are us."

Ice crawled down Zephyr's spine. "I refuse to be you. I'll destroy us all first."

The two laughed, "How?"

Teeth bare, Zephyr unleashed his fury – shattering both mirrors. Countless shards pierced the sand at his feet. Sapphire eyes watched – but not greedily. Or amused. They just watched.

Now what...? His heart slowed. *That was too easy...* There wasn't time between that realization and the grating laughter to react. Hands grabbed him from either side – dragging him back.

"Thank you." The chained one chuckled.

"Why hate us for your actions?" The masked reflection tightened his grip – sending shooting pains up to Zephyr's neck.

Ice settled in Zephyr's gut. "My actions...I have no right–"

"Then why hate us?" The masked one interrupted.

"All three of us." The veiled figure clarified.

"Consider carefully." The elf woman approached – face giving away nothing. "Your answer determines your future."

Looking from one self to the other, Zephyr searched. Seconds ticked by. But no answer came. The reflections leaned in – pressing down on him. Two sets of onyx eyes got closer. *Ferdinan's eyes.*

Memories of when he was the maddest flashed around him. Completely out of control. Dizzy. Disoriented. Zephyr fought to escape. Escape the memories. The reflections. Himself.

"Why do you hate us?" The reflections crowded in.

They have his eyes... Which means...I do too...

They grabbed him and repeated their demand.

Please don't make me say it... He knew. Had known for some time. But saying it... "I'm...I'm a failure..."

Those nearly inaudible words screamed across the twilight beach. They weren't loud. But...saying them. Giving them existence... That act made them powerful beyond his control.

Zephyr turned to the veiled, chained reflection. "You were created 'cause I'm a failure."

Turning to the other, he added, "you were created to hide him from me. That's why I hate all of us."

The chained one smiled and both released him before fading out of existence. A delicate hand mussed Zephyr's thick black hair.

"I'm responsible for my cousin...I made him what he is."

The elf nodded. "Why do you hate him?"

I feel sick... "'Cause he believes he failed me..."

"What're you going to do about it?"

222

Chapter 34

Nothingness filled him. A nothing so complete there wasn't room for despair. There was only one option to stop the destruction, the deaths, and the lies he'd set in motion and let grow out of control.

Classes just started. There was plenty of time. And this was the only option. Even if he hadn't earned it.

His heart hurt. It stung. It burned. Ready to disintegrate. It wasn't enough, but it was what he could offer. *I'll suffer 'til the end.*

Taking a glass from the cupboard, Ferdinan poured in a little water then carried it to his room. Grabbing a small container from his bag, he sat at his desk. Measuring out the powder...

This wouldn't just kill him. It'd dissolve him...with the right concentration... He needed to suffer, but no one could find him before there was nothing left. *I deserve this. It's the only way to pay for any of my sins...no matter how little.*

The spoon didn't fare well when he mixed it. Watered down milk. That's all this was. A sharp burning stabbed at his chest forcing tears to his eyes. *Finally...* The cup moved closer to trembling lips.

It's finally over.

I'm finally free.

"I'll never pay for my sins, but at least I won't commit any more." He just had to hide the corrosive powder, lock his door, and step into the tub. That's all. The drink would do the rest.

"You aren't doing that."

◊

Exhausted, Zephyr hobbled out of his room. *Ferdinan's here...? Why?* His cousin rarely spent time in the suite.

The elf's question drifted through his mind. *What will I do...?*

Swallowing, Zephyr considered it. He needed to fix this. But how? *Leaders take action.* He approached as Ferdinan opened a container and mixed some white powder into a glass. And... Infected blood streaked down his cousin's head. That hole ate through the skeleton's chest. Stepping back, Zephyr observed silently. *This is wrong...or...am I? Do I need to stop this? What is he doing...?*

With baited breath, he watched Ferdinan remove the spoon... What was once a spoon. *What...?* He needed to move. Needed to do something. But...he didn't know what. None of this made sense. Why would a Scientist take something like that out of the labs?

A stick-thin arm waved the glass around – constrained by too small clothing. His cousin lifted the glass to thin lips.

"I'll never pay for my sins, but at least I won't commit any more." A boney hand reached to close the bedroom door.

I'm not seeing this. This isn't happening. This can't be happening... "You aren't doing that."

Jolting back, Ferdinan nearly dropped the glass.

"Why!?" Shocked disbelief chilled him – driving him forward.

Transparent blue crystals tripled in size. The glass hit the desk – tottering on its edge before deciding it wouldn't spill after all.

Those selfish, lifeless eyes bore into him. Zephyr felt his breathing become quick and irregular. He recognized the failure in them...but there was something else. *Why would you do this?! I feel like that to, but I'd never!!* "How selfish are you?! Think about someone beyond yourself! I thought there was hope for you...! But no! No!! You're worse than ever!"

Red tinged the room. The Prince felt his veins would burst! Lurching forward, Zephyr grabbed the skeleton. Pulling Ferdinan away from the desk, he threw the Tinkerer to the ground. Leaping on top, he rammed a fist into his younger cousin's face. Again. And again. *I'll soften your hard head! I'll make you stop this! How dare you! How DARE you do this! How dare you hurt our family!*

Hurt me...

A sob escaped him. *Stop this! It's always...* Zephyr blinked. *It's always been this way...* And he failed every time to change it...

Pulling his cousin up, he drove the Tinkerer into the wall. His cousin didn't resist...just allowed him to smash that too thin neck into the wood stud. *His pulse...it's too fast.* Claws tore through his heart. His very soul. There Ferdinan was in his grip... Yet it felt like his cousin was being swallowed by an abyss. One Zephyr was powerless to overcome. *Why?* Grabbing the Tinkerer's too-small shirt, Zephyr pulled his cousin so their faces were inches apart. Their eyes met.

All the fire turned to ice.

Those eyes...

They're begging me...

They want me to kill him!

He wants me to kill him...?

The tension left Zephyr's body. Horror and shock filled his cousin's face - pleading the Prince not to stop, not to give up. Saying it's the only way. *I'm not seeing what I say I am. It's not selfishness...*

I can't fix this...

"No more..." Voice high, Zephyr released his cousin. *How can you want that?!* His hands moved roughly - nearly as uncertain as the rest of him. "I don't care anymore! Do this selfish thing. Be your usual selfish self. No one ever wanted you anyway!"

Zephyr rammed a hand through the wall as he left. He didn't stop when choked and battered words screamed out behind him.

"Why?" Ferdinan's voice was high and strained and alien. "If no one wants me, then why does it matter?! WHY!!!?"

~

Golden fingers clawed at his hair. Zephyr screamed. *What happened? He can't possibly...!*

Painful thoughts surged through him. There wasn't an object in his room safe from his wrath. He kicked over the nightstand - shattering the lamp sitting on top. A hole exploded through his armoire. The desk was ripped from its spot to fall forward. Taking a glass, plate, and screen with it and adding more shards to the floor. Throwing knives embedded in walls. The mattress was torn and tossed aside. Everything. None of it survived.

The final act of his dying tantrum was hurtling his pillow against the bathroom door.

Panting. Goo filled him to bursting - as if someone were pumping it in.

What is this?

Whatever it was, he was useless to stop it. The Prince was entirely out of his element. He sat on his bedframe - the only thing that survived - and cradled his head. *What am I supposed to do? I can't tell anyone about this... What am I supposed to do?!*

◇

He stopped himself...good. If only he chose better words... But Oya couldn't fully fault Zephyr. Those words reflected how deeply he felt. They provided an opportunity for a new lesson as well...after he stopped tearing apart his room.

While Zephyr calmed down, she tended to her friend. Ferdinan laid motionless on the floor - curled into a ball.

How did I let this go so far? Black swirled among the green discoloring his soul. His heart wept again, and the belly wound was rotting. Uncertain about what came next, Oya sat beside Ferdinan and muffled his will to do anything. Neither did she move until Zephyr's door opened two hours later.

From behind, she tapped his shoulder, making him jump.

"Who?!" Golden hands danced - two fingers swaying side to side. "You're the girl I saw him running with."

"Indeed," she smacked him upside the head.

"What was that for?" Startled, Zephyr stepped into a defensive stance, but stopped when he realized she wasn't going to attack again.

"Telling a person who wants to die to kill himself is murder."

"Excuse me?"

"I watched the whole thing."

Surprised onyx eyes looked up before dropping to the floor. He drew a line across his chest. "You're right. I'm sorry."

"There're so many invisible seeds."

"What?"

"Good and bad. The bad ones are infesting you." She latched onto his need to confide. To speak. To be heard. "But there's a good seed trying desperately not to be choked out. It's the same for him."

"You're his friend?"

"Yes. He's my dear friend."

"I'm sorry. But he's always wanted to die. I hate him 'cause he wants to die and nothing I did ever helped." Zephyr's face twisted – trying to stop, but his hands and tongue kept moving. "I hate him for what I've done to him...'cause it's easier than hating myself."

"You don't have to stop hating him. You can continue as you always have," Oya tested.

A bitter, tear-stained laugh rang out. "I drove him to this. There's no repenting for such heinous–"

Oya grabbed his hands and forced him to look straight at her. "Stop. Or you'll become just like him."

"That'd be sad to see?"

Not particularly. "What kind of General will you become if you allow this to eat away at you?"

"I shouldn't be General."

"Then who? He says it's a position for a Prince, not a Lord."

Zephyr froze – eyes doubling in size. "That's why?"

What's why? "Your life is not your own, Zephyr." She repeated the elf's lesson from many months before. "Running away. Using this as an excuse to hide...that's not taking responsibility."

The Prince held out his hands – shaking them. "What do I do?"

Freakishly green eyes sparkled. "Taking responsibility hurts. Admitting to hard things...or holding your tongue when necessary... But if you want to become a man who deserves to be called 'General' by millions, and 'cousin' by one...start now."

The golden boy withered. Looking at her was too painful. "I don't deserve to face him."

"It's not about you." Oya pointed to the huddled Ferdinan, "As a leader, it's never about you. And this, right now? It's not about *your* needs or desires. It's about *him*. What does *he* need?"

"You're taking pleasure in this." Zephyr sniffed, trying for a more lighthearted complaint.

"Greatly."

"Thanks." Tapping his chest, he walked over and knelt beside his cousin. Ferdinan didn't flinch – just stayed curled up. "Ferdinan."

What'll you do, dear friend? Oya released his will, slipped back into the shadows, and watched.

Glazed-over blue crystals came to life, spilling out blood when they connected with Zephyr's. Scrambling back, Ferdinan placed five paces between them and brought his face to the ground. "I-I'm–"

"I'm sorry," Zephyr closed the space between them – bringing his head down just as far. "The damage I've done...I...there's no fixing it. But I *am* sorry."

Ferdinan stuttered, fumbling for words.

Zephyr interrupted him. "It's not your fault. What I did to you was wrong. I don't know how to do anything right... But...maybe... I'll start with one simple command. I expect you – I beg you..."

Ferdinan stayed frozen – eyes on the floor and at a total loss.

The flat of Zephyr's hand tapped his chest before balling into a fist and pointing upward. "Live."

Neither boy looked at the other.

Neither could stand seeing what they'd done to the other.

And Oya was the only one who realized.

Neither boy could breathe. Ferdinan – because of all the horrible things he'd done to hurt his Prince. And Zephyr – because he'd broken his cousin irreparably.

Both boys knelt, saturated with dark emotions.

All of this is new to them, isn't it? Does either know how to express what they feel? Think? Fear? Oya watched Zephyr's lips move – searching for words. *Is this something I can teach?*

"I command you to live. I command you to not die."

Silence stretched forever until a strangled "Why?" clawed out of Ferdinan's throat.

"'Cause I want you to live."

Chapter 35

"This is impressive, Elbie." Ferdinan accentuated his praise with a bright – if forced – smile. "A little tweaking and it'll be sound."

"Yes, sir." Elbie looked out the window then back to his mentor. "Um...are you going anywhere this break?"

"I haven't been summoned yet and have no personal plans."

"If you stay, can we work on this over the break?"

Ferdinan smiled bigger and nodded. *Live. Don't die...how are they different?* And what should he do from here? Ignoring his growling stomach... *Mentoring. It's all I'm remotely capable of...* "If I don't get called away. I'm excited to see how it turns out."

Mismatched eyes lit up. Screen in hand, Elbie looked timidly at the blueprints he designed. "How do you make those micro boards? The circuitry...it's so tiny. It looks printed on, but..."

He agreed to not ask about the disks yet. "You'll learn that in Master Ludwick's Circuitry and Design class your eighth year."

"Um..." Elbie blushed sheepishly. "My printer... Programing it to print graphene circuits could be more beneficial than gems..."

"Amazing..." *Why didn't I think of that...?* The near perfect conductor of graphene circuits. The improved efficiency and battery life alone... "Keep finding more ideas for your printer."

Pink tinged Elbie's cheeks, but the young Tinkerer beamed.

"Elbie." The words stuck – not for pride, but for fear.

"Yes, Master Ferdinan?"

"I..." Shaking, the skeleton knelt and bent forward. "I'm sorry. I've failed as your mentor. I haven't been here. Haven't been attentive. I've made you worry. I'm truly, very sorry."

"I know." Elbie jumped off his stool and stood before Ferdinan; even bowed and on knees, they were nearly face to face. "Please keep teaching me. You're in high demand...and that can't be easy... I want you to teach me. Just...not if I'm a burden."

Those words slashed at his heart. Hiding his face, Ferdinan mussed the boy's hair. "You've *never* been a burden. Teaching you and Yuyu is the only joy I've had. You're a good child and a wonderful student. Thank you for putting up with me."

* * *

"What's a Dual?" Oya appeared on the desk beside Jon, nearly knocking him out of his seat.

"Oya...! I apologize." Swallowing his heart, Jon faced her. "Duel? A fight to the death between two people, I think...it's an *old* term."

"No." Bare toes danced in the air. "The kind of Dual someone is described as being."

"A Dual? Someone with two different abilities...but-"

"Ah, I see." Oya grinned - interrupting the rest of Jon's answer. "Is it a bad thing?"

"No. Just rare. The last Dual was an Energist with Healing abilities. She lived over a hundred years ago."

"How rare are they?"

Jon considered his answer. "They're kind of a freak happenstance... There's only been three known duals."

Green eyes aimlessly scanned the room. "In how long?"

"The first person with abilities was nearly a millennia ago."

Her usual wicked grin beamed at him. "Thank you."

Before he could press for more, she vanished. "A Dual? Where did she hear about that?"

* * *

Once Elbie left, Ferdinan's smile disappeared and he turned to the screen with forbidden research. Living meant keeping that voice in control...and himself. Dose by weight was significantly less than by height. *Maybe if I split the difference?* That drop was less extreme and it'd stretch his supply another three weeks per batch.

All the extra energy was nice - for the most part - but the mood swings and insatiable appetite had to go. However, even those were better than that voice. Gathering his supplies, Ferdinan went to work cooking the next batch. But the dose...

Pulling out his mint tin, he opened the bottom compartment and looked over its contents. Nearly a month's supply left.

Chills and electricity ran up his spine. *How should I do this?*

Carefully he studied. Going by weight... *No. I can't risk taking too little. Maybe splitting the difference really is the best course. Will that be enough? Will it work?*

Chewing on his lip, Ferdinan returned his attention to the tin's contents. *I should keep these in case the lower dose doesn't work.*

He wants me to live? Doesn't he understand I'm dangerous?

A chime demanded his attention – forcing a deep sigh from him. Regret and a strange kind of melancholy weighed down his heart. "I was looking forward to staying..."

Elbie's carbon printer... Figuring out the medicine... *Why the Artimuses? Why keep summoning me there?* Being in that home – surrounded by Jon's family – it hurt. It tore at his soul, crushed his heart. He didn't belong there. No matter what they wished.

But he couldn't refuse. The order was from his General and a personal request from the Queen Mother. *No, the request came from Evelyn. She's too young to understand she shouldn't want me around...* Even if neither his General nor strongest ally was involved, how could he turn down the five-year-old hero?

"Focus on Evelyn. Ignore everyone else and you'll be fine."

But it was physically impossible to ignore the Artimus family.

"There's no winning."

* * *

"You won't last long like this." A floppy fisherman's hat blocked her view of the moon.

"I'll keep all my promises. One way or another." Breathing out, Oya laid an arm across her eyes. *I really am tired...*

"As much as I and your keepers want to help, there's only so much we can do. You understand this?"

Soft twilight sand gently cradled her. *Can I sleep in the realm of dreams?* "There's no such thing as an infinite energy source."

"As long as you understand." There was a pause before the man spoke again. "But I'll do what I can to ease your burden."

Oya sat up and looked at him. "And how'll you do that?"

"I'll approach Ferdinan again. Maybe he'll listen after what his cousin said."

"And Zephyr?" A delicate hand played with her steel locket.

"It's possible he'll overcome on his own."

Oya turned her eyes to the starless sky. "It didn't look minor."

"True. But unlike Ferdinan, Zephyr has the will to change."

It was tempting to laugh. Her dear friend was an immovable object in a world desperate to move him.

Chapter 36

How is this real? Those were fun dreams, but...they were dreams... Until they weren't.

Sitting on a pier, Yuyu looked out over the ocean. It reached on forever. Where the oceans ended, rivers and streams and lakes and ponds began. No matter how hard the earth tried, it couldn't be contained. Water jumped and tickled her bare feet.

I'm sorry. I want to play, but I'm waiting on a friend. Yuyu spun the ball bearing. A wave reared up and splashed against the pier – leaving her left side soaked. *Haha! I wasn't ignoring you!*

The light *thud* of running feet grew louder until her island brother stopped beside her. "What happened to you?"

"A wave got me..." Yuyu giggled, looking up at Elbie.

The brow above his green eye rose. "You can play in the water?"

Yuyu grimaced. "No, but walking along the shore..."

"How does a wave only get half of you?"

"I don't know! It just did." She smiled brightly and motioned for Elbie to sit beside her.

Kicking off his shoes, he sat. They enjoyed the sea breeze, warm sun, and a pleasant conversation about nothing until Elbie's eyes focused on his hands. *Why is he staring at them?*

She should ask. But the shell demanded her attention. It was tiny, but not rare. And after it appeared the ocean became alive. Or it'd grown a personality. A mischievous one. It'd splash high or rush toward her when there weren't any waves around. And returned a pen she'd lost to its depths nearly two years ago.

But always it called – telling her it was there. Comfort beyond description filled her when she looked at it. It was like having a mother to hold her and a friend to pick on her at the same time.

"What do you think of this?" Yuyu showed Elbie the shell.

Mismatched eyes glazed over as he became perfectly still. *What?*

This isn't your place, little one.

But...I'm just curious...I meant nothing bad.

I know.

Giggles that didn't exist filled her soul. But before she could put the shell away, Elbie spoke.

"It's cute. I haven't seen one marked like that."

What? But I thought...?

"If you'd like, I can make it into a necklace for you."

"Um..." Water splashed up – wetting both their feet, but Elbie didn't seem to notice. "I don't want to risk it being damaged..."

"No, I'd protect it." Tiny hands drew a circle just below his collar bone. "Master Ferdinan taught me how to use the glass machine. I'll make a pendant that'll protect it and look cute on you."

I forgot about that! "You finally got to it? It's lots of fun, isn't it?"

Elbie scratched his cheek and nodded.

He wants an excuse to play with it. But she searched for excuses to program new things into it also. "Thank you. I'd love that."

* * *

There he is. The one Xhou wanted to talk to. He watched and read everything he could... He saw. He understood the sacrifice. The suffering. Now he'd finally thank the scientist who found the cure.

Oya appeared from thin air, but Ferdinan didn't flinch. Wasn't even surprised. And the boy was laughing... A sincere, genuine laugh.

It matched that smile as Ferdinan gave her a mock lecture. But she smacked his arm and bolted. Chuckling, the skeleton dropped his bag and gently placed a box on top of it then ran off after her.

He can run? Xhou blinked. *When did he learn how to play?*

Is he ok? Xhou thought Ferdinan would be inconsolable. So much death. After all the people who died... The skeleton saved Evelyn and Yuyu and Elbie...but was too late to save Rura.

How did he learn to smile? To laugh? After all that...? But he *was* laughing and running and playing. He was having fun. For the first time... Approaching now, Xhou would only upset that joy...

This is good enough.

* * *

A familiar voice stopped him a few feet from the gangplank.

"Zephyr?" Worry cloaked his friend. "I have something to say."

"About what, Denila?"

"I'm worried about you. You've been miserable this block. Don't deny it, you can't hide that from me." She took his hand. "I want to help you. It hurts seeing you so sad. Seeing my friend hurting...I can't stand it. How can I help you become happy again?"

Putting down his bag, the Prince embraced her. "I'm sorry. When I return, I'll be a person who deserves your friendship."

When she tried pushing herself back to look at him, he held her tighter. "You've always deserved it."

If only that were true. Giving her one final squeeze, he painted a smile on his face, and stepped back. "Thank you."

* * *

Ferdinan tapped her shoulder and bolted before she could turn.

"*Cheater!*" Oya laughed – struggling to catch up.

"What're you two up to?" Jon smirked – carrying their luggage.

Ferdinan turned bright red and stopped. *Don't do that...*

"Playing before you leave on a grand adventure. Without me. A *second* time." Oya scrunched her nose up at Jon.

"I'm sorry. Maybe next time." Mussing her short, unnaturally red hair, Jon shifted the luggage away from Ferdinan.

"Yay! I want to see your land of giants!"

Jon rolled his eyes. "It's not a land of giants."

"*Will you be ok alone?*" Ferdinan tried snagging his bag again.

"*Only if you call.*"

"*I will.*" A fresh blush stained Ferdinan's face. "*Do you have everything you need? A month was too much for you last time.*"

"*Probably not. But I'll play with Xhou when I'm bored.*"

A truly amused laugh escaped the skeleton.

Oya grinned. "*Ah! Dear friend, I love hearing your laugh! I love it as much as the stars above...the consolation they give.*"

"I'm still here." Jon cleared his throat and shifted the bags again.

Purpling, the Tinkerer turned away. "We better get going."

"*Hug Evelyn for me.*" Oya grinned at Jon. "Enjoy the coddling."

Jon rolled his eyes. "That's the nicest thing you've said to me."

"You're welcome." With a dramatic bow she winked at them. "*I expect a new song before you get back!*"

* * *

The lower dose was working though the hunger was still stronger than he liked. Ferdinan could sit for short spurts and slept a couple hours the last few days. But when the chemical's level evened out... When that happened... *What can I expect?* Laying back, he considered this...until he was standing before the Fisherman.

"Fisherman." Ferdinan bowed. "How may I help you?"

"That's my question." The Fisherman continued when Ferdinan turned away. "You know the infection's still there. If it wasn't, you wouldn't be scared of not taking that chemical you made."

"It's keeping the voice under control. That's all I need."

"I'll clean out the infection again, repair the tears it caused." Stepping closer, the Fisherman offered his hand. "Please. Let me clean your wounds. You won't last the break if I don't."

"Thank you for your offer. But I don't care."

Frowning, the Fisherman stood as Ferdinan turned and walked away. "If you don't care, then why not let me help you?"

"Help someone who deserves it."

Ferdinan didn't see the man frown. Or reach out and force him to sleep. Gently laying the boy down, the man hovered glowing hands over Ferdinan's chest.

Epilogue

"I shouldn't be surprised..." Oya sat on the twilight beach staring at the little rope's worth of connections wrapped around her palm. *How many resources does maintaining relationships take?* Even on her beach she was weary. But she didn't have the luxury of stopping. Of giving up. Glowing orbs danced on the edges of her vision and she winked to them – but they didn't distract her thoughts for long.

How did such evil spread so far...? Inhuman green eyes turned to the full moon commanding a starless purple sky. Sighing, Oya laid back. Evil was a constant blight of humanity. But how did it reach this level without her mother's notice? Or her own? Cautious and ambitious was a terrible combination to be up against. But that woman couldn't fight or defend against the unseen.

Defeated giggles rolled out of her. Assuming she could gather all the connections in time. But this was her birthright – her responsibility. Just as it had been every time. *Can I get the rest of them while my dear friend is gone...? Or most, at least?*

Blowing out a breath, Oya jumped to her feet.

Or she tried.

Halfway up, she fell back onto the ground. Laughter burst out of her. *I refused to accept new limits!* Not right now. It didn't matter what she could do. What mattered was what she *had* to do.

The doorless opening to the silver road appeared. Holding up the rope, she rolled to her feet. *Zephyr...will still need looking after, but not constant attention. Yuyu... Û-ya ̂ın will watch her for now. How will they fair together?* Though she wanted to look over those little sprouts until she had to leave. *Iitano's heir...I can't reach her yet, but she's safe. Ferdinan...*

Ferdinan was traveling to the family of giants. The family who loved him. That was more than she could offer. Stepping onto the roads, Oya made her way to the woman and the void she created to work in. Squeezing the rope, she pulled one person after another into existence, starting with the Kōjomǎ and ending with the lowest workers she'd found so far.

They stood like the roots of a tree – all spreading out from the woman with silver-streaked hair. Too bad only a portion of the roots were discovered. *I did this much in a block while tending to several people and disasters, how much can I do in a month with few distractions?*

Oya walked to the last she'd left off with. Giving a wink to the orbs dancing in her peripheral, she placed a golden-brown hand over their heart and searched for the next person to claim.

About the Author

Psychologist, writer, crafter, and colored hair enthusiast…when CR Saxon isn't coming up with new and terrible things to subject various characters to, she can be found attempting projects with more ambition than skill, getting lost in random research, or catching up on chores. Her life is generally one of chaos and glowy screens – all while mentally living many lives in the name of fun, adventure, and storytelling.

Mirrors and Dreams
Copyright © 2021 C R Saxon

All rights reserved.

ISBN: 9781955644037